# Matador

A Jessica Watts Southwest Suspense Novel

Kathryn Dodson

Renegade Reads

# Contents

# Chapter 1

Jessica glimpsed her mother through the large windows of the cottage, the inside bright and cheery and full of housewarming party guests. Tela, Jessica's dog, sat beside her in the cold pickup and whined in anticipation. If only Jessica could muster the same enthusiasm for Clarice's move to the area.

Her mother's new home, nestled under a giant tree, sat at the edge of an impressive commercial pecan grove located a few miles north of El Paso, near the tiny town of La Union, New Mexico. She'd seen the house once before, the day Clarice decided to lease it from her art dealer.

Jessica would have leased it in a second, just for the peaceful feeling of the grove of massive trees. Tonight, they made the night even darker, but the bright light shining from the windows welcomed her. A decorated tree leftover from Christmas glowed with lights and tinsel.

The second Jessica opened the door, the dog bounded across her lap and raced toward the house. Jessica followed with slightly less enthusiasm. Her mother had lined the walkway with luminarias, the old-fashioned kind with candles nestled in lunch bags filled a third of the way with sand. Jessica inspected one to make sure her mother had used LED lights instead of real candles. No reason to burn down the pecan grove and half of southern New Mexico. Cool light flickered in the bag.

Still hidden in darkness, she paused at the door, unsure whether to knock, try the knob, or turn around. Despite time spent working on their relationship, a barrier remained between mother and daughter. Screw it. Jessica needed to bury the hurt part of herself and just move forward.

She swung the door open, and the sounds of the women inside buffeted her. She recognized her good friends Luz and Sarah, once her landlords, and her attorney Alma. These women raised Jessica after her mother abandoned her at sixteen. But it was time to get beyond that. She had to leave the past behind.

Tela burst into the room, wiggling her whole body. She ran up to Sarah and spun around her feet, the Catahoula Leopard dog creating a blur of chestnut and white.

"Tela, stop," Jessica yelled. "I'm so sorry. She's just a little excited."

"Who's a good girl?" Sarah baby-talked the dog, ignoring Jessica entirely.

"You need to come around more often," Luz said. "We miss you and the dog."

"I know. Sorry. It's just been so busy with the new job and my classes." Jessica had lived in a tiny building on Sarah and Luz's ranch for years. It wasn't until recently that her life turned around. Marrying Angus, purchasing her own home, starting law school, all the stability she now enjoyed didn't exist back then. She'd leaned on them, hard sometimes.

"Here, honey. Have a margarita." Her mother handed her a cobalt blue glass frothing with what looked like a lime-green Slurpee. Oh, dear. How could her mother not know how to make an authentic margarita? Jessica could have taught a class on that.

"Thanks, Mom." Jessica looked at her mother, arms wide, waiting for a hug. She set the glass on the counter. Jessica wasn't a hugger, but she wouldn't snub her mom in front of guests. She stepped into her mother's arms. A little awkward, but bearable. Tela jumped on the two women, giving Jessica the chance she needed to back out of the embrace.

"No." She addressed the dog, then turned to her mom. "I'm sorry, but this little monster needs to go on a walk and burn off some of this energy. I'll be right back. The place looks great, by the way."

It looked better than great. Her mother had adorned the cream stucco walls with her colorful desert paintings. Thick rugs sat atop a burnished terracotta floor. A wreath of chiles hung over the mantle where a fire crackled. Plates of tamales and sweets almost hid the green and red patterned tablecloth thrown over the bar that separated the living area from the kitchen. Jessica inhaled the aroma of her mother's famous chili as she spied the large pot on the stove. It smelled especially good tonight, overlaid with the scent of piñon wood burning in the fire.

"Just a quick walk," she said to the dog. "I want to get back here for the food and company."

"I'll go with you," Sarah said. "I miss both of you."

They headed outside. Jessica hadn't thought to bring a leash. Who knew Tela would be on fire tonight?

"Hey, let's walk along the irrigation ditch instead of the road since I don't have her leash." A dirt track ran beside the dry ditch. A whole network of ditches connected the Rio Grande to the many agricultural fields between El Paso's mountains and New Mexico's mesa. Jessica had seen the pecans completely flooded in the past, the water hued silver under broad branches and dark trunks.

The dry dirt beneath their feet meant the grove hadn't been irrigated in some time. Still, the dirt remained soft, and she hoped Tela wouldn't stray too far off the track, find a puddle, and come back muddy.

The dog ran ahead of them into the darkness and occasionally tore back to make sure they hadn't left. Jessica appreciated the quiet of the night and crossed her arms to keep warm.

"How's the new job?" Sarah asked.

"I really like my boss. I've already learned a lot from her, and she's an unbelievably slick negotiator." Jessica had only worked as a paralegal with Linda, a local attorney, for a couple of months, since she'd left Alma's firm after an altercation with a client.

"Are you keeping out of trouble?" Sarah asked.

"Well, our clients are all alive, although I'm only sixty days in." She wished she could see Sarah's face in the night to make sure she'd caught the joke. Sarah worried more than most people, and frankly, Jessica had done plenty to earn her concern over the years, what with dangerous jobs and her penchant for hard liquor and other vices. Fortunately, these days she wanted only enough excitement to stave off boredom.

"Tela. What have you got? Did you find a stick?" Sarah asked as the dog danced around them, something white and muddy protruding from her jaw.

"Oh, no. You're filthy. You're not going back into mom's house." Jessica lunged for the dog. "Drop it," she said, her hand firmly on the stick. Only it wasn't a stick. The dog opened her jaws, and Jessica examined the dirty treasure. She noticed the knobs at each end.

Jessica dropped it. "No, Tela." She placed her boot atop it to keep the dog from picking it back up.

"What's wrong?" Sara asked.

"I think that's a bone."

"Oh. Gross. Probably a cattle bone given its size."

"Maybe." Tela had run back into the night, and they heard her barking not far off. "Let's go see."

Jessica followed the dog, shining her phone's flashlight in the direction she'd run. When the light hit the dog's spotted coat, Tela turned and barked once, then resumed digging. Jessica jogged toward her.

"Wait, are you sure this is a good idea?" Sarah asked, fear in her voice. "It's dark, and no one knows exactly where we are."

"We have to find out what's going on. You can stay here if you want." Jessica turned her head toward Sarah, half-shouting the words as she trotted toward the dog.

"Um, no." Sarah's footsteps quickened to a jog.

"Tela, no. Leave it." Jessica's reprimand did nothing to stop the dog from digging furiously into the dirt next to the irrigation ditch.

When Jessica reached Tela, she hauled her back by her collar and shone her light downward. Oh, no. A human skull. Tela had only partially uncovered it. A section of lower jaw had scrape marks across it from Tela's paws, and a few teeth lay scattered in the dirt.

"Sarah. You might want to stay back. There's a skull here."

Sarah's footsteps stopped, but her labored breath continued. The dog whimpered and pulled at her collar.

Back at her mom's, Jessica called the Doña Ana County Sheriff's Department. More guests had arrived, filling the once festive studio. The spooky find had put a damper on her mother's party. Jessica hadn't buried that skeleton under the pecan trees, but trouble followed her like a bad smell.

Fortunately, one of the women who'd arrived, Robin Saunders, owned the property. Jessica would happily turn everything over to her, although when she'd first mentioned the bones, Robin's eyes had filled with tears. She'd hardly said a word since and had only nodded when Jessica offered to call the sheriff. Fortunately, he would arrive soon. Doubly fortunate, her mom lived just across the state border in New Mexico, meaning a completely different sheriff's department than the guys who'd arrested Jessica just a few months earlier.

Luz, who worked for the City of El Paso, took command of the room and asked that no one leave until law enforcement dismissed them. That announcement stifled the partygoers like a weighted blanket.

Finally, bright lights signaled a vehicle pulling up outside, followed by a rap on the door. Jessica checked to see if her mom or Robin would answer it, but neither moved.

Jessica swung the door open to a man who might have had the lead role in a TV western. His full white mustache covered his upper lip, and a black cowboy hat topped his head. He towered over Jessica and must have been six-five to her five-ten. He wore the khaki sheriff's department uniform, but a tooled leather pair of cowboy boots covered his feet.

"You the sheriff?" she asked.

"Deputy Lefty Griswald at your service. I hear you ladies found some human remains out here." His eyes left Jessica and scanned the room behind her. "This looks like a party."

"Yes sir, officer. This was my housewarming party," her mother said. "May I get you a cup of coffee?"

"I'd sure appreciate that."

Jessica tried hard not to roll her eyes. The politeness would mean more delays. "I can take you to where the bones are. My dog found them in the pecan grove."

"Well, sure. I'd like to hear the story first. So how long have you lived out here?" He addressed the question to her mother, and Clarice puffed up like a prize hen, seemingly eager to tell her story.

Jessica sat through her mom and then Robin speaking with the officer. Robin mentioned that her father, Paul Brown, had bought the orchard in the 1950s. He had brought her out here often when she was a child, and she'd built the studio on the property to remind her of him.

"He disappeared when I was fifteen."

Jessica choked on the sugar cookie she'd just shoved in her mouth. "What do you mean, disappeared?" She asked the question before Lefty could get a word in.

Robin's eyes filled with tears for the second time that evening. "No one knows what happened to him. They never found a body or anything. Maybe . . ." She broke down into sobs. Jessica's mom wrapped an arm around her and told her it would be all right.

"I wouldn't jump to any conclusions," Lefty said. "The medical examiner should be here any minute, and we'll figure out what happened and who those bones belong to."

As if the words had conjured him, another vehicle pulled up outside. Through the window, a thin man with curly dark hair stepped out of a truck. He wore a puffy jacket against the chill but pulled a white doctor's jacket from the truck. Comically, the lab coat didn't fit over his jacket, and after struggling with it, he wadded it up and threw it into the truck. Jessica opened the door for him before he had the chance to knock.

"Hi. Joe Ruiz, Medical Examiner," he said, extending a hand to Jessica.

"Jessica Watts. I found the body." She reached her hand toward his and shook it firmly.

"Where is the body?" he asked. He looked around as if he expected the bones to emerge like a party trick.

"Out in the orchard. I can take you there." Anything to get to the next step of tonight's fiasco.

"Lefty, have you visited the crime scene yet?" Joe asked.

"Just getting to that. Ladies, will you all stay here until I get back?" The deputy pulled himself back from the women, several of whom seemed to be fawning over his tall cowboy persona.

Jessica exited, hoping the men would follow. Soon, Joe and Lefty stood in the yard with her. "It's about a quarter of a mile down the irrigation ditch." She pointed across the yard into the darkness.

"Does it look like a recent crime scene?" Joe asked.

"No. The bones look old," Jessica said.

"Did you notice any fresh tire tracks near the site?" Lefty asked.

"Not at all. It's not much more than a dirt track."

"We'll take the trucks down, then. You ride with me." Lefty motioned her toward his SUV.

Jessica feared she wouldn't be able to find the site from the truck, but the high-beam lights lit up the dirt like midday. She recognized the freshly uncovered mound yards before they got there.

"It's where that pile of dirt is. The big white bone is the one my dog brought me. I'm afraid I touched it."

"Not to worry," Lefty said. "We'll get this figured out."

As much as Jessica loved being a part of the action, it thrilled her that these old bones were someone else's case. She'd talk about finding them. Make a statement, whatever. Then go home to Angus.

# Chapter 2

When Jessica and Lefty returned to the studio, the party had restarted without its earlier festive flair. Now, sagging faces and occasionally tears accompanied the clinking glasses and overlapping words. The stage where everyone should have gone home had long passed.

While Lefty spent a little time with each woman, documenting their account of the evening, Clarice bustled Robin over to Jessica.

"Honey, you remember Robin, don't you?" her mom asked, almost shoving the red-faced woman in front of her. "She owns the gallery that shows my work, and she leased me this studio."

While Jessica had only met Robin a few times, her mom droned on about her incessantly. Plus, this studio gave her mother a place to live other than Jessica's house. Not only did Jessica feel like she knew the woman well, she owed her a huge debt of gratitude.

"Of course. I'm so sorry about what happened here tonight. Have you ever had something like that happen out here before?" Maybe this place was a Native American burial site. The Rio Grande had attracted people for millennia. El Paso, the pass, had long been a crossroads for travelers along both the north-south and east-west axes of North America. The bones had looked old, although they were disturbingly close to the irrigation ditch.

"No, certainly not that I know of. What if it's my dad?" Robin burst into a fresh round of tears.

"Can you help her?" Clarice asked. "I've told her how wonderful you are at finding people."

Yeah, live people. And so far, she'd only found a woman who wanted to stay lost and four girls. Memories of that last grisly night in the desert flitted before her. Not everyone had survived. And even those who did carried permanent mental scars.

Jessica had meant to ask for donations tonight for the two Guatemalan immigrants from that night. The cousins now lived at a detention center; their family had been murdered on their trip north seeking safety and freedom. She wanted to do something for them—provide food and gifts. She also wanted to find the evil men who'd left them orphaned.

Jessica refocused on Robin. Her husband might be a key to what happened to those girls. Dick Saunders, ex-mayor of El Paso, ran with some of those involved, although Jessica didn't know how to approach him about something so explosive. She had made little progress on exactly what had happened and who was responsible.

"I'm sure the local law enforcement will do a good job of figuring out who those bones belonged to," Jessica said. She had no reason to get involved.

"I'll pay you," Robin said. "Even if that's not him you found tonight, it's time for me to learn what happened to my father."

Jessica stared awkwardly at the woman. What exactly had her mother told Robin? She had no idea how to find someone who'd disappeared years earlier. "That's not what I do. Besides, I have a job." The last thing Jessica needed was to get sucked down the vortex of helping her mom's friends.

"I'm sure Ms. Reed would understand," Clarice said. "After all, you've only worked there a couple of months."

Jessica cringed at her mom's comment. Spoken like a woman who'd never had a real job. Jessica needed to show up for this job, prove herself worthy. Besides, Linda had helped her track the immigration journey of the Guatemalan cousins, so Jessica already owed her. Unfortunately, they'd yet to find any relatives to care for the girls.

"Linda Reed?" Robin asked. "The attorney? I know her. I can give her a call. I'm sure she'll be fine with it."

"Please don't." The last thing Jessica needed was her mom and her friends getting involved in her work life.

Robin laid a hand on Jessica's arm. "Please. I need your help. I'll pay you five thousand dollars just to look into my dad's disappearance. This has haunted me since I was a teenager. If I only knew what happened to him, I could let go. But part of me believes he's still alive, that he abandoned us. I just want to know the truth."

Damn. Nothing like playing on the heartstrings of someone who understood abandonment. Although Jessica had always known where her parents resided, they'd left her in El Paso and seemed fine with their decision. She'd punished them by not speaking to them for a dozen years. To not even know what had happened to her parents, that would have thrown her into an even deeper level of hell.

Also, the money would be useful. Her job with Linda didn't pay as well as the one she used to have with one of the city's largest law firms. Plus, looking for someone who disappeared long ago probably wouldn't put her life in danger like the last two jobs had.

She sighed. "Let me think about it. It's late, and this has been a hell of an evening."

———

The next morning, Jessica arrived at work early. Linda had to be in court, and Jessica hoped to catch her before she went to the courthouse.

Last night, Jessica had brought her mother home with her. Finding bones, even old ones, near the studio had been more than Clarice could deal with. Jessica had roused Angus from a deep sleep after they'd arrived, mostly to warn him not to walk around naked the next morning. She'd ended up telling him the whole story, including Robin's offer. Angus's eyes had lit up at the five thousand dollars. It would definitely ease the tight financial situation she'd caused.

The key in the office door's lock jerked her out of her memories. Linda's normally wavy almost platinum hair lay smooth and had new golden undertones, signaling a visit to the salon. A skilled plastic surgeon had rolled back a few years, which Jessica only knew because she'd finally broken down and asked the woman her age. Chronological age—sixty. Visual age—early fifties. But when you looked into her eyes, centuries of experience seemed to stare back at you, much of it hard won.

"You're early," Linda said.

"I wanted to talk to you before you went to court."

Linda dropped into one of the chairs in front of Jessica's desk. The law office had been converted from a home built early in the last century. Jessica sat behind an impressive wooden desk in the once living room now reception area. The space still had a homey feel, and somehow, despite her Armani pantsuit and stilettos, Linda fit right in. "What's going on?"

Jessica relayed the finding of bones near her mom's new home. "The place is owned by Robin Saunders, the ex-mayor's wife. She thinks the bones could be her missing father. Either way, she'd like to hire me to try to figure out what happened to her dad."

"So, they think they finally found old man Brown. I'll be damned." Linda leaned back in the chair and shook her head. "That one's been a long time coming."

"You know the story?"

"I lived the story. And I know Robin. Her brother Colby was my high school boyfriend. Maybe my only true love. If you believe in that stuff." Linda's response caught Jessica off guard.

"Were you dating him when his father disappeared?" she asked, trying to do the math in her head.

"Yes. It was our senior year of high school. It would be good to get the truth out there after so many years, although really, it's too little too late." The energy drained from Linda.

"Why?"

"Just promise you won't believe all the BS about Colby killing his dad. Colby was the gentlest person I've ever met." Linda's blue eyes went soft, as if she'd gotten lost in the past. "Are you going to take the job?"

"I haven't decided. She's willing to pay five thousand dollars. I could run it through the firm." Jessica realized she needed to have a more detailed conversation with Robin. Five thousand dollars for what, exactly? Would she only be paid if she proved what happened to her father? That could be a lot of work for nothing, given all the years that had passed. Her thoughts moved to the many articles and cases she needed to read for this semester's law school courses.

"You don't need to run it through the firm. You should do it. Consider it your New Year's bonus."

A crick in Jessica's neck loosened. They needed the money, even though it would mean some late nights. "Maybe I will. You know, I still think Robin's husband had connections to what happened with that preacher and the Guatemalan girls. And speaking of them, I'd like to figure out how to get them some funding for whatever's next for them."

Linda stood. "I've got to get ready for court. Maybe when you're researching Robin's dad, you'll run across something on Dick Saunders. You never know. As for the girls, contact Casa Sagrada. They do more to help migrants in this area than anyone."

Jessica looked up the organization as soon as Linda left the room. Founded in the seventies as a temporary home for immigrants, in recent years, it had focused on supporting those detained in the region. It operated on both sides of the border and at least tried to ensure that the poor seeking refuge had enough food and supplies to make it through their detention, if not in comfort or with dignity, at least with the hope that someone cared. It would be the perfect organization to help the girls.

She delved into their website and emerged an hour later with a far greater understanding of the refugee crisis. Texas alone imprisoned over fourteen thousand migrants in detention facilities. Far too many arrived as children, like the young women Jessica had encountered in the desert.

People had crossed the border since the government had decided there should be one, and the border patrol caught many of them and returned them to Mexico. The ones who made it through usually found work in El Paso or elsewhere. Only recently, when certain politicians claimed immigration was America's greatest problem, had it become a big deal.

Recent rule changes made detention at the border for weeks, months, or longer the standard practice. For kids with no parents like the Guatemalan girls, this had to be especially hard. The US government wanted to deport them to Guatemala, but unless and until they found any living family members, the girls faced an uncertain fate in the US.

Jessica's research cemented her decision to take Robin's job. She'd dedicate some portion of the money Robin paid her to helping the girls and other immigrants. And perhaps she'd find a way to learn what Robin's husband knew about the men in the desert who preyed on migrants. It seemed like the least she could do.

# Chapter 3

Jessica arrived home to her mom and Robin having a conversation in her living room. She assumed Clarice being there that late meant she'd spend another night at the house. Jessica didn't blame her. It had been creepy to find human bones in the pecan grove. The beautiful studio her mom rented didn't have other houses near it, and it would have given even Jessica the heebie jeebies to be out there.

"Hey, sweetie," Clarice said when Jessica opened the door. "I've got a proposition for you, and Robin wanted to talk you into finding out what happened to her father."

"Sounds good," Jessica said. She perched on one of the chairs across from the sofa where they sat. Tela, who'd been curled at her mother's feet, got up and ambled over. Normally, she'd have bounced and barked until Jessica opened the door and then sprang at her, demanding attention and love.

Jessica reached for the dog's head and began massaging her ears, a favorite treat. The dog let out a soft whine and stared at her with those strange eyes, one ice blue, the other peridot green.

"I want to borrow Tela for a while." As she heard her mom's words, Jessica clutched Tela, fingers digging into fur.

"Why?" Jessica asked.

"Frankly, I'm afraid to be alone at the studio right now. I know it's silly. Lefty said those bones looked old, but if I had Tela with me, I'd feel safer."

"Well, she's probably as likely to lick someone to death as bite them, but she does have a good bark." Jessica loosened her death grip on the dog. She didn't want to lose her dog, but her mother's plan made sense.

Jessica had lived alone with the dog for years, and her bark scared just about everyone who didn't know her. "Maybe you should look for your own dog, a real guard dog."

"I think I will. Robin says it's fine."

"Actually, I'd feel a lot better if she had a dog out there. The studio was always a refuge for me, but I never spent many nights there."

Jessica looked down at Tela. "Do you want to go spend a little time with Mom?"

Tela barked in response, and Jessica took that as a yes. "She's all yours, at least until we get you another dog, but I get full visiting rights."

"I wouldn't have it any other way. Besides, then I'll get to see you more."

Jessica glanced over at her mother's comment and saw a grin and sparkling eyes. She liked this teasing side to her mom instead of the over-earnest, clinging woman she'd gotten to know over the past two years.

Jessica turned to Robin. "We need to work out the details, but I'll take your job."

"Oh, thank you! Let me send you the money right now."

Sometimes Jessica loved people who thought it was no big deal to pay someone that kind of money without even thinking about it. She watched her phone, incredulous, as the money showed up in her account.

Now she needed to get to work. "Robin, tell me what you know about your father's disappearance. Any information you have might be relevant."

"Of course. By the way, Lefty called today and said they wouldn't get the DNA results for a month or so. I don't know if those are my father's bones out there, but I have a strong feeling they might be. He wasn't the type of man who would have left his family with no explanation."

"I haven't had a chance to look up anything yet."Typically, Jessica would have prepared for a client meeting but, normally, clients didn't just show up at her house. "What year did your father disappear?"

"It was 1986, when I was fifteen. Friday, April 25, to be exact. At least, that was the last day anyone saw him. He went to work at the insurance company, like always, but never came home. We weren't sure anything was wrong at first. No one had cell phones back then, and my dad used to travel a lot, especially on weekends. I remember my mom asking if I knew where he was. By Sunday night, we knew something was wrong. He never missed work, and when he hadn't shown up by Monday morning, well, I think that's when my mom got the police involved."

As Robin told the story, her lack of emotion surprised Jessica. Maybe too much time had passed, leaving the rote recitation sounding practiced and dull.

"What happened next? Did the police investigate? Was there speculation about what happened to him?" Jessica asked.

"The police looked for him. The local news stations broadcast that he was missing. It made the front page of the newspapers, but nothing was ever found. Not his car, not him, nothing." The emotion Robin had lacked earlier came to her voice. Her forehead wrinkled, and she shook her head slowly. "We, his family, had no idea what had happened to him. But that didn't stop everyone in town from spouting theories. This town is full of gossips."

"Tell me about it." Jessica's mom exhaled in frustration.

Yep, Jessica knew all about that too. Her father had been the district attorney in El Paso when he was arrested and convicted of destroying documents in a case. His guilt had followed Jessica since she was sixteen and still came up today. People thought it fine to offer their opinion on his motives, or worse, their thoughts on whether his daughter had inherited his dishonesty. At least Robin's father hadn't done anything illegal. Probably.

Jessica looked at Robin with new eyes. She'd thought of the woman as an El Paso elite, wealthy, wife of an ex-mayor. She'd also seen her as a potential savior, the woman who had provided her mother a place to live and a means of income.

Now she saw a kindred spirit despite the perfect blond bob, designer jeans, and Chanel jacket. Jessica looked down at her own uniform of black slacks, fitted T shirt, and wool blazer. Only the color of her shirt and the weight of her jacket ever varied. She'd cultivated the practical and professional image years ago as a way to protect herself from an infamous family.

She briefly turned her attention to her mother's brightly colored tunic over yoga pants. Artsy comfort. Each woman dressed perfectly for her role. Grieving daughter, betrayed wife, those definitions lurked beneath the surface, but not so deep that gossip didn't hurt.

"It might help to know what the rumors were, although I'm most interested in what you and your family members think happened. Did you notice any unusual behavior in your father before he disappeared?"

Robin leaned forward and rested her elbows on her knees. She clasped her hands together under her chin, and Jessica wondered if she'd start praying next, but she'd clearly engaged, as if her hands held back barely contained energy and motion. "Let's start with the rumors. I don't think any of them are true. Some people said my brother killed him, but that's impossible. Colby was the gentlest person I ever met."

Her comment mirrored Linda's, both women convinced of the brother's innocence. Jessica had no reason to doubt their intuition, although she wondered what truths might have sparked that particular rumor.

"Others said my dad had a second family, but I think those people were just being mean to my mom. He was a great dad. He showed up for school events and encouraged my art. He always told Colby he had a place in the company, and he and mom almost never fought. They spent lots of time together hosting parties, going to the symphony and events at the local university. From what I could see, they had a great marriage. My mom would probably be happy to talk to you about him."

"Oh. Does she live in El Paso?" Learning about the mother surprised Jessica. She hadn't heard a word about her until now.

"Yes. She's in her eighties and doesn't get out much anymore. She's actually turned into a bit of a recluse, but I can set up a meeting with her if you think it would help."

"Yes. It would help tremendously. Are there other people close to your father whom I should speak with?"

"I'll think about it, and I can ask Mom. Maybe Charles Gordon, his business partner from back then, although I'm not sure where he is or if he's still alive."

"That would be great," Jessica said. "So, the rumors were that your brother killed him, or he had a second family."

"Those were the minor rumors, although they hurt the most. The big one was speculation that my dad was involved in the drug trade and was killed over a deal gone wrong. Back in the eighties, there was a ton of drug activity here."

"There always has been," Jessica said. How eerie that this woman's father might have been caught up in the same activity that brought her father down. "Do you think there's any truth behind that speculation?"

"I really don't. My dad ran an insurance company. From what my husband tells me, he ran the company very conservatively. Dick tries to carry on that tradition now that he runs the firm."

Robin had given Jessica the perfect opportunity to turn the conversation toward her husband, but she'd become curious about her father. "Do you know if he made any big investments outside of the firm or had any windfalls of cash?"

"Not that I know of. He saved for our college education. Oh, he did invest in a racehorse once. We all thought that was hilarious. He even used to joke about how his friends must have gotten him drunk the night he did that."

Robin sat back on the sofa, much more relaxed. She cocked her head as she seemed to pull memories from the past. "He had a group of guys he hung out with. They went hunting and fishing together on the weekends. Those are probably the ones who convinced him to buy the horse. I didn't really know them well, and I don't remember them coming around the house much. Maybe my mother will remember their names."

"It sounds like speaking with your mother is the next step. Is there anything else you remember about the rumors or his behavior that seemed unusual?"

Robin closed her eyes for a moment. When she opened them, her brow creased in thought. "You know, sometimes I would hear him speaking in Spanish on the phone. It was odd. I never even knew he spoke Spanish."

"Do you know what he was saying?" Jessica asked.

"No. Spanish wasn't my best subject at school. Also, I think I had a hard time hearing him, as if he spoke softly. In fact, I remember once standing outside his study door and listening. I'm sure he didn't know I was there."

Robin seemed caught in a dream, and Jessica hoped she'd remember more. Many kids in El Paso grew up with at least a passing knowledge of Spanish, and it spoke to Robin's privilege that she didn't know any at all.

"Huh," Robin said, seemingly still mired in thought. "I don't know why he spoke Spanish or hid that ability. But I really can't imagine him being involved in illegal drugs. My dad was a family man with a successful business. The thought of him having ties to the drug trade seems very far from my memories of him and the life we lived growing up."

"I think we need to look into it. When I was fifteen, I'd never have guessed in a million years that my dad was involved in that stuff." Jessica moved her eyes to her mother.

Clarice's lips pressed into a fine line as if trying to stifle any comment. Finally, she broke. "Jessica. Your father wasn't involved in drugs. He deleted some files to protect people in the office he ran. That was it."

"It was a drug case." Jessica crossed her arms and stared her mother down. The conversation had brought up their biggest mother-daughter argument. Her father had admitted his guilt and apologized. Her mother wanted to sweep away the details of the case.

"It's not like he was involved in drugs or used drugs," Clarice said.

"I don't think Robin's father used drugs. But any involvement with the drug trade can get you killed." Or worse, although Jessica didn't say that last bit. Torture, having to flee whatever life you had, Jessica could imagine many things worse than death.

Robin reached down to grab her purse. "I apologize, but I need to get going. My son is coming home from college today, and I'm picking him up from the airport. Can we continue this conversation later? Perhaps over lunch this week? My treat."

"Sure, just let me know what works for you." Jessica said.

"That's great timing." Clarice rose from her side of the sofa. "Jessica, I'd love for you to go to the studio with me and help get Tela settled. I'd be especially grateful if we could get there before dark."

Jessica sighed. She'd have to put off her studies until later, but her mom and her dog needed her.

# Chapter 4

Jessica followed her mother's minivan to the pecan orchard, her second visit in as many days. Tela sat beside her in the truck's front seat, excited to be going somewhere. The evening sun was already dropping below the western horizon, and she combated the night's chill with the truck's blasting heater.

When they reached the pecan grove, Jessica stepped out of truck, her vision filled with huge tree branches stretching toward the evening sky. A Halloween party or haunted maze would have fit this location perfectly, with rows and rows of black trees extending until nothing but shadow remained. And now she knew bones lay beneath them.

"Hey mom, I'm going to take Tela for a walk. If she doesn't get some exercise soon, she'll bounce and bark the rest of the night."

"That sounds good. Would you mind checking out the studio with me first?"

Jessica hadn't realized the depth of her mother's fear. Clarice dropped the keys twice before slotting them into the lock and opening the door. Perhaps it made sense, because her mother had never lived alone. She'd gone from her parents' house to the sorority house to marrying her father. Jessica had lived alone almost half her life, and while her mother held some responsibility for that, that didn't lessen her mother's fear.

"Are you sure you want to stay out here? You're welcome to crash at our place a little longer." Angus would certainly agree to Jessica's offer, he always wanted to take care of people.

"I need to do this. I need to be on my own," her mother said. "But I do appreciate the dog."

Tela had run inside the studio and sniffed every corner and now stood in front of them waiting for her next adventure. Jessica took a quick tour of the place to make sure no bogeyman hid behind the shower curtains or under the bed.

"All clear," she said after checking the bedroom.

Her mom bustled around the small kitchen, putting away dishes from last night's party. "Do you need any help with that?"

"No. You take Tela for her walk, then you should probably get back home to your husband."

Jessica laughed. "Angus won't be home for hours, and he's plenty capable of taking care of himself."

Her mother turned toward her and leaned against the counter. "I know I wasn't there to teach you this stuff, but if you want a happy marriage, you need to keep your man happy."

The comment started a fire in the pit of Jessica's belly. She hated the way her mother fawned over men. Had she always been this way, or was it a result of being trapped in a house, caring for her father for so many years?

"Angus married me for who I am. If he'd wanted Suzy Homemaker, I'm sure he could have found her." Jessica slipped out the door before her mother could respond.

She headed back down the irrigation ditch to where they found the bones. Now marked off with caution tape, Tela's original hole had grown much larger. Someone must have come back and excavated the rest of the skeleton.

It took all her strength to hold Tela back from the pit. Dogs didn't recognize police tape. Jessica finally turned her in a different direction and let her scamper through the trees in the growing darkness. As day turned to night, the orchard slipped into eeriness. Shadows seemed to move behind the trees, and the hairs rose on Jessica's arms. She called for Tela and jogged back to the studio.

She opened the door to her mother sipping tea in a plush armchair under a red and green crocheted throw. Warm light filled the room, and the smell of cinnamon hung in the air. Tela lapped water from a dish on the floor, then curled into a ball at her mom's feet. The cozy scene could have jumped out of a magazine or painting.

"You're sure you're okay here?" Jessica asked.

"Completely. Tela will protect me." Her mom bent over to pet the dog's silky ears, and Tela raised her head and licked Clarice's fingers.

Traitor, Jessica thought, but in the very best way possible. "Lock the door after me," she said as she left them behind.

---

Jessica returned to her quiet house and opened her laptop. On the drive back she'd thought about the coincidence that her father and Robin's might have connections in the drug trade because of its prevalence in the region. The El Paso/Juarez border had crossed goods of value for centuries. Drugs had likely been part of this cargo from time immemorial.

Her father's stint as district attorney had occurred during likely the most dangerous part of this saga. The rise of the Juarez drug cartels and subsequent violence that erupted in the streets of the Mexican city had headlined many newspapers. She knew little of that earlier time before Robin's father died. Back then, stories of the drug trade focused on Miami, or at least that's what she remembered from reruns of *Miami Vice*. But of course, it had been here as well.

She fell into a research hole about the drug trade in the seventies and eighties. The newspapers told stories of people shot in their El Paso offices, planes landing in the desert at night, drugs hidden in car tires or human bodies. An alleged drug kingpin hired an actor's father to kill a judge the day of his sentencing. El Paso had been the wild west, not just in the late 1800s, but a full century later.

None of those articles mentioned Paul Brown. Searches on him tended to bring up the society pages. His marriage, a stint as president of the chamber of commerce, support for the symphony and Episcopal Church.

Jessica's phone alarm beeped. Nine o'clock. Angus would be home soon. She called Clarice. "Are things quiet out there?"

"Very quiet. Tela is wonderful company. Thank you for lending her to me. I hope you don't mind that I gave her some roast beef as a snack along with her dinner."

"She's going to come home spoiled, isn't she?" Jessica smiled as she said the words. She couldn't resist that dog's pleading eyes either.

"Well, since you haven't given me grandchildren to dote on, she'll have to do."

Jessica almost hung up the phone. Her mother always had to push things just a little too far. Heck, she'd only been back in Jessica's life for two years. She hadn't been a good mother, and Jessica doubted she'd be one either. Neither of them deserved the responsibility of raising a child.

Changing the subject seemed a better course of action than hanging up or starting yet another guilt-fueled argument. "Did you know Robin when you were younger, and do you remember when her father disappeared?"

"She was a couple of years older than me, and we went to different high schools, so I didn't know her back then. Later, though, we met at the junior league. We became friends, although we weren't particularly close back then. I'm not sure why. I think she's wonderful now. A real life-saver."

"What about her dad?"

"I remember when he disappeared. It was in all the papers. I always thought her brother did it. He committed suicide just a few months later, so it made sense."

"Wow. That's tragic. Did you know her brother?"

"Oh, no. He was much older than me. I think I was twelve when this all happened, and he would have been eighteen? It's a big difference when you're that age."

"Okay. Should I check in with you in an hour or so?"

"No. I'm fine. Besides, Tela and I are going to bed soon."

"Good luck with that. Remember to make sure she sleeps in her bed. If you let her in yours, she'll wake you up all night long."

"We'll see. Good night and thank you again. I'll take good care of her."

Jessica ended the call with a promise to visit the shelter to find a new dog for Clarice. She already missed Tela, although her dog's important job tonight made her proud.

She dipped back into her research, this time focusing on the days just after Paul Brown's disappearance. It took two weeks after the date Robin had given her for the first headlines to show up. *Local Man Missing.* An ongoing investigation, a number to call for anyone who had information, but no rumors or speculation. The articles mentioned the distraught wife and teenage children, as well as Charles Gordon, Brown's business partner.

According to the papers, no one had any idea where Paul Brown had gone. The last person to leave Brown Insurance that Friday had seen him in his office and waved goodbye. He'd never gone home. His tan Cadillac Seville remained missing.

Maybe he'd gotten in that car and driven away. Jessica had certainly thought about doing that a few times in her life. But most people stayed put, especially those with families and successful companies.

The articles tailed off, and then, six months later, Colby Brown committed suicide in his parents' home. While the newspapers mentioned his father's disappearance when reporting on this latest tragedy, blatant speculation linking the incidents hid between the lines.

Seven years after his death, Jessica found a notice in the back of *The El Paso Times* that Paul Brown had been declared deceased. Later that same year, the family made the papers again, this time for a more joyous occasion, the marriage of Robin Louise Brown to Richard Derek Saunders.

Jessica pushed the laptop away and sat back. Foul play had to be involved. Except why didn't they find the car?

She heard a car door slam, then footsteps trudged up the steps. Normally, Tela would have rushed to the door, bouncing and barking.

Jessica missed her dog. But the man coming in the door would make everything better.

Angus pushed the door open, bringing a blast of cold air with him. He slid his jacket off and rubbed his hands together before running them through his shaggy brown hair. "Man, it is getting cold out there."

"There's supposed to be a storm on the way in a few days. We'll have to keep each other warm." Jessica winked at her husband.

A smile lit his face, carving deep dimples into his cheeks. Jessica still couldn't believe her luck. Her best friend since kindergarten, she'd gone years refusing to believe they belonged together. An optimist, he'd always appreciated life's gifts, while she spent years broken and searching for fulfillment in the darkness of booze and strangers.

Some people hit rock bottom. Jessica smashed into it with a fury that shattered the barriers she'd built around her heart. Newly liberated, her heart wanted Angus, and somehow, he'd waited for her, forgiven her, even married her after she'd asked. Who knew she'd get a happily ever after?

"Hey, sit a minute. I've got a few questions." Jessica patted the couch.

Angus sat close beside her on the sofa. She snuggled into him, trying to provide some warmth. "I can't decide whether Paul Brown ran out on his family or something nefarious happened. He disappeared without a trace, and they never found his car."

"Did he have a reason to leave?" Angus asked.

"Not that I know of. His daughter didn't notice anything unusual. As far as I know, there weren't any financial problems, although I'll have to look into that. But if someone had killed or kidnapped him, why did his car disappear too?"

"Without the car, no one knows what happened. That's a good reason to make it disappear."

"Good thinking," Jessica said. "But how easy is it to make a vehicle disappear?"

"In El Paso in the eighties, hell, you could leave it on a street corner, and it would be gone in a few hours. Leave it in a convenience store parking lot with the keys in it, and it would vanish in seconds. That happened to my uncle's truck down in the valley. Or you could always drive it into Mexico or out to Los Angeles. Making a car disappear is easy. A body, not so much."

"Well, the body may have come back to haunt us. Although, it's probably just as likely that the body Tela found is unrelated to Robin's father."

"I've been wondering about that. Why does Robin think the body they found is her father?"

"I think she's wanted to know what happened to him for years, and it brought up a lot of emotions. She wants me to figure out what happened to her father regardless."

Angus gently took her face and turned it until she stared directly at him, her nose just inches from his. "Can I tell you how happy I am that you are working on a case where the guy died forty years ago? You've almost died twice tracking down people. This case seems far safer."

"I hope so. But it's going to be a lot harder to solve." Jessica closed the gap between them and pressed her lips to his.

# Chapter 5

Fifteen minutes before noon, Jessica left the office and strolled toward the heart of downtown El Paso to meet Robin for lunch. She passed the massive federal courthouse, a modern structure in desert colors. To her left, a building from the early 1900s with graceful scrollwork, arched windows, and balconies spoke to a more genteel era. Ahead, the smokey glass of the county courthouse cast an eighties glow on its surroundings. This mish mash of buildings happened in most downtowns. Through luck or poverty, El Paso had kept a much larger portion of the graceful, historic buildings than most cities.

That included One Texas Tower, the building where Jessica headed. Robin had requested they meet at Café Central, perhaps El Paso's most expensive restaurant. She'd said she'd treat, so Jessica agreed.

Jessica had dined there before, back in her real estate days when corporate clients from the Midwest and East Coast wanted to meet the Mexican landowners and entrepreneurs they'd need to partner with to move their factories to Ciudad Juarez, just across the border from El Paso. Jessica had rarely bought meals then either, not with the games of one-upmanship men from different nationalities played with each other.

She passed through a small triangular plaza best known for its exact replica of the Aztec calendar. She glanced at the colorful monument as she strolled by. A man on a cell phone caught her eye. Something about him seemed familiar. A couple of steps further on, she stopped and turned around. His phone no longer at his ear, the man stared openly at Jessica.

She had noticed his light shirt and dark pants, but now realized he wore an El Paso Sheriff's uniform. Tall and broad shouldered, his bulk seemed familiar. He was the sheriff who'd arrested her at Dominion, the ranch owned by a twisted pastor and his wife.

Fury slammed into Jessica. If this guy had listened to her, they would have gotten to the Guatemalan girls earlier. So much heartache would never have happened.

She stomped back to him. He looked surprised but didn't back down. Instead, he put his hands on his hips and stood up straighter.

"You're the deputy who arrested me. Why didn't you listen when I told you I heard voices in that locked building?" Her words flew at him like spikes of anger.

"Ma'am, you were trespassing on someone's property."

"What are you guys trying to hide? I suppose you know what went down out there. You could have stopped that." She wanted to pound his chest with her finger or fist, although he might consider that assault. She'd already spent enough time in jail.

"I don't know what you're talking about." His eyes changed from the hard stare of when she approached. They seemed to soften, perhaps with guilt. Or maybe that's what happened when he lied.

She crossed her arms, making it harder to throw a punch. "I'm going to find out what's happening in the desert. And I will discover what the Sheriff's Department's role is."

He shook his head but didn't respond. She noticed his name badge, T. Guerra. He didn't look like a bad guy. Probably about her age, he had dark eyes and wore his black hair in a buzz cut.

She tried a different tack. "If you know of anything that would help me find out what's going on, I'd appreciate hearing about it."

He actually rolled his eyes at her. Jessica fumed. She'd much rather solve this mystery than go meet Robin for lunch. But clearly, she wouldn't get far with this guy. "I wish someone in your office would take these crimes seriously."

"We take all crimes seriously." He said it with conviction.

"Deputy Guerra, if that were true, you would have helped those girls that night. You didn't."

"You . . ." He started to say something but stopped himself. He ran a hand over his shorn hair. "You have a good day, ma'am." Then he turned and left.

Jessica stared after him as he crossed the street and walked toward the county courthouse entrance. She wondered if he could feel her gaze following him. Asshole.

The detour made Jessica late for lunch. She swung open the large glass door and stepped into the elegant, tiled entryway. The tiny restaurant had a bar to the left and a dozen or so white-clothed tables to the right. She spied the door to the private dining room down a short set of stairs. She'd often wondered what kind of deals had gone down in that room over the years.

Motion caught her eye, and she turned to see Robin waving at her from a table near the window. Jessica waved back, then removed her coat and handed it to the host before joining Robin.

"Thank you for meeting me here. I love this restaurant and don't get downtown often enough to enjoy it." Robin gave her a warm smile and picked up the leather-clad menu.

Jessica smiled back, somewhat out of place sharing a table with this woman in her fuchsia wool dress and matching jacket. Chunky, expensive-looking jewelry decorated her throat and wrist. Jessica's black pantsuit and cream blouse made her look more like the help than a lady who lunched.

She shook her head, dispersing the thoughts. Just because she was here to work didn't mean she couldn't enjoy the meal. She opened the menu and quickly decided on a sandwich. Would Robin have cared if she ordered the $120 wagyu steak?

How much money had she inherited? Jessica hoped Robin wouldn't mind her delving into her family's finances. Money rooted many crimes.

When the waiter arrived, Robin ordered a glass of chardonnay and an ahi salad. Jessica asked for the French dip, which blessedly came "El Paso style" with green chiles and jalapeño au jus.

"Don't you want a glass of wine?" Robin asked.

"No, thank you. I've got to get back to work after this." Jessica wondered how close Robin and Linda had been back when Paul disappeared.

"Your mom says you're a paralegal."

"Yes. I'm working on my law degree."

"That's wonderful. My son, Taylor, is thinking about becoming an attorney too. Although, his dad expects him to take over the family business. Taylor is who I went to pick up last night, and he was so excited about learning what happened to my dad that he insisted I set up this lunch immediately."

"There's no guarantee I'll be able to find the answers you want. Your dad disappeared a long time ago."

"I have a good feeling about this. Besides, your mom says you have a sixth sense about finding people."

"My mom tends to get carried away. I've found people in the past because I'm ridiculously persistent, but I'm unsure what clues are left in a case this old."

"Well, I'll answer any questions you have. I've asked my mom to talk to you as well." Robin sighed and her perky demeanor faded. "She's not happy about it, but she'll come around."

"Doesn't she want to know what happened to her husband?" If the mother wouldn't talk to her, Jessica would have little to explore.

"She's in her mid-eighties, and frankly, age has made her grumpy. I'll get Taylor to talk to her. She'll do anything for that kid."

"How much do you know about your family's finances from when your dad died?"

Robin took a sip of the recently arrived wine and seemed to think about the question. "That's hard for me to answer in any detail. I was only fifteen at the time and didn't think much about money. I guess that tells you something though. Money wasn't ever anything I had to worry about. Neither before my dad disappeared nor after."

Must be nice. Jessica banished the ungrateful thought. No kid controlled things like that. "Was your mother very involved in the business?"

"I don't think she had anything to do with it at all until after my father disappeared. She definitely started keeping an eye on things after that. Dad's partner ran the day-to-day stuff, but he met with my mom quite a bit."

"And now your husband runs the business?" The questioning led Jessica down a path she wanted to follow. Where had Dick Saunders come from and how had he become so powerful?

"Yes, for years now. I think Mr. Gordon, left the company just a few years after Dick started there."

"Would you walk me through the timeline?" Jessica asked.

"Sure. Dick and I met in college. He was a year older than me. We met at a frat party, and I think I fell for him the moment my eyes saw that rugged face."

Jessica thought about the man just this side of portly whom she'd met on occasion. Rugged didn't fit him today, but time could be hard on people.

"You look skeptical," Robin said. "Believe me, he was both handsome and a gentleman, and that combo was hard to come by at the University of Texas in the nineties."

"Oh, I'm sure he was great." Jessica chided herself for not keeping a poker face. She didn't like the guy, but if she wanted information about him, that couldn't show. "When did you marry?"

"Pretty much the second I graduated. He had such a kind heart that he decided to move to El Paso for me. He had all kinds of prospects, and I've never forgotten this sacrifice."

"And you were an artist?"

"Well, I had dreams of gong to New York and making it as a sculptor. There were times when I thought I'd never move back to El Paso. The city became such a dark place after dad disappeared and Colby died. But being with Dick helped me understand the importance of family."

Jessica kept quiet, hoping Robin would share more. Dick didn't sound like any twenty-year-old man she'd ever met and seemed nothing like the person he embodied today.

"We came back here after college. That's when I built the studio. I used to go out there while Dick worked. But then I got pregnant, and raising a family takes a lot of time and effort." Robin seemed lost in her own story, her eyes no longer focusing on Jessica. The wistful moment passed, and she refocused and smiled. "Anyway, I learned I'm better at determining talent in others than producing art myself."

Perhaps she spoke the truth, but she seemed to have left a part of herself behind. People chose their paths for a reason.

"Tell me about when your husband went to work for your dad's company."

"It happened immediately. I think he was a godsend to my mother. She wanted eyes on the family business, and I certainly wasn't the person for that. She used to spend a lot of time looking at financial reports over the kitchen table. I think it's how she stayed connected to my dad after he was gone."

"But I thought you said Charles Gordon ran the company after your father."

"He did. I mean he was president of the company, but my mom held sixty percent of the shares. She wanted me to change my major from fine arts to business." Robin shook her head. "That would never have worked. Math isn't my strength. Fortunately for the business, Dick is a math whiz. Mr. Gordon only stayed for a few years after Dick and I settled in El Paso—just long enough for Dick to learn the ropes."

"Do you know where he went? He might be a good person to speak with about your father's disappearance." To find the truth, she needed to talk to people outside the family. He probably wouldn't have shared with his wife and children his involvement with drugs, mistresses, or other nefarious reasons one might disappear.

Robin sighed. "I don't know what happened to him. I don't think he left on the best of terms. Mom supported Dick becoming the company president instead of Mr. Gordon. He wasn't happy about that."

"I bet not." Jessica waited for more.

"Dick wanted to fire him, but mom demanded they give him a payout. It was one of the few times they argued. Dick hates to leave a dime on the table, but mom said Charles deserved the money because he'd held the company together after dad went missing. They had a terrible row." Robin picked up a fork and stabbed her salad.

"How much money were they talking about?"

"Oh, I don't remember. You can ask Dick about it. Or Mom."

Clearly, Robin didn't want to return to that memory. Which made the situation even more curious to Jessica. She needed to talk to Robin's mother and find Charles Gordon.

"I'm so glad your mother came back to town," Robin said, leading the conversation in another direction. "Her artwork is astounding. I'm featuring it at our annual winter party. You'll have to come. I'll send you an invitation. Bring your husband."

"Um, thank you." Jessica took a bite of her sandwich, mostly to fill her mouth so she wouldn't say something stupid like she couldn't imagine anything worse than socializing with Dick Saunders. She'd already thought him shady, and hearing Robin's story made him appear ungenerous as well.

"The party is a lot of fun, and everyone in town is there." Robin droned on about the fete while Jessica finished her meal.

"Oh, and we always make a big donation to a charity. I want to make sure the gallery gives back to the community."

Jessica's ears perked up. "Have you thought about donating to Casa Sagrada? They help the immigrants in detention centers, many of whom are women and children. The Guatemalan girls I found at Jeremy Wright's ranch are there, and I want to find a way to help them."

Robin stalled for a minute, and Jessica could almost see the thoughts crossing her mind. She likely donated to organizations like the symphony or a museum. Jessica kept her face still but delighted in watching the struggle.

"You know, I think that sounds like a wonderful idea. Can you send me some information on them?"

"Absolutely." A huge grin spread across her face, and Jessica put all the warmth into it she could. "Thank you."

Robin waved at someone behind Jessica. Jessica turned to see Dick Saunders striding toward them.

He leaned down and kissed his wife on the cheek. "You didn't tell me you were going to be downtown today," Dick said.

"I'm here to have lunch with Jessica Watts," Robin gestured toward Jessica. "I've hired her to help me find out what happened to Dad."

Dick's bulk turned toward her. "Hi. Dick Saunders," he said, thrusting a hand in her direction.

"I know. We've met before," she said, shaking his outstretched hand.

Dick squeezed her hand with more pressure than necessary, then dropped his head toward his wife. "You know I would have hired a real private investigator for you."

Jessica heard every word clearly. Asshole.

"She's found people before. I think she'll be great at this." Robin backed up Jessica immediately. Her voice didn't challenge her husband, just showed her excitement about the project. "Oh, and she had a great idea for this year's holiday party charity, Casa Sagrada." Robin's eyes stayed focused on Jessica.

A storm cloud passed over Dick's features. "I thought we were donating to the symphony again."

"We gave to them last year. It will be good to mix it up. And I hear Casa Sagrada is really helping refugees.

Dick sighed as if exasperation leaked from his very soul. He looked at his watch. "We should probably look at this more tonight. I have a client meeting right now."

His tone reminded Jessica of scolding a small child. Robin seemed to brighten, as if she'd just won a point in a game. A game Jessica didn't want to get trapped in.

Before they left, Jessica asked Robin about interviewing her mother. "I'm sure it's unpleasant for her to revisit your father's disappearance, but it's critical I speak with her to have a shot at solving this mystery."

"Why don't we meet at her house tomorrow morning. She gets up extremely early, so we could meet before you go to work. Say seven o'clock? She's less grumpy in the mornings."

"That sounds great," Jessica said.

"Mom is . . . well, she might not be happy to see you or to talk about that era." Robin's voice dropped as if she feared her mother would overhear them.

"It would really help. Also, did anyone ever look at your father's old bank records?" She hated suggesting that it might expose unusual sources of funds, gambling debts, or a wad of cash leaving to start a new life, but if the mom wouldn't talk, she would have to get the information somehow.

"I think there are records dating back to the ice age in my dad's study. That's another good reason to meet at my mom's"

Jessica took down the mother's address. Rim Road, one of the most exclusive streets in El Paso. This case was about to get interesting.

# Chapter 6

When Jessica returned to the office, it surprised her to hear someone in the back. Upon entering the kitchen, she found Linda, who'd spent the last few weeks at the courthouse working on a big lawsuit. Her boss back in the office meant the case settled early.

Linda poured herself a cup of coffee from the pot Jessica had brewed hours earlier. She placed it in the microwave and set the timer to four minutes. It would come out bitter and burned.

"I'm happy to make you a new pot. And four minutes is a long time to heat a single cup of coffee." Jessica had learned early that coffee merely delivered heat and caffeine to her boss, not flavor.

"It'll be fine. How was your meeting with Robin Saunders?

"It went well. I'm meeting her mother tomorrow. Hopefully, she'll have more information since Robin was just fifteen when her father disappeared."

"You're meeting with Barbara Brown? Don't tell her hello for me." Linda crossed her arms but kept her gaze on the microwave window.

Jessica's eyebrows slid up her forehead, surely conveying her shock at the statement. "Not your favorite person?"

"That woman is an ice queen." Linda pulled her coffee out of the microwave before it beeped. She leaned back on the counter, wrapping both hands around the mug.

"Please, tell me more." Jessica leaned against the opposite counter, mirroring her boss.

"My interactions with her were a long time ago, but both she and her husband always pressured Colby to be someone he wasn't."

"I think most parents do that. Except for mine." Her parents hadn't even bothered being around, although given her current volatile relationship with her mother, maybe that hadn't been all bad.

"Yeah. Mine were all over me too, but not like the Browns were with Colby. I don't know about you, but I aimed for the perfect, studious, self-motivated daughter. My parents pushed me, but not nearly as hard as I pushed myself."

"I was not that person. Mostly I was confused in high school and thought everyone who looked at me saw a criminal's daughter."

"That must have been tough." Linda's voice softened, unusual in the petite blond who consistently projected toughness. "Colby didn't know what he wanted to do with his life, but he knew for certain it didn't include taking over his father's business. Mostly, at eighteen, he just wanted to have fun. I'm sure he would have figured life out eventually." Linda took a sip from her mug and screwed up her face like it tasted awful. She took another gulp.

"Colby opened up a whole new world to me. I'd never skipped school before I met him, never rafted down the Rio Grande, never made love under the stars in the soft desert sand."

Jessica giggled. She'd never seen this side of Linda before.

"That's probably more than you wanted to hear. But truly, I would be the world's most boring human but for Colby. I've never seen a smile so filled with joy. When you mentioned him the other day, it brought all of this back to me. I still miss him." The wistfulness in Linda's voice hit Jessica like a desert breeze. It made her want to grab Angus and take him out to the furthest dunes for a night of romance.

"I wish I'd met him," Jessica said.

"He'd be someone different now. I think we all are. Anyway, good luck with Mrs. Brown."

"Hey, I've got a question for you. Did you know Paul Brown's partner? A Charles Gordon?" Jessica asked.

"No, I don't remember him. We were kids when his dad died, and I left for college soon after. Once Colby died, I almost never interacted with the family. I run across Robin occasionally at events in town, but that's about it."

"Speaking of events, I guess Robin throws a big party at the gallery every winter. She told me they donate to a local charity each Christmas, and I asked her to consider Casa Sagrada. She said she would."

It was Linda's turn to laugh. "Man, I bet Dick will hate that. He doesn't seem like the pro-immigrant type."

"I agree with that. He's one man who truly lives up to his name."

"True." They both chuckled, but then Linda stilled. "Be careful with that one. We don't know how deeply he's involved with that gang the Guatemalans ran into in the desert."

"I'll be careful." But Jessica also wanted to know how deep those relationships went. And she planned on finding out.

———

The next morning, Jessica drove along Rim Road as the sun rose. The street had earned its name because of the way it skirted the southern edge of El Paso's mountains. As she drove higher, the south side of the road fell away to an astounding view of downtown El Paso and the giant city of Juarez stretching toward the horizon. The sun glinted off the glass of buildings, making the entire valley glow in the morning light.

To her right, some of El Paso's early mansions sat far above the riffraff below. Broad lawns led to stately multistory homes, many with balconies where the wealthy could view the economic churn of the cities but not get their hands dirty. More recently, much grander mansions began scaling the mountain's side. Their modern architecture, with concrete slabs and soaring panes of glass, caught the light of the desert in far flashier ways than the adobe and brick of Rim Road. It signaled the difference between new money and old.

Her phone navigated Jessica to a home set back on a lot with a large semicircle drive. Tall pines shaded the driveway and cast shadows on the home. The house itself reminded Jessica of something from an eighties rerun, *Dallas* or *Falcon Crest*. Dormers punctuated the high-pitched roof which dropped to a series of white columns fronting a deep, shaded porch that ran the width of the home. Grand double doors painted slate blue matched the shutters on the windows running along the front of the home. Two thigh-high flowerpots on either side of the door overflowed with multicolored pansies, setting off the white-painted brick exterior.

Jessica pulled in behind a Mercedes SUV, hoping it belonged to Robin. Nothing she'd heard so far made her think speaking with Barbara Brown would be easy. Her ancient white truck didn't exactly fit in up here. The gardeners probably drove better vehicles.

She rang the bell, and Robin answered it in seconds, as if she'd waited on the opposite side of the door. While yesterday the woman had been at ease, today her eyes darted nervously.

"Please come in." Robin led her through the foyer. On one side, a room stuffed with ornate wooden furniture upholstered in blue velvet sat atop a faded oriental rug. Across the foyer, a wood-paneled study lay behind closed French doors.

Moving forward, they entered a great room, the first that seemed like it had been updated this century. Leather-clad sofas formed an L, one facing a fireplace, the other a large screen TV. Jessica noticed a kitchen and breakfast area off to the left and a long hallway on the opposite side of the room.

"Why don't you wait here," Robin said. "Mom's not quite ready." Tension emanated from the woman.

"She doesn't want to see me, does she?" Jessica asked.

"Not exactly. She says she doesn't want to relive that time. It has been a long time for her. She remarried, to a local dentist. He died over a decade ago. Recently she's just been holed up here. It's like she's waiting to die. But he was my dad, and I want to know what happened."

When Robin spoke the words, Jessica could see the fire building in her. It was like watching herself as she struggled with how to handle her mother.

"You know what?" Robin said. "Come on back. It's time you met my mom."

They traveled down the long dark hallway. The carpet, strangely, matched the blue of the exterior door and shutters. Perhaps that was a trend in the seventies or eighties. They hooked a left at the end of the first hallway and entered another. Through an open door, Jessica caught a glimpse of the arroyo that backed up to the Rim Road houses. Halfway down, Robin entered a door on the left.

"Mom, I'd like you to meet Jessica Watts."

Jessica stepped into the room. Likely once a bedroom, the space had become a sort of ladies' dressing area. One wall held an open closet. Shoes lined the lower rack, above them hung clothes sorted by length and color, and handbags and hat boxes sat on the top shelf. A large vanity with an enormous mirror surrounded by bulb lined the back wall. The middle of the room contained a sitting area with a matching pair of rose-colored velvet sofas facing each other.

Mrs. Brown, or whatever name she went by now, sat on one of the sofas. Its twin sat opposite a cherry coffee table. Jessica had stepped back in time.

The woman before her wore a wool plaid suit that Jessica imagined Jackie O would have worn. She also had on stockings and pumps. Her hair had been teased within an inch of its life and surrounded her head like a football helmet. Her perfectly applied makeup included lipstick that Jessica swore matched the rose velvet upon which the woman sat.

"Robin!" The woman's voice cracked like a pistol in the small space. "I said I didn't want visitors today."

"Mother. This is important to me. I want to know what happened to my father. If we wait much longer, anyone around when it happened will be gone. Then I'll never know. Please talk to Ms. Watts."

Robin turned to Jessica, her eyes now steely with determination. "Jessica, meet my mother, Barbara Brown Porter."

"Hmph." Ms. Brown signaled her displeasure. "Mrs. Brown is fine."

Robin grabbed Jessica's wrist and pulled her further into the room. "Jessica, please have a seat." Robin sat on the empty sofa, and Jessica perched beside her.

"I'm sorry to have to reopen old wounds," Jessica said. "But you are key to my having a chance of learning what happened to your husband."

The woman's icy gaze tracked first her daughter and then Jessica. "I don't know why you have to dredge all this up. What is it you want to know?"

The loaded question stumped Jessica. If she asked the wrong thing, this lady would throw her out. She might, no matter what. "Robin told me some of the rumors that swirled around your husband's disappearance. I'd love to put some of those to rest and . . . "

"Colby had nothing to do with whatever happened to Paul. He was a wonderful boy." Barbara's comment interrupted Jessica.

"Yes, I've heard that." Linda's description of Colby brought compassion to Jessica's voice. "I'd love to prove that rumor wrong. Will you help me? I'd like to hear what you remember from the time of your husband's disappearance. What do you think happened?"

Barbara's sigh seemed to carry forty years of sadness with it. "I thought he left us. He was gone more weekends than not, hunting and fishing. He loved to be out in the woods by himself or with a group of buddies. I tried to build a good home for him, supporting the business by throwing dinner parties and making connections at the tennis club. The kids always tried to please their father. For a long time, I thought his leaving was my fault. Nothing I did was enough."

"Mom." The shock in Robin's voice turned both women toward her. "You never told me any of this."

"You know how it is with successful men. I'm sure you've felt the same way about Dick." Barbara's voice seemed weary, as if it carried the burden of wealthy women everywhere.

The comment forced Jessica to think about her own mother. Why did these women always sacrifice for their husbands? Didn't they want to lead their own lives? Angus wanted her to be a whole person. They helped each other succeed.

Robin withered under her mother's gaze, and red creeped into her cheeks. "I'm fine. Really. I love my work at the gallery. Can we please focus on what happened to Dad?"

"The gallery has been good for you, and wonderful for the community." Barbara's voice softened. She paused before returning her gaze to Jessica. "I think Paul probably went out to the mountains in New Mexico. He loved to hunt out there. A mountain lion could have gotten him. Maybe a bear." She said the words without passion, as if she'd spent forty years deciding on this version of the truth.

"What about his car? No one ever found it in all those years?" Jessica asked.

"He wouldn't have taken the Cadillac to the mountains. Maybe he rented a truck. He did that a time or two. Perhaps he went with a guide, and whatever got Paul killed the guide as well."

"Did the police look into those scenarios?" Jessica asked. It seemed like an easy thing to follow up on.

"Not to my knowledge, although I'm not sure. That was a really horrible time, and I tried to focus on the kids. It's terrible when your dad disappears. You can see how it's affecting Robin all these years later."

"Yeah. I understand that." Jessica had lived it.

"You're Joe Watts's daughter, aren't you?" Barbara asked.

Jessica nodded.

"So, you do kind of understand. Although, you knew what happened to your father."

"Yeah. Me and everyone else."

"I never understood why your mother went with him. A mother's place is with her children." Disdain flooded the woman's voice.

Jessica refused to take the bait. "Did Paul say he was going hunting that weekend?" Jessica didn't remember the papers mentioning that.

"Not that I recall. Usually, he let me know when he'd be gone, but you know men. Sometimes he just got the urge to leave." The woman looked down at her hands and rubbed the crepey skin. When she looked back up, a tear threatened to fall from suddenly red eyes.

"Oh, Mom. I never knew you thought that." Tears leaked from the sides of Robin's eyes as she reached for her mother's hand.

"That's why I don't like bringing any of this up," her mother said, patting Robin's outstretched arm. Her comforting voice didn't match the icy stare she gave Jessica.

Despite the glare, Jessica tried to make her voice as gentle as possible. "Do you still have your husband's records from that time? Things like diaries and financial information? Perhaps we can find something that proves your theory. That way, you and Robin wouldn't have to live with the rumors about Colby or your husband's potential involvement in the drug trade."

Jessica watched as the woman's gray eyes went cold. "Stop this. Paul wasn't involved in drugs. We'll never know what happened for sure. Leave well enough alone. I refuse to go through any more of this nonsense." Like a switch, anger quickly replaced compassion.

Robin stood, swiping a finger under each eye to smooth away the tears. "Come on. Let's let Mother get some rest."

Jessica stood as well, having no idea how to handle this situation. "It was nice to meet you." She bobbed her head, since the regal woman probably wouldn't shake her hand and curtseying seemed out of the question.

"Well, that didn't go as badly as I thought it might," Robin said as she led Jessica through the hallways.

Barbara hadn't thrown anything except eye daggers and an icicle voice, but Jessica hardly considered their interaction good. Plus, the meeting provided almost no new information about the case.

Robin paused at the foyer. "I guess this is it for the day. Hopefully, you can find something to go on."

Jessica stared over her shoulder into the office. Records either existed or they didn't, no forgetfulness or feelings.

"Was that your dad's office?" Jessica asked.

Robin turned and peered into the room. "Yes. It's hardly been used since he went missing. I've seen Mom in there a time or two, but she wouldn't let her second husband use it."

"Do you mind if I take a look? Maybe I can find some paperwork that would give us a lead."

Robin blew out a big breath. "I don't think my mother would appreciate it. At least not in her current mood."

Jessica took stock of the woman in front of her. She'd seemed to desperately want answers when the body was found. Barbara might not want to unearth the past, but Barbara hadn't hired her.

"If you want to know what happened to your father, I need to use every lead I can get my hands on. Some of them may be in that office." She stared Robin down, waiting to learn whether this case would be impossible or just difficult.

Robin stood a little taller. "You're right. I do want to know, even if no one else does. The keys to the file cabinets are in the upper left hand desk drawer. I'm going to keep Mom occupied. I can probably give you ten or fifteen minutes. Let yourself out when you're finished."

"That's a start," Jessica said and headed for the office. She closed the French doors behind her to cut down on noise, then surveyed the desk.

She opened the drawer Robin had mentioned and found a key ring with three small silver keys and one brass skeleton key. The drawer also held boxes of pencils but nothing else. The center drawer had a selection of pens, paperclips, and other assorted supplies. The one on the right held eyeglass cases and a Mont Blanc box. She opened it and found a gold pen and pencil set. The next drawer down had notepads and a box full of business cards. And a gun.

She slid the drawer all the way out and stared at the wooden-handled black revolver. It looked like something that would have been used in a Western movie, but with a shorter barrel. It had a round cylinder for bullets, and Jessica wondered if it was loaded. She closed the drawer without touching it.

The bottom drawer contained envelopes and yellow legal pads. She moved back to the left side of the desk and the single remaining drawer. It didn't budge when she pulled the handle, but the skeleton key fit neatly into the lock, and she slid the drawer open. Inside, she found hanging files. If she'd owned the desk, she'd have locked the gun drawer instead.

Labels across each tab had years scrawled on them, 1987 through 1996. The ten years after Paul Brown's death. Each file contained two documents, the tax returns for that year and a ledger. Jessica quickly scanned the ledgers. They showed the monthly income and expenses for Brown Insurance. Nothing seemed out of the ordinary.

She returned the files to the drawer and moved quickly to the file cabinet. The drawers wouldn't budge, but the remaining keys unlocked them. The top drawer had no business information but contained the family documents: marriage license, birth certificates, school report cards.

Jessica hit paydirt on the middle drawer. A large section titled *1986* contained credit card receipts, bank information, and other documents that might tell her more about Paul Brown. She quickly leafed through them.

The Browns had several bank accounts, one which contained regular household expenses like groceries and gas. The other had larger expenses, such as tuition to St. Clement's Episcopal School and car payments. A healthy savings account had a deposit of over twenty thousand dollars and monthly thousand-dollar withdrawals. The only note said RG—expenses.

Voices and footsteps interrupted Jessica's search. She quickly shoved the file drawer closed with a metal-on-metal clang.

"What is going on?" Barbara's raised voice carried through the wall right before she swung the office door open. "What are you doing here? Why are you going through my things?"

"I told her she could." Robin stormed in after her mother. "I want to find out what happened to Dad, and Jessica is going to help me."

Barbara turned on her daughter. "I told you to leave this alone. Do you want more heartache? Your father left us. Isn't that enough shame on this family?" Rage filled her words.

"Whoa." Jessica hadn't meant to speak.

Barbara turned at the sound of her voice. "You're one to talk. Daughter of a criminal. Get out of my house."

If Barbara had meant to shame Jessica, it hadn't worked. It had taken her years to forgive her father. He'd made a mistake, and yes, he committed a crime and had been punished. You couldn't change the past, but you could learn to look at it in a new light. "Ma'am, why don't you want to know what happened to your husband?"

Barbara looked at Jessica for long seconds before turning and leaving the room. "Get her out of my house." The words wafted in through the open door as her footsteps faded away.

Robin dropped her head into her hands, seemingly defeated. But then she lifted her head and straightened her spine. "I'm sorry. I thought you'd be gone."

"I should have paid closer attention to the time," Jessica said. "But there's a lot here."

"Like what?"

"Do you have any idea what RG stands for?" Jessica asked.

"Not really. Perhaps something about the pecan grove? Dick always calls it Robin's grove. Why?"

"Maybe that's it. Does your family make regular payments for something related to the grove? I've found monthly $1,000 payments to RG."

"No. We actually lease the pecan grove to one of the larger growers in the valley. They pay us. The only thing we have to pay is annual property taxes."

"Huh. I don't understand this payment. And I haven't even gone through the credit cards yet. There might be payments to a hotel or hunting guide. We should really find out."

"Why don't I get you copies of the credit card statements? Can you show me where they are?"

Jessica unlocked the middle drawer and pulled it open. "They have an American Express card and a Mastercard. I'd love to see the statements for all of 1986. It might give me a good idea of people I can contact as well as an indication of where your father might have gone."

"Fine. I'll drop them by your office. You should probably go now. I might leave too." Robin cast a wary glance toward the door.

"Sometimes it's easier than staying," Jessica said. Although everyone must face their parents eventually.

# Chapter 7

At lunchtime, Jessica drove to the studio to visit her dog. And to see her mother.

While some women might have daddy issues, Jessica had a mother issue. As a little girl, she'd idolized Clarice. They'd argued like most teenagers and moms when she hit those years, but it escalated as the house became a powder keg. Jessica hadn't known why at first, then one night, her father didn't come home.

Through tears, her mom told her he'd been arrested. She'd also told her everything was fine and he'd be home soon. Jessica hadn't realized how traumatic school would become until the next day. Everyone knew. It started with the teachers and spread through the kids like a virus. Her dad was a criminal.

Friends abandoned her. Two or more adults meant whispers and glances. Pity headshakes. Teachers occasionally made snide comments. Bullies had a reason to torment her. Only Angus stayed by her side.

Just when Jessica thought it would never end, it got worse. Her dad's guilty sentence and house arrest were quickly followed by her parents begging her to move with them to Fort Davis, Texas. For a teen, it sounded like a death sentence. She refused. And they left without her.

Alma, then a young attorney, moved in with her and became her guardian. She hadn't known that her parents had also incentivized Jaime Castro, a police officer, to move in next door. They'd kept her safe from bullets, but her parents' abandonment had ripped her insides apart.

Jessica blamed her father for breaking the law, but her mother bore the blame for leaving her. For choosing her husband over her daughter.

Even now, after she understood they'd left to keep her safe from the Juarez drug cartels who didn't like the loose end her father represented, the scars from that time still stung. Yes, she'd dug the knife in some herself, refusing to communicate with them for over a decade.

By the time she'd gotten back in touch, it was almost too late. Her father could barely speak because of a stroke. That had gutted Jessica, but she'd made good on her promise to do what she could to help them. She listened to her father as he slowly formed the words to tell his story and plead for forgiveness. She'd given it freely. When he died, she wished she'd had more time with him.

Things hadn't gone as well with her mom. Tears sprang from Clarice every time Jessica tried to have a true conversation with her about what happened. Jessica hit back with comments that hurt her mom, especially since her father's body had already damaged him beyond repair.

Each time she and her mother reconciled, one of them blew it up. First Clarice, who'd stood Jessica up after promising to meet her, abandoning her all over again. Jessica responded with her own mean streak and a solid fear that letting this woman into her heart might be more dangerous than facing criminals in the desert.

She pulled up to the studio, spying her mom's minivan parked next to it. After seeing Barbara Brown in action this morning, Jessica realized she didn't have the worst mother around. Clarice loved her, even if her heart was too torn apart to do it properly.

When Jessica shut the car door, Tela's head appeared in the window. The dog howled and bounced, making a complete spectacle of herself. When her mom opened the door, Tela raced out and leapt into Jessica's arms. Which would have been fine, except that Tela weighed seventy-five pounds. Jessica fell onto her butt while Tela whined and licked her face.

"I guess I really am going to have to get my own dog," Clarice said.

"Get off, you ridiculous mutt." Jessica pushed Tela aside so she could get up, then rubbed the dog all over her body. Man, she missed this dog. She'd have to change her dirt-caked pants before going back to work, but seeing Tela was worth it.

"Come on in. Let me make you a grilled cheese." Her mom waved her toward the door.

"That sounds great. Thanks. Let me play with Tela for a few minutes and burn off some of her energy."

Jessica chased the dog around a few of the nearest pecan trees. She ran out of energy long before Tela did. The uncomplicated joy of the dog erased the unease that had stayed with her since the encounter with Robin's mom.

When she entered the studio, she walked into the smell of childhood. Her mom slid the sandwich from pan to plate, then cut it on the diagonal. Jessica never cut her sandwiches in half. Her mom placed a small bunch of grapes on the plate, taking her fully back to being six years old.

"Thanks, Mom," Jessica said, trying to suppress a sudden choked up feeling. Allergies, perhaps.

"Of course, sweetie. Come have a seat at the table. Would you like anything to drink?"

Jessica asked for water, which her mother brought over with her own cup of tea. Tela leaned on Jessica's leg as she ate.

"Why don't we go dog shopping at the Humane Society on Saturday morning?" Jessica asked.

"You miss your girl, don't you?" Her mom reached down and stroked Tela's head.

"Sure. But it would also be nice to spend a little time together." Why did offering an olive branch seem so risky?

"Sure, honey. That sounds good." Her mom patted Jessica's arm but didn't seem to pick up on Jessica's emotional vulnerability.

Jessica took a deep breath. Would this relationship ever seem normal? It had to be better than no relationship at all, something that had left Jessica brittle for too many years. Tela rested her head on Jessica's thigh, and she stroked the dog's silky years. Uncomplicated love.

When the time came to say goodbye, Jessica thanked her mom, then gave the dog her biggest hug. She looked up to see the sadness in her mom's eyes.

"I love you too," Jessica said as she stood and wrapped her arms around her mother.

The sound of a truck coming down the gravel drive interrupted them. Jessica grabbed Tela's collar as she barked and lunged forward.

"I wonder who that is?" her mother said.

The county sheriff's truck rolled to a stop and Lefty Griswald stepped out. "Good afternoon, ladies. How are you today?"

"Oh, Mr. Griswald. So nice to see you." Her mother's voice went up an octave and sounded a little breathier than before.

Lefty looked like he almost reached out to hug Clarice, but then stopped and shoved his hands in his back pockets. "Nice to see you again, ma'am."

"Please, call me Clarice."

Uh oh. Jessica watched her mother's cheeks redden. Her mom liked this guy. Jessica wondered if he visited regularly.

"I have an update on the bones we found here," Lefty said. "The medical examiner says they belong to a male. He hasn't been able to figure a time of death, but he thinks the body has been there for several decades."

"Does he think it's Robin's dad?" Jessica asked.

"We won't have the DNA test back for several weeks, but it's a possibility. The most important thing he found is a crater in the skull. He says it looks like blunt force trauma, but the bones are too old to determine whether it happened before or after he died."

"Does he know what kind of instrument made the wound?" Jessica asked. The timing made it much more likely the bones belonged to Paul Brown.

"He said it might have been a shovel or something else with a flat blade. If the wound happened before he died, it would have been enough to kill him."

"Wow." Jessica guessed a body wouldn't have ended up out here all alone unless something had gone wrong. She'd bet the guy had been killed out here. And if it was Robin's dad, maybe she could figure out the who and the why.

"That's frightening," Clarice said. "Robin hired Jessica to try to find out what happened to her father."

Did you find a shovel or any other potential weapons at the scene?" Jessica asked.

Lefty cocked an eyebrow as he looked at Jessica anew. "Why are you involved in this?"

"Oh, Jessica has a reputation for finding people. It's a talent," Clarice said.

Jessica wished her mom would stay quiet. The officer would probably think she was some kind of wacko. "I'm just doing a little research."

"I'm doing the investigating here, but you be sure and let me know if you find anything useful." His tone of voice said he'd just as soon pat her on the head as take her seriously. Fine with her. She didn't need cowboy sheriff here keeping tabs on her. "Hey, I need to get back to work. Hold on to Tela while I leave, and you be a good girl," she said to the dog.

Her mom grabbed the collar as Jessica headed to the truck. She nodded at Lefty as she walked by.

"Would you like to come in for some iced tea?" Her mother's voice floated by as Jessica closed the truck's door. Just how close had her mother and Lefty become?

# Chapter 8

The next day, Jessica procrastinated starting her law school home-work by looking into Charles Gordon, Paul Brown's partner at the insurance company. Money could motivate criminal activity. Perhaps Mr. Gordon wanted more of the company's profits. That would also explain why Dick kicked him out of the company as soon as possible. Not that Dick could possibly be the good guy in any story. Fortunately for him, he hadn't known the Brown family when Paul disappeared.

The search engine had plenty of information on Charles Gordon from El Paso. Some of the articles dated back to the time of Paul Brown's disappearance, including one noting that he'd taken over the company. Whenever a reporter asked what he thought happened to his partner, he said he didn't know but hoped someone found him soon.

Gordon had served on the board of directors of the local community college and the El Paso Mission Trail Association. Jessica also found a number of addresses for him. She plugged the most recent one into a mapping app. Just a few miles away, Copia Tower looked like a large apartment complex. Jessica had seen the building from the freeway.

She couldn't find a phone number for Charles Gordon, so on her lunch break, she jumped in the truck and drove there. She pulled into a parking lot surrounded by a high chain link fence. Unattractive when viewed from the freeway, the building deteriorated as she drew closer. Dirt filled areas meant for grass surrounded the building, and only a few sparse clumps of green pushed their way through. Paint peeled from the trim surrounding windows and doors, and a glass side panel at the main entrance had a crack along its length. The sign on the door indicated the building was a retirement home.

Jessica opened the door to a linoleum-clad reception area with two plastic chairs, one of them filled by a gray-haired woman in a lime green sweatsuit. A young Latina woman with black lipstick and fake eyelashes the size of caterpillars sat behind the lone desk. Double doors to her right opened to a room with tables and chairs, a quarter of them filled with people. The scent of pea soup wafted in from the room and turned Jessica's stomach.

"Can I help you?" the woman at the desk asked.

"Yes, I'm looking for Charles Gordon. I believe he lives here, but I couldn't find a phone number for him online." She approached the desk with a smile, hoping the receptionist would cooperate. The woman in the green scurried from her chair and into the room with the tables after Jessica spoke.

"I'm sorry, but we don't give out information on residents." The receptionist's sullen voice said she didn't give a damn about Jessica's smile.

"So, he does live here?" Jessica asked.

"Again, I'm not allowed to give out any information."

"But what if it's something he'd like to know? Can I leave him a note?"

The woman stared at her but didn't say anything. Jessica decided to outwait her. After a long moment, the receptionist opened a drawer and withdrew a notepad and pen. She shoved it in Jessica's direction.

Jessica quickly scribbled a note to Mr. Gordon asking if she could visit or call him on behalf of her work for Mrs. Saunders. She laid her business card on top of the note and slid it back across the desk. The woman nodded at her and turned back to her computer, giving Jessica no indication of whether the note would reach the man. She shook her head and turned away, the trip a bust.

Just then, she heard a man's voice. "Are you here to see me?"

Jessica turned to see a stooped man in the doorway to the side room. Behind him, the woman in green grinned. Jessica could have sworn she saw a twinkle in the woman's eye. Jessica gave her a quick wink.

"Are you Charles Gordon?" she asked the man.

"I am. How may I help you?"

"I've been hired by Robin Saunders. She wants to find out what happened to her father."

He escorted Jessica to his apartment on the eighth floor of the building. She might not have followed him had she known he lived in a tiny studio apartment. It contained only an unmade bed, a reclining chair facing a TV, and a card table with two chairs.

"Please, have a seat." He gestured to the table. "Would you like something to drink? I can offer you a glass of water."

The sparse kitchen took up about six feet of one wall and featured a microwave, a hotplate, and a dorm fridge. She heard the ding of a game show from the adjoining apartment's TV. Mr. Gordon had fallen far from his perch atop one of the area's largest insurance companies. "No, thanks. I'm good."

Jessica sat at the rickety table. "I'd love to hear your thoughts on what might have happened to Paul Brown."

"That was a very long time ago. Why is it coming up now?"

She debated telling him about the bones but decided to keep that to herself for now. "I think Robin has wondered what happened to her dad for a long time."

"Well, I guess that's not really a surprise. That poor girl." Mr. Gordon shuffled over to the table and rested his cane on it before taking the other chair. "What did you say your name was again?"

Uh, oh. She hoped he didn't have dementia. She'd introduced herself downstairs. "I'm Jessica Watts."

"That's what I thought you said. It just occurred to me that you're Joe Watts's girl. Damn near the spittin' image of him with all that dark hair and blue eyes. We used to carry your parents' insurance. That is, until he was convicted and all."

"Yep. I'm his daughter. I'd really like to focus on Paul Brown." She'd love to focus on anything other than the court case that brought her family infamy. People always seemed to delight in pointing out her father's crimes. It worked like a reverse celebrity—all the gossip, none of the popularity.

"What do you want to know? I can't promise I'll remember much, but I'd like to help Robin if I can."

His affinity for Robin interested Jessica, especially since it didn't go both ways. "Were you close with Paul and his family?"

"I'd say we were fairly close. We were partners in the business and worked together for years." Charles raised a hand to smooth the still-dark fringe of hair around his smooth dome.

"But Paul owned the majority of the company, correct? Did you two get along?"

"We got along fine. He was the face of the business, met with the customers, went to chamber of commerce meetings. I ran the numbers on the back end. That's an important job in the insurance business. Insurance is based on risk. Run the numbers wrong, and you can lose a lot of money."

"When was the last time you saw him?"

"The Friday he disappeared. For all I know, I was the last person to see him. Our offices were next to each other. We were both the last ones in the office, as usual, but I left a little early because I had something important to attend to."

"Oh. What was that?"

"I have no idea. It was such a long time ago." Charles stared straight at Jessica.

He'd just lied to her. He'd stared straight at her and concentrated on every word. She'd have bet money he remembered exactly what he'd had to do that long ago evening. The lie alone made her want to know more.

"Did Paul's behavior seem odd that day?"

"Not at all." Charles's shoulders sank and the lines around his eyes smoothed a bit. "I don't remember anything unusual about that Friday. I had no idea anything was wrong until he didn't show up for work on Monday."

"You didn't know he was missing before that?"

"No. I called Barbara when he missed his first meeting, and she said she hadn't seen him all weekend. That's when I insisted she call the police."

"Robin told me he traveled a lot on the weekends. How did you know something was wrong that particular time?" She may have hit the mother lode with this guy. He seemed to have plenty to say about the weekend his partner disappeared, but the police had likely interviewed him back then.

"Because he never missed work." He let out a heavy sigh. "I'll tell you the truth. Paul could be a real ass, and he should have been there more for his family, but the business meant everything to him. He wouldn't have missed work unless something was wrong."

A line caught Jessica's attention. "What do you mean he should have been there more for his family?" She tried to sound casual, but her senses lit up.

"Outside of the business, Paul found it difficult to focus on what was important. He had it all, a beautiful wife, popular kids, money, respect. But instead of taking care of those things, he squandered them by spending time away from home. And it wasn't just the travel. His personal finances were all over the place too. He bought the pecan orchard, invested in a racehorse, imported goods from Mexico." Paul gesticulated with his hands as he spoke, the narrative driving some kind of furor in him.

"Wait. What kinds of things did he import from Mexico? If Paul Brown's investments included drug running, Jessica wanted nothing to do with it.

"Pottery, leather goods, textiles. That sort of thing."

"No drugs?"

"No, not Paul," Charles's vehement response put Jessica at ease. "He wasn't that kind of guy. I don't think he would have done anything illegal. He was just never satisfied with what he had."

"Huh. I'd like to know more about his extracurricular activities." Paul may have run the business, but Charles didn't have a ton of respect for the man.

"You've got to be careful when you turn over stones in the desert." Charles's voice dropped an octave and became almost scary. "Have you ever seen a vinegarroon?"

"No. What's that?"

"It's like a scorpion, but bigger, blacker. They have huge pincers in front, but instead of a scorpion tail, they have a long whip coming off the back of their bodies. I found one under a rock once. Scariest thing I've ever seen."

Jessica wondered if the story was supposed to make her think of something in particular. Is that what had killed Paul? How would he know that?

"Do you know what happened to Paul?" she asked.

Charles waved a hand in her direction as if dismissing her. "Of course not. Maybe he ran away. Maybe somebody killed him. I had to stay around and pick up the pieces. I had to keep the company going and be there for his family. For a while anyway." Bitterness seeped into his voice.

Jessica grabbed at the opportunity. "What happened when Dick Saunders started working at the insurance agency. You didn't stay too long after that."

The man in front of her seemed to shrink, but he looked at her with defiance. "I did. I stayed on another few years. I felt responsible for Paul's family and needed to make sure they were okay. After that, well, Dick and I didn't always see eye-to-eye, but he was the one who married into the family."

Interesting that he chose that phrase. Almost as if he had wanted to marry into the family. She took a shot. "Do you mind if I ask a personal question? I've heard rumors that you were interested in Barbara."

"Barbara is a fine woman, always has been."

Jessica waited, hoping he'd keep talking. He waited her out, until she would either have to ask a different question or leave. She wondered what might open him back up. "You were married before Paul disappeared?"

His eyebrows rose and his cheeks colored as he visibly angered. Jessica had made a mistake with the question.

"Are you here to accuse me of something?" He puffed up like a rooster about to go on the rampage.

"No. Absolutely not." Jessica raised her hands in surrender. He looked ready to fight, and the last thing she needed was to take down an octogenarian.

"I'm just trying to get the lay of the land," she said. "Robin asked me to look into her father's death, and I wasn't even born when it happened."

"You tell Robin she can come talk to me any time. Why would she get you involved?"

Why the hell had she gotten involved? She had a job and didn't need this kind of trouble. But it had found her, just like it always did.

"I'm a family friend, and I have a little experience finding things." Missing women. Philandering priests. What a track record. She stared at him, his head shining under a fluorescent light, his eyes a cloudy brown. He stared straight back as if daring her—to what? Press further?

"There are rumors that perhaps Colby Brown killed his father. What are your thoughts on that?" she asked.

"Colby couldn't find his way out of a paper bag. I doubt he could outwit someone as smart as his father. I'm sure you heard he died of an overdose?" Charles deflated a little, no longer ready for a fight.

"Yes. I thought maybe he overdosed because of the guilt." No one she'd talked to so far thought it could be Colby, yet that had been the prevailing rumor.

"Colby did not get along with his daddy. Paul wanted his son to be just like him. He kept threatening to send Colby to the army if he didn't straighten up. But Colby just wasn't that guy. He was a sweet kid but not too bright. Got involved with marijuana. After his father died and his girlfriend left, he started using the harder stuff. I was around the family then, and I'm sorry about what happened to him." He sounded like his heart hurt thinking about young Colby. Jessica's did.

Stories about Colby reminded Jessica of Angus. At eighteen, he'd aspired to play in a band, hang out with his friends, and get high on weekends. And often on weekdays. Slowly, over the years, he became more serious. He opened a record shop and eventually a music school for kids. But he wasn't the kind of guy who ever wanted an office job. In high school and college, he'd smoked his fair share of pot—they all had. Hell, this was El Paso. What else was there to do? Most kids felt that way.

She looked at Charles. "Is there anything else? Do you have any other ideas about what may have happened to Paul?"

"I have no idea." He rubbed his face with both palms, stretching and scouring the wrinkled skin. "I sure wish it had never happened. I'd be a lot better off if Paul had lived a long and happy life. He'd have put Dick in his place, that's for sure. And he definitely wouldn't have left me in the poor house living off of Social Security. But he just couldn't stay focused on the things he had. He always had to push for more, and I think he probably just pushed someone too far one day. It's a real shame, him leaving that beautiful woman and family. They deserved better."

Another strange sentiment. There definitely seemed to be a lot of emotion under the surface with this one. And he talked about everything as if it had happened last week, not almost forty years earlier.

She remembered Linda saying that Colby thought his father had cheated on his mother. "One more question. Do you think Paul could have had an affair?"

A long sigh emanated from Charles. "I really don't want to speak ill of the dead."

Jessica waited, hoping he'd say more. Instead, he stood and started clearing dishes off the counter. She wondered if she'd talked him out.

Once he'd put the dishes in the sink, he turned and rested against the counter. He crossed his arms but didn't speak.

"Thank you for your time. I'll leave my business card in case anything else comes to you."

He didn't even say goodbye. She let herself out the door and into the run-down hallway. What a sad old man living in a decrepit building. She never wanted to live in a place like this. She wouldn't want her mom to either. Although, her mom looked younger every day now that she was no longer trapped caring for an invalid in the middle of nowhere Texas.

She thought about Charles's last words, all but confirming that Paul had an affair. What if those bones belonged to someone else, and Paul had lived happily ever after with a different woman, maybe even a different family?

She needed to get back into the Browns' house. If something like that had happened, there had to be a money trail.

# Chapter 9

Jessica swung the waiting room door open and stepped inside. Her favorite police officer, Jaime Castro, and her boss Linda huddled together on two hard plastic chairs. Their heads bent close, and their words didn't carry across the small, sterile room.

It surprised Jessica that they'd beat her here. She'd purposely arrived early, excited that she'd finally get to speak to the two Guatemalan cousins she'd rescued from the desert.

The door swooshed closed behind her and Linda glanced up. Her eyes widened, and she quickly straightened. Jessica could have sworn Linda whispered "she's here" as the woman's cheeks turned crimson.

"Hey, you two. What's so interesting?" Jessica asked.

Jaime rose and wrapped her in a hug. It seemed suspiciously like overkill, but she went with it. He'd done too much to help her not to reciprocate.

"How are you doing? How's Angus?" Jaime asked. He wore his police blues, and his heavy belt with all its contraptions rested on his hips. Jessica had pressed against the unforgiving bulk of his bulletproof vest as they'd hugged. They loaded these police officers down like burros.

"I'm good, Angus too," she responded.

"I spent years trying to chase that boy away from her when she was a teenager. He's the only one who wasn't scared of me." Jaime turned his attention to Linda when he spoke.

"Oh, I'm pretty sure he was terrified of you at first, but you eventually came around," Jessica said.

"Yeah. He's a charmer. You sure ended up with the right guy."

"I'm going to let the receptionist know we're all here," Linda said, skittering away. Jessica had never known the woman to skitter.

"What were you talking about when I walked in?" Jessica asked, more curious than ever.

He looked at her, hesitated a moment. "An old case. I told you she used to be on the police force before she was an attorney."

"Ahh." They'd been talking about her father. The sudden certainty of this and understanding Jaime would know she'd want to avoid the conversation, put her at ease. She appreciated the small kindness of not having to address her father's crimes, for once. She glanced at Linda's back as she talked to the receptionist behind the glass. "It's hard to imagine anyone with such a tiny frame carrying all the equipment you have to wear."

"It does seem like they add something new every year," he said. "But make no mistake, that woman is tough as nails."

"I believe it," Jessica said. And she did. She'd seen Linda eviscerate people in the courtroom, not to mention the amount she could drink and the disgusting coffee she could tolerate. Even now her voice rose as she asked to talk to the supervisor.

Within minutes, they were led into a different room. Bare, except for a table and six chairs, the room had scuffed beige walls and a worn green carpet. She hoped its dreariness didn't reflect where the girls lived.

"What was the issue?" Jaime asked once they'd settled into chairs.

"The girls are being moved soon. I'm not surprised. They've stayed here unusually long already."

"Where will they go next?" Jessica asked.

"The government would like to repatriate them to Guatemala, but they haven't found any relatives yet. They may end up in foster care here, or in a facility."

The door opened, and the two girls came in with a thin middle-aged woman who looked exhausted. The cousins had shiny hair, scrubbed faces, and clean clothes. They looked entirely different from the terrified young women from a few months earlier.

When she found them, they'd spent weeks traveling north to the border, then days walking through the desert, only to have most of their family killed the moment they thought they'd found safety. Jessica still didn't know exactly why the girls had been saved, or what horror might have awaited them had she not found them while trying to save a friend.

She smiled at them. The older one, Mari, pressed her lips together and gave Jessica a curt nod. Someone had cut her once long hair to shoulder length. It suited her high cheekbones and cheeks that had grown a little fuller than when they'd first met. Angela, only ten years old to Mari's twelve, kept her eyes downcast. Her shoulders slumped toward the table, and she remained rail thin.

Jessica fumed at the injustice in the world. If that first sheriff, the one who arrested her, had listened to her instead of whatever baser instinct drove him, it would have spared these girls some trauma.

She'd promised Mari and Angela she'd find out what happened to their family. It would help if they had any idea where they'd crossed the border or come across the men with pickup trucks and guns. Unfortunately, they hadn't remembered anything yet.

That wouldn't keep Jessica from trying. She addressed Mari. "¿Has recordado algo del paseo? Quiero encontrar a los hombres que . . . lastimaron a tu familia." She probably shouldn't have asked the question. She wanted to know if they remembered their trip, convince them she wanted to find the men who—she couldn't say mataron, killed—their family, so she went with "hurt." The disingenuous word didn't fool anyone. Mari's eyes filled with tears, and she shook her head.

They could have crossed anywhere in the massive and almost empty land east of El Paso. It was like searching for a cactus spine in the vast Chihuahuan desert.

"Había una charca." Angela's voice came out in a whisper.

Mari looked at her cousin. "¿Qué dijiste?"

"A mami y papi los mataron cerca de una charca." Angela's voice remained soft, but she didn't cry.

Mari did cry. "No lo recuerdo." Her voice sounded despondent at the missing memory. Or, perhaps, Angela had misremembered the men killing her parents near . . . something.

"What is a charca?" Jessica asked, unfamiliar with the word.

"Maybe a pond?" Jaime answered. "We use estanque around here, but I think I've heard that word before."

"¿Cerca del agua?" Jessica asked if she meant near water. The girl nodded.

"¿Recuerdas algo más?" Jessica asked.

Angela shook her head. Maybe she didn't remember anything else, or perhaps she couldn't speak of the remaining memories from that grisly time.

"I will find them. Los encontraré." Deep in her bones, Jessica committed to finding the killers. And then she'd prosecute them. She'd chosen courses in criminal law to help her understand the crimes particular to the border. She also had much to learn from Linda and Jaime. If this case alone ended up as her life's work, it would be enough.

Jessica glanced at the girls again. They'd survive this, but the sadness in their eyes seemed permanent. She toed the large bag at her feet. It contained two backpacks filled with clothes, snacks, and toys. She and Lucía, the teenage family friend who'd also been in the desert that night, had picked out gifts like bead kits and coloring books. "Toys that create beauty," Lucía had said, since these girls had so little left in their life right now.

Jaime and Linda questioned the supervisor. Linda tried to ensure the girls would be placed in the best situation possible. Jessica hoped they'd go into foster care with a family instead of being transported to an agency full of traumatized kids. But so many children, formally called unaccompanied minors by the US government, crossed the border to escape something far worse than a dangerous journey. They threw themselves on the mercy of people in a country with rhetoric and systems determined to shove them away and send them back to the danger they'd fled. The whole system sucked.

Jessica shook her head. She could easily descend into the depths of depression thinking about the immensity of the problem. But if she focused on these two girls who had lost everything yet still had a future, she could make progress.

She wanted to comb the desert, find the place where the girls' families had been shot. She'd start looking for the mystery pond as soon as possible. There had to be bodies and bullet casings. But the huge desert could hide many things. The girls didn't know where they crossed the border, didn't know how much time they'd spent in trucks before reaching the ranch where Jessica eventually found them. But she'd figure it out.

Jaime asked the girls a few questions. Like her, he worried about a bigger conspiracy. He'd mentioned cases all along the border where crimes ended up implicating law enforcement officers from one jurisdiction or another, both Mexican and American. In this case, Jessica suspected the sheriff had some involvement in at least covering up the crime. The case had no leads, and too many, all at once.

She didn't know how long it would take to pull all the threads together on this one. She might be a full-blown attorney by the time they figured it out. But they would. She would. This was her home, and she'd welcome those who needed help and destroy those who defiled her house.

Her heart grew big, looking at these girls and knowing there were hundreds, thousands, like them who needed help. Jessica was good at finding things, at getting the desert to give up its secrets.

The formal questions finally ended. "¿Todo está bien aquí?" Jessica wanted to move the conversation away from crime but wished she hadn't asked if everything was fine here. How did she expect them to answer, holed up here with no idea what would happen next? They probably thought they'd never be fine again.

"Sí. Gracias," Mari said, her eyes now dried from her earlier outburst.

So polite. Jessica doubted everything was fine and didn't want to waste time on pleasantries. But that's what she did, continuing the conversation in Spanish. She learned the staff were nice, the kids were nice, they were fine. Nothing deeper. What had she expected? Girls with nothing learned to tread lightly and not upset anyone.

Jessica reached across the table. Both girls reached their hands toward hers. She hadn't expected this from Angela. The softness of their fingers, despite all their troubles, gave Jessica hope. They were just kids. They had a hard road ahead of them, but they'd make it. And she'd do everything in her power to ensure that.

# Chapter 10

Jessica sank into the couch next to the big glass window overlooking the front yard. She glanced outside just as an El Paso Sheriff's Department SUV drove by. A dark-haired man drove the vehicle, and she wondered for a moment if it was Deputy Guerra. She shook her head. Hispanics made up over eighty percent of El Pasoans. Most people had dark hair.

She hauled her law textbook off the coffee table and opened it. Torts covered private wrongs, such as acts of negligence, assault, and defamation, not exactly her favorite class. She loved "Water Law and the West." Sometimes she felt split into a million pieces, studying for classes, working full time, taking on special cases like trying to figure out what happened to Robin's father. But always in the back of her mind, she thought about the Guatemalan girls and the insidious group that killed their family and seemed to have ties to important El Pasoans.

The law book couldn't hold her attention. Just the word *private wrong* conjured up images of a desert night and frightened border crossers. What did you call it when so many wrongs piled up on each other? People spouted vitriol about immigrants. It sounded like defamation to her ears. Assault had happened that night and would likely have continued with whatever plan the men in trucks had when they drove the girls away. She shuddered.

Earlier in the day, she had looked for water along the border using an online satellite mapping program, thinking the task would be easy. It surprised her how many cattle tanks, runoff reservoirs and tiny bodies of water the desert held. She'd tried to narrow it down, but since no one could lead Jessica to the site where the murders happened, she would have to work the problem in the opposite direction. The men in trucks, the killers, took the girls to Jeremy Wright's ranch. Jeremy had an in with the El Paso Sheriff. That's one of the reasons Jessica had been arrested. Well, that and the trespassing.

Dick Saunders also had some connection to Jeremy Wright. He'd praised the pastor to Jessica's mom, and his position on the school board granted him oversight of the Christian youth group that employed Jeremy.

Could she do honest work for Robin and get close enough to Dick to learn more about the men in trucks? She had to try.

She sighed and slammed the book closed. Normally, Tela would have been curled at the opposite end of the couch. The book closing would have given her an excuse to bark, then come snuggle. Jessica wanted her dog back.

She pulled out her phone and texted her mom, asking if she had time to go to the animal shelter. Then she texted Robin.

*Spoke with Charles Gordon. Still need more info, especially financial data. Any chance I can come back?*

Robin responded first. *Let me look around.*

*Thxs. Did Colby keep records?* She wondered what impulse made her ask about the brother. But really, both requests queried the dead for information. That's what it would take to solve this case.

Fifteen minutes later, her mom responded to her earlier text. *Meet me there in an hour?*

———

Jessica met Clarice at the animal shelter. Her mom spoke into an intercom at the door and said she wanted to adopt a dog. It surprised Jessica when they asked if she had an appointment. That hadn't occurred to her.

They were buzzed in, the sound almost prison-like. Who were they trying to keep out? They entered a covered area and could see chain-link cages and a grassy yard beyond them. Jessica walked toward the dogs, but a woman came out of a side door and asked them to come in and register first.

Two women sitting behind a long counter welcomed them. About her mom's age, they immediately began talking to Clarice about what kind of dog she wanted. Thoughts of prison fled. These friendly women should staff the detention facility she'd visited earlier.

Soon, a young dark-haired woman who interned at the shelter led them back outside. As soon as they reached a place where the dogs could see them, the shelter erupted with barks.

A long row of kennels stretched before them. Large dogs voiced their concerns about the intruders, most of them running forward to confront them. This was exactly the type of dog her mom needed—big, loud, and protective.

Clarice covered her ears. "Are they always this loud?"

"Usually," the young woman said, almost shouting to be heard above the din. "They get excited when they see someone new."

It turned out most of them were excited to see the intern. When the woman approached, tails and bodies wagged, and the dogs quieted.

"They like you," Jessica said.

"They're good dogs. They'll warm up to anyone."

Jessica turned to her mom, who walked down the aisle slowly, pausing in front of each dog for a few seconds before moving on.

Jessica already had a few favorites. A brown Doberman with uncut ears and a long tail. He'd scare the hell out of anyone. A scruffy Australian Shepard mix with one blue eye and one green one, just like Tela, barked especially loud despite his smaller size. He'd be another great deterrent.

Her mom reached the end of the row without approaching any of the dogs. Several large dogs lay in the grassy area beyond the cages. These dogs, seemingly happy in their roomy environs, neither barked nor approached them.

"Is this it?" Clarice asked their guide.

"We've got smaller dogs on this side," the woman said as she led them around the corner. This row of kennels backed up to and mirrored the one they'd just seen. A range of medium and small dogs stretched before them. If possible, they barked even louder than the large dogs.

Clarice resumed her walk. She eyed each kennel and then moved on.

"Hey, Mom. I think a big dog would be better protection." Jessica followed her mom as she walked to the end of the row, then turned around and started back. They'd seen every dog in the place. There had to be forty dogs here, and several would be excellent guard dogs. Her mom didn't seem drawn to any of them.

Suddenly, Clarice stopped. Jessica picked up her pace to see which animal had finally caught her mom's attention. At her feet, a small blond dog looked up at Clarice, wiggled her entire body, and didn't bark once. Wiry hair stuck out everywhere like badly overgrown grass. Her mahogany eyes never left her mother.

"Mom, she's the size of a cat." And she didn't bark. This had to be the worst possible dog for Clarice. Jessica looked into the next kennel where a basset hound mix flopped on the concrete, uninterested in anything around him. Okay, second worst.

The guide joined them at the cage. "This is Sir. She's a terrier/chihuahua mix."

"Sir? As in 'thank you, sir?'" Jessica heard the derision in her voice and gave the woman a smile. It wasn't the guide's fault her mom had stopped at the wrong dog. Although the name was ridiculous.

"Can I see her?" Clarice asked.

"Of course." The woman grabbed a small leash hanging nearby and went into the cage.

As if distressed that another dog might be chosen, the barking inched up a notch. The beginnings of a headache pounded through Jessica's brain. She should have come here on her own, picked out a dog, and presented it to Clarice. The goal was safety.

"Sir, it's your lucky day," Clarice said. "Although we'll have to change your name."

Jessica shook her head. Her mom would choose a cute dog over one that would guard her home. She was too soft-hearted. The thought stopped Jessica. When had that happened? Her mom definitely hadn't been too soft hearted when she'd chosen to leave her sixteen-year-old daughter behind and go into exile with her husband.

Jessica closed her eyes, then spun away from where her mother bent, petting the wiggling dog with both hands. She walked to the larger open area and looked at the dogs sunning themselves on green grass. When would this hurt go away? She'd chastised herself for months. The problems with her parents had happened a lifetime ago. Things had changed. She'd reconnected. Why couldn't she leave the past, and past hurts, back where they belonged?

She ran a finger under her eye where a tear threatened to fall. What the hell was going on with her? She was badass Jessica Watts, a woman who could take on evil in the desert and live to tell about it. Someone who could solve crimes and save people. Not some sniveling little girl who still wanted her mommy.

She took a deep breath, letting anger replace shakier emotions. Her tears dried. What did she care if her mom adopted the wrong dog? Some problems couldn't be solved.

# Chapter 11

Jessica had just sat down at the reception desk with a fresh cup of coffee when the door slammed open. Robin entered balancing several files atop a blue shoe box with an Adidas logo. She dropped the pile on top of Jessica's desk with a thump.

"Here. You wanted more stuff, and I got it. Thank god Mom has a weekly hair appointment. She doesn't even know I was there." Robin arched an eyebrow, and a triumphant look crossed her face.

Jessica smiled. "You might be cut out of the will for this kind of work."

"What's going on in here?" Linda asked, coming in from the back of the office.

"Hey, Linda. It's nice to see you," Robin said. "Jessica asked me to get some files from the house, and to see if there was anything interesting in Colby's room."

"Oh." The noise Linda emitted sounded like someone had punched her in the chest. She walked forward almost in a trance, her eyes on Jessica's desk. She sighed heavily before lifting the files off the blue box. Three white stripes crossed the top of the box, and Linda ran her fingers along them. Someone had sketched the Millenium Falcon and several other spaceships from Star Wars onto the box in ink.

Robin looked at Linda, her eyes glassy. She placed a hand gently on Linda's back. "I found this in Colby's closet."

"I haven't seen this in so long." Linda's voice barely rose above a whisper. She slid a finger under the lip of the lid and lifted. A chuckle escaped, and she reached into the box, pulling out a small green glass bong. "This is Colby's all right."

Linda lifted the device to her nose and sniffed. "It's been too long."

Jessica wondered if she meant it had been too long to maintain its aroma, or whether Linda thought it had been too long since she'd smoked.

Linda set the bong on Jessica's desk, then pulled out three cassette tapes. "Rock mix, love mix, chillin' mix." She set them each on the desk as she acknowledged them. The covers had drawings: an electric guitar, the silhouette of a buxom woman with long hair, and an image of the bong along with a pot leaf. Subtle.

"Was he the artist?" Jessica asked.

"He loved to draw." Linda and Robin said the words simultaneously. They glanced at each other, and Robin slipped her arm around Linda and pulled her into a hug.

"I miss him so much," Linda said.

"Me too." A tear made its way down Robin's cheek.

Linda reached back into the box and pulled out a keychain with a silver peace sign and several keys still attached. Finally, she pulled out a cloth-covered blue notebook. "He kept everything in here," she said. "Poems, musings, drawings, you name it." She ran her hand over the cover but didn't open it.

"Linda," Robin said, pointing at the box.

"Oh, no." Linda placed the notebook under her arm and lifted an envelope from the box. She held it in both hands, breathing heavily. Tears filled her eyes but didn't fall. Then Linda turned the envelope around and slipped a finger under the seal. As she did so, Jessica read Linda's name on the front.

"I can't do this here," she said, before looking at Jessica and then Robin. "May I take it?"

"Of course," Jessica said. Robin nodded.

Linda pressed the envelope and notebook to her chest and disappeared into the back of the office.

"Well, that was intense," Robin said. "I hope you find some answers in those." She pointed at the files, but her eyes darted to the hallway where Linda had gone.

"Thanks for bringing these. I know it's hard to go against your mother's wishes." The memory of Barbara Brown's anger hadn't faded. Heck, she'd probably have disowned her daughter had she found her sneaking out records.

Robin's attention refocused on Jessica as she sank into the chair across from her. "Jessica, you have to give your mom a chance. She's really trying to restart her life here. She needs your support."

Jessica prickled at the reprimand. She had tried. Hell, she'd given the woman her dog. Jessica inhaled slowly before responding. It wouldn't do to piss off a client. "I am trying. I think we're doing a lot better."

Robin nodded, seemingly proud of herself for bringing up the topic. The little, self-righteous tip of her head pushed Jessica over the edge.

"You know," Jessica began. "It would be like if your father was out there living his own life, knowing you and your mom were here, but never reaching out. You might have a few knots to work out before your relationship returned to normal."

That wasn't exactly fair. Her parents had abandoned Jessica, but her mom had written hundreds of letters. Jessica threw each of them away without opening them. She'd thought that would keep the wound from festering. It hadn't.

Robin inhaled sharply and scraped the chair across the tile floor as she stood. "I've got to go." Two steps toward the door, then she was gone.

Jessica shouldn't have chastised Robin. Clarice really seemed to be trying, now that she had her own place. And Jessica had Robin to thank for that. She must be nicer to the people who paid the bills.

When she went to check on Linda, she found her at her desk, resting her chin in her palms. The notebook and letter, still in its envelope, sat on the desk. Linda gazed at Jessica with red-rimmed eyes.

"Are you okay?" Jessica asked.

"Colby was a wonderful guy. He had the kindest heart of anyone I've ever met." Shiny tears and bloodshot eyes made Linda's irises glow like aquamarines.

A pang slipped through Jessica's heart. This eighteen-year-old whom people clearly cared about couldn't defend himself against the rumors. Unlike Angus at that age, Colby didn't have a strong family that always had his back. And Angus had Jessica. She never let him fall.

But Angus's dad hadn't disappeared. His kind and loving mom was Barbara's opposite. He hadn't combatted swirling rumors, and his girlfriend—or whatever they were back then—hadn't left for college. She could only afford UTEP.

"I want to prove he's innocent," Jessica said.

Linda wiped away the tears under her eyes. "I want you to do that. If you need help from me, let me know. Make this your biggest priority."

"Will you let me know if there's anything in the notebook that might help the case?"

Linda lifted the journal from her desk. "Here. Take it. I don't think I can handle this right now. I remember him writing and drawing in it."

Jessica stepped forward and reached for the notebook. Linda's fingers stayed attached for a second before she released it. "Will you keep it in the top drawer of your desk? I'd like to go through it when I'm not so emotional."

"Of course." Jessica wished she could say something to take away Linda's sorrow. The air between them pulsed, heavy with loss. She'd never seen her boss this way. Defeated. Usually, her fierceness scared other attorneys, jurors, anyone she faced. Now, she'd slumped back into her small frame, seeming as frail as a bird.

Jessica would solve this mystery for Linda. For Colby. As well as for Robin. She'd right this wrong and figure out what the hell had happened when Paul Brown disappeared.

She returned to her desk and opened the ledgers. She easily identified most of the expenses. A few she googled. Weekly payments to a car wash company still in business in central El Paso. An accounting firm. The only regular payment she couldn't identify went to RG—the same initials she'd seen earlier. RG received one thousand dollars the first of every month until Paul went missing.

Unfortunately, when she looked up RG, she found a raft of companies. RG Enterprises, RG Products, RG Boots, RG Auto Sales. She wrote each name down on a legal pad. One by one, she looked them up online. She found an investment company, a manufacturer, a boot maker, and a used car dealership. The investment company had formed in the 1990s. The plastics manufacturer had moved to El Paso in 2003. The used car dealer had been in El Paso since 1954. The man she spoke to at the dealership, the son of the original owner, said he couldn't imagine why anyone would make years' worth of thousand-dollar payments to them, although he sure wished someone would. He promised to ask his father about it.

She left a message for the boot maker. The phone rang just before she sent the phone to the answering service so she could leave for the day.

"Linda Reed Law," Jessica said as she answered the phone. "This is Jessica."

"Jessica. Rick Gilbert. You left a message for me."

She couldn't recall a Rick Gilbert, then his initials hit her. "Rick—you're the boot maker?"

"Yeah, but I didn't know this was a law office. Is someone suing me?"

"No." She wondered what kind of person would jump to that conclusion. "I'm trying to find a person or business with the initials RG who worked with or for Paul Brown in the 1980s."

"Man. That was a long time ago. Let me think."

Again, his response surprised her. Maybe she'd hit paydirt. "He used to pay someone one thousand dollars a month, but the initials RG are the only reference in his ledger."

"Whoa, that's a lot of money. My company was a lot bigger back then, and we had sales that big to some of the retailers, but I don't remember a Paul Brown. Did he own a shoe store or boot shop?"

"No, he had an insurance company."

"Hey. Is this that guy who disappeared?"

"Yes. I'm trying to find out what happened to him for his daughter. Would any of the stores you sold to place an order for an exact amount every month?"

"No. Orders were hardly ever for exact amounts like that. Also, I don't know why we'd have had recurring orders from him unless he owned a store."

"I guess it's another dead end then." Jessica had hoped the initials would turn into a clue, but that hope faded with each disappointing piece of information.

"You know, there used to be another RG. The El Paso Saddleblanket Company got our payments mixed up once. I think they tooled leather, saddles and belts and stuff like that. I'm pretty sure they were from Mexico."

"Really?" Hope flashed back into existence.

"Yeah. Now that I remember it, they branded their stuff RG, but just letters, not a logo like I have. They did good work."

"Do you have any idea how I can find them?" she asked.

"Not these days. El Paso Saddleblanket closed ten years ago. Maybe try some of the other boot and bridle stores. I wish you luck."

"Thank you." She'd have hugged the guy if he'd been in front of her. The lead wasn't much, but next to nothing, it shone like a diamond.

Back at her desk, Jessica opened the notebook. A pencil sketch of a woman filled the first page. A younger version of Linda stared back at her. No wrinkle lines marred the face, and Linda's fierceness had gone missing. This girl looked sweet and innocent, words no one today would use with Linda.

Jessica's heart went out to her boss and the artist so clearly in love with his subject. She turned the page. Another drawing. This time, characters from the original Star Wars movie. Luke, Leia, Han, and Chewy. Girls and Star Wars, typical teenage boy obsessions from the early eighties.

The next page held only words in large block letters.

*I HATE HIM. I will not carry on his legacy. I want more from life than running a company I despise. He only cares about money. Mom only cares about appearances. I'm done.*

So, his life wasn't all sweetness and roses. But these musings came from a teenager. At that stage in her life, Jessica hated her parents and might have written something similar if she'd had a journal. She turned the page.

Another drawing. Jessica recognized the sand dunes in the desert outside of El Paso. Evidently, they'd been a refuge for teens long before her time. The scene included a bonfire and trucks spraying sand as they attempted to summit the steep hills. She could almost smell the desert at night—creosote and mesquite.

The next page contained a drawing of a ring. Clearly an engagement ring, it had a modest diamond. Pencil marks around the stone denoted its sparkle.

*She'd never accept. Her future is brighter than me. I won't hold her back.*

Then, in tiny writing at the bottom of the page: *she is my lifeline*

Jessica wanted to rip the page from the journal. Why should Linda have to read this when Colby had taken his own life? Would she blame herself? Jessica would have. But the journal wasn't Jessica's to manipulate. She turned the page.

*I confronted him, told him I knew everything. The asshole. He denied it. He has a son my age. He's lied to us all for so long I doubt he knows the truth anymore. I wish he was dead.*

Damning words. Colby hadn't mentioned names, but it had to be his father. Why else would he care so much? All the remaining pages were blank.

Jessica closed the notebook and slipped it into the desk drawer. She hoped Linda wouldn't look at it tonight, wanted to hide its contents from any prying eyes. Colby's words had neither the power to convict, nor the ability to quell suspicions. That Paul Brown might have another child, another family, left her flummoxed. The monthly payments made sense in light of this new information, but how should she proceed? Her only remaining lead, two initials, didn't give her much to go on.

Still, thoughts that Paul Brown might still be alive and living with a completely different family flitted through her head. The thought stretched reality—he'd be so old now—still, it made her pause. What would Robin think of her dad then? What about Barbara? Could Barbara have known? And if he was alive, whose bones had Tela uncovered?

# Chapter 12

The bootmaker was right. El Paso Saddleblanket had ceased operations years ago. Jessica sighed in frustration. The sound made Tela whimper, and she reached across the couch to pet the dog's head. She loved having her dog back but worried about her mom and the pixie dog she'd adopted.

"What's next?" she asked Tela.

She knew El Paso Saddleblanket had sold Mexican blankets, Native American ceramics and jewelry, western boots, and all kinds of curios. She'd visited the store in downtown El Paso long ago with her parents. It had seemed the size of a football field, with narrow aisles lined with stacks of goods. Now, she might think of it as a tourist trap, but back then she'd found it spectacular.

She typed "leather goods in El Paso" into her computer and the search came back with a list of companies. Most of them manufactured boots, bags, or saddles, although one specialized in gun holsters. Jessica needed a store that would sell leather goods, not manufacture them.

The boot maker had mentioned saddles, so she typed that into the search. Bingo. Images of half a dozen stores packed with southwestern goods and souvenirs appeared in rows on her screen. She started with the first one, calling and asking if they worked with a supplier with the initials RG who made belts, saddles, and other leather goods. On her third call, she got lucky.

"Sure. That'd be Rancho Gamboa," said the woman on the other end of the line.

"Fantastic!" Jessica couldn't contain her excitement. Perhaps she'd broken the case. "How can I get a hold of them?"

"I'm not sure," the woman said. "Abel makes his deliveries the first Tuesday of every month. I can ask the owner for a phone number if you'd like."

"Yes, please," Jessica said. "Would it be possible to speak with the owner directly?"

"I can give him your number if you'd like."

Jessica left her information with the woman. She couldn't contain her excitement that she might actually solve the ancient case. She grabbed the dog and fluffed up her ears, scratching in all the right places. Who'd have thought at eight-thirty on a Saturday morning she'd have made so much progress?

She decided to meet Angus at the music shop where she could work on the books for him. She let Tela into the backyard for some exercise while she showered. As she headed toward the front door, her phone buzzed. She looked down to find a text from Robin.

*Lefty wants us to meet him at the orchard.*

So much for good intentions. She texted Angus that she wouldn't be in today and headed for New Mexico.

———

Jessica pulled into the drive and parked near Robin's Mercedes, Lefty's SUV, and her mom's minivan. Despite the bright sun, the pecan trees looked ominous with their leafless branches reaching for the sky. She zipped her jacket against the chill.

The atmosphere changed as soon as she opened the door to the studio. The aroma of fresh-baked cookies and cinnamon wafted through the air, drawing her into the room.

Lefty and Robin sat at the kitchen counter next to a plate of cookies that rested atop ivory and turquoise Talavera tiles. Her mom's smile brightened when she saw Jessica.

"Come on in. Can I get you a cup of coffee?" Clarice asked.

"I'd love it." Jessica reached for a cookie. "Oh, my god. These are delicious. What are they?" Butterfat, sugar, and sharp cinnamon melted on her tongue.

"They're chocolate chip cookies, but I left out the chocolate chips and swirled in cinnamon sugar instead." Clarice's face lit up at her daughter's compliment.

"They're extraordinary," Lefty said. Jessica caught the wink he gave her mom. Not for the first time, she wondered what kind of relationship those two had. She might have to talk to her mom about it.

"Why did you call us out here?" Robin asked. Her hand tightly grasped her coffee cup, and frown lines crossed her brow.

"Well, I've got some news about the bones," Lefty drawled. No wonder Robin was uptight. Her property, and perhaps her family, were in the crosshairs of Lefty's news.

Jessica turned toward Lefty, who was staring at her mother. "Well?"

"Well. We got the results back from the lab. Robin, those are your father's remains."

"Oh!" Robin's hand flew to her mouth, and her eyes brimmed with tears.

Jessica laid a hand on her back. "I'm sorry."

"Oh, honey," Clarice flew to Robin's side and wrapped her in a hug.

Jessica pulled a paper towel from the holder and handed it to Robin once she'd pulled away from Clarice.

Robin dabbed at her eyes. "It's okay. At least now we know what happened."

"About that," said Lefty. "The medical examiner determined the cause of death was blunt force trauma to the head."

"What?" All three women turned toward him in unison.

"I'm afraid your father was murdered."

Robin's voice hitched in a gasp. Other than that, the room stayed eerily silent. Finally, her mom's dog whimpered at Jessica's feet, breaking the spell.

"As I'm sure you'll understand," said Lefty. "The sheriff's department will take over the investigation." He looked at Jessica as he spoke.

"Of course." For some reason, Clarice responded.

Jessica said nothing. She'd been asked to find out what happened to Paul Brown. Lefty and the medical examiner had solved the what, but not the why. Deep in her bones, she believed in Colby's innocence. If Lefty found his notebook, they could easily blame the murder on him.

But this offered her the chance to set this case aside and get back to her studies. She should have looked at it as a gift, but instead, she wanted to find the truth more than ever.

Lefty turned to Robin. "I know you hired Jessica to look into this for you. We'll need any information you've given her. I'd also like to set up interviews with your family."

Jessica tried to stifle her smile. Lefty would be no match for Barbara Brown.

Robin nodded at him. She hadn't said a word, just sat stiffly on the stool with tears running down her cheeks. Clarice reached across the counter. Robin did not offer her hand in return.

"I'm so sorry," Clarice said. "This has to be a terrible shock, but I promise it will be okay. Lefty will figure out what happened to your dad." She patted Lefty's arm with the hand that had reached for Robin.

"I've got to go. I need time to process this." Robin stood, tears still trailing down her cheeks.

"Ma'am, I need to talk to you about those interviews."

A fire lit in Robin's eyes, and she turned on Lefty. "I said I needed time. You have my number. And speaking of that, what made you think it was okay to tell me this here? This is my family's business."

In the long silence that followed, Jessica watched Lefty shift on his feet, start to talk, then shift again. She enjoyed watching him squirm. Kudos to Robin. Jessica would have hated being in her situation, forced to deal with and share information in front of acquaintances.

Robin pulled her purse strap onto her shoulder. "You know where to find me," she said to Lefty with ice in her voice. Then she left.

"Yeah. I'm going to go too," Jessica said. "I'll leave you two to—whatever."

"Jessica!" Her mother's reproach was like a slap.

Jessica raised her eyebrows at her mom, then followed Robin out the door. She couldn't be sure why it pleased her to see Lefty's staged announcement blow up in his face. Perhaps she still didn't trust sheriffs after her recent run-ins with a few from El Paso. Those deputies had protected an especially awful man. But Lefty worked in New Mexico and had no connection to the El Paso Sheriff's Department . Plus, he didn't seem depraved, the way she thought of the others. Maybe he just wanted to impress her mom. Still, the awkward, poorly handled meeting made her think less of him.

Her mom didn't seem to feel the same. Too bad.

# Chapter 13

By Tuesday, she still hadn't heard from the shop owner about RG. She asked Linda for the morning off to work on the case and headed to the shop's location in far east El Paso. The person on the phone had mentioned "Abel made deliveries for Rancho Gamboa on Tuesdays," and Jessica guessed that happened early.

Linda had just nodded and waved when she'd asked. Each day that passed, Linda's mood seemed to fall deeper into a well. She'd probably seen Colby's journal, and that wouldn't have brightened anyone's day.

It surprised Jessica that Robin hadn't called and asked for the ledgers and Colby's box of belongings. She hadn't heard a word from her since Lefty made his grand announcement about murder.

Jessica drove into the morning sun on the wide freeway that wound through El Paso. She passed shopping malls, hotels, the building where Charles Gordon lived. That man knew more than he'd let on. Maybe when, if, Jessica identified the mysterious RG, she could talk to him about it.

Of course, according to Lefty, she no longer worked this case. But she would, at least until Robin told her to stop. She'd do it for Linda and for Colby.

Twenty minutes later, she pulled onto the service road and then stopped at a burnt orange building with a huge sign advertising art, gifts, and jewelry from Texas and Mexico. The bottom of the sign read "saddles, blankets, and boots." The words "western wear and cowboy hats" accompanied the image of a buxom cowgirl. With so much going on, the sign was a hot mess designed to lure tourists off the interstate.

She stepped inside to a barrage of color. A wall of shot glasses and displays of Mexican pottery took up her immediate right, while jewelry counters stretched in front of her. The clothing department lay to her left with jeans, hats, and plaid western shirts on display. She could see cowboy boots on the back wall and rows of pottery, brightly colored blankets, and saddles stretching toward them. The store was like a Target geared toward people obsessed with the Wild West.

Two cashiers sat behind registers, but other than them, Jessica seemed to be the only person in the store. She wandered toward the back, trying to formulate a plan. An older man, perhaps in his seventies, walked in through a pair of swinging doors in the back corner. He carried a large brown box which he set at a junction of belts and boots.

Lanky, with sinewed muscles bulging out of his short-sleeved western shirt, he differed from any seventy-year-old she'd ever seen. He looked tough, like Clint Eastwood's meaner cousin.

Jessica walked straight up to him and stuck her hand out. "Jessica Watts."

He gave her a suspicious glance but shook her hand. "Conrad White. What can I do for you?"

"I'm looking for one of your suppliers. RG?" Jessica hoped he was the owner, or at least a manager. He certainly didn't look like any stock boy she'd ever seen.

"Rancho Gamboa. You're in luck. Abel just dropped off a delivery." The suspicious light returned to the guy's eyes. "What do you want with him?"

Jessica had to think fast. "I work for Robin Saunders. She owns an art gallery in town. She's interested in his work."

"I know Robin. She carries paintings and sculptures. Abel works with leather." The glare in his eyes told her his suspicion had turned up to eleven. He'd probably call Robin the second she left the store. El Paso might have almost 700,000 people, but that just made it the biggest small town in America. Relatively few people ran the city, and they all tended to know each other. Between the length of time Robin's family had been in El Paso and her ex-mayor husband, most long-time businesspeople probably knew her.

"I'm not sure exactly why she wants to talk to him. Perhaps she wants to commission something."

The man shook his head, then he shrugged. "You might as well come on back before he leaves." He turned toward the back doors and Jessica followed.

Behind the doors, a cement-floored warehouse held racks of boxes. There were three dock doors, two of them closed. The third let in a bright shaft of light and a stiff desert breeze. Jessica tightened her jacket around her. A ramp led from the dock-high door to the parking lot, where a bright blue dually pickup waited. A man who looked to be about Robin's age, in his fifties, leaned against the truck door. He wore jeans and a white guayabera shirt. Jessica couldn't see his eyes through the shade cast by the rim of his baseball cap. She recognized the chihuahua on the cap—El Paso's minor league baseball team.

"That's Abel," Conrad said, before picking up another box and heading back into the store.

Jessica made her way down the ramp, careful not to slip in her slick-soled boots. "Hi, I'm Jessica Watts," she said as she approached the man.

"Abel Gamboa." He offered his hand. "Is Conrad coming back? I need to get my check and head home."

"I don't know." She wasn't sure whether to ask him the next question. Surely, he was too young to have done business with Robin's dad. He'd have been a teenager when Paul died. Was murdered. Still, this was her last lead. "Did your company used to have a contract with Paul Brown?"

Jessica watched shock hit the man like the blowback from a nuclear explosion. His eyes went wide, and he jerked his hand away from her.

"Who are you? Why did you ask me that?"

"Robin Saunders—she used to be Robin Brown—hired me to find out what happened to her father. I think you know something about that." Or at least she guessed so from his reaction. "I'd like to hear your side of the story."

"I don't know what you're talking about," Abel said. He pushed himself off the truck and opened the door.

"Please don't leave. I know he was paying you a thousand dollars a month. Please, just tell me what for."

He didn't even look at her. Instead, he climbed into his truck and slammed the door shut.

"Are you his son?" Jessica asked.

The truck started, then sped out of the parking lot. Jessica noticed the Chihuahua, Mexico, license plate as he drove away.

"Where the hell did he go?" Conrad asked, joining her. He held a check in his hand.

"I don't know," Jessica said. "But I need to find him."

---

When Jessica pulled up to the law office, the empty driveway surprised her. Linda had called in sick yesterday, the first time she'd done that in the months Jessica had worked for her. Linda had texted, asking Jessica to cancel any meetings and handle any new business that came in. Fortunately, their rash of court cases had slowed this week.

It had relieved Jessica to see Linda back at her desk this morning, before her visit to the saddle store. Now, Jessica needed to figure out how to follow up with Abel, since Conrad refused to give her any information on him. He did take her card and told her he'd pass on the information.

She'd hoped to ask her boss for advice but it looked like Linda was gone, Jessica worry from yesterday returned. Had Linda stayed home because Robin's finds stirred up memories of Colby? She checked to make sure the blue notebook remained in her desk drawer. She'd seen it yesterday, but today when Jessica opened the drawer, the notebook was missing.

She glanced at her phone. No missed messages from Linda. She checked the firm's phone messages. The sole message was a client calling to reschedule a meeting.

The kitchen remained exactly as Jessica had left it the night before. Jessica stopped by Linda's office and found a note on her desk.

*Jessica,*

*I'll be out dealing with personal business. Please reschedule any meetings.*

*Linda*

Why had Linda left the message in here instead of putting it on Jessica's desk? The erratic behavior concerned her. Of all the people she knew, she'd have expected Linda to break down last.

Jessica trudged back to her desk, concerned for her boss. She loved working here, partly because the small firm meant she had her hands in lots of different cases and constantly learned on the job. But she also loved working for a fierce and fearless woman. She'd watched Linda tear through a man in the witness box who thought he could avoid paying his housekeeper because she didn't have papers. When Linda threatened legal action against him for knowingly hiring an undocumented worker and then holding the woman in virtual servitude, he'd started visibly shaking.

Whatever trauma from the past had returned after Linda discovered Colby's mementos, Jessica needed to help however she could. She quickly rescheduled Linda's remaining meetings, sent the phone to the answering service, and headed toward the west side of the city.

Linda lived high up the mountain in an older development called Casitas Coronado. The condos in the gated community backed up to Franklin Mountains State Park, home to the dry desert mountains that bisected the city. Jessica drove up a two-lane road past low-slung homes from the sixties and seventies punctuated by red and ochre cliffs and the soaring mountains rising behind them. In the spring, she might have seen the spikey arms of ocotillo filled with deep green leaves, or perhaps the orangey-red of claret cup cactus blossoms. But deep in the El Paso winter, leaves became a luxury on everything but scrubby sage. The ocotillos' skeletal arms reached skyward, covered by sharp gray hooks.

Jessica shook her head. The bright sun glowed overhead in a deep blue sky. That should keep the ominous thoughts at bay. Still, something was off today, from the way Abel Gamboa sped away to Linda's no show at work.

At the housing development, she faced yet another problem. A gate stood between her and the condos beyond. She told the man in the booth she needed to see Linda Reed.

His gaze turned questioning. "Ms. Reed is usually at work."

"She didn't come in today. I'm Jessica Watts, her paralegal."

His suspicion didn't ease. "Just a minute." He picked up the handset and punched numbers into a keypad. "Ms. Reed?" Jessica heard him say. "I have a visitor for you, a Ms. Jessica Watts?"

He punched a button, and Jessica heard a click, then the gate started its slow swing away from her. "You can go in," the man said.

Jessica arrived at Linda's condo and noticed the open garage door. She walked through it, past Linda's BMW, and found the door to the house ajar as well.

"Linda?" she called, walking into the laundry room. She continued through to an open living room and dining area with large abstract paintings on the walls. Through an open doorway, she spied an all-white kitchen. Linda sat at the table in the breakfast area wearing an ice blue fleece robe knotted around pajamas.

Her boss didn't look at her as she walked in. Instead, she stared at the blue notebook splayed in front of her.

"Hey, are you all right?" Jessica asked.

Linda nodded. Finally, she looked up and focused on Jessica. "Would you make me some coffee?"

Jessica opened cabinets until she found the coffee, then started it in the ancient Mr. Coffee on the countertop. Next, she scrounged around in the refrigerator until she found bread, butter, and jam. She'd never seen her boss without makeup and an Armani suit. Today, Linda looked ten years older and as fragile as a baby sparrow.

Jessica toasted the bread and then slathered it with butter and jam and set it on a plate next to Linda. As soon as the coffee had brewed, she filled two mugs and sat across from her boss. Jessica faced the large window and had a stunning view north along the wild mountains. The housing developments below crept ever farther up their sides.

"Talk to me," Jessica said. "Tell me what's going on."

Linda picked up her mug, wrapping her hands around it like she needed the heat. "Not staying in El Paso to help Colby is one of the big regrets in my life." Her eyes settled on Jessica. "Sometimes I think he was my shot at happiness, and I chose success instead."

"But you were eighteen. You went to college. It's not like you abandoned him."

"I did abandon him. He hated his father, and then his father disappeared. That does a number on a kid. I left him here with his evil mother and swirling rumors that he'd killed his dad. I couldn't have stopped the rumors, but maybe if I'd stayed, or convinced him to escape with me, he would have survived. Maybe we could have had a happily ever after. Not that I believe in that stuff."

Jessica didn't know what to say. She'd come close to throwing away her own happy ending, back when she hurt so bad she couldn't let the one person in who loved her. But a brush with death and a missing woman had shown her what was important just when she'd tried to throw her happiness away on booze and anonymous guys.

"You are not responsible for what happened to him." It was far too late to save him now anyway, but that thought seemed too cruel to voice. "I don't think he killed his dad, but those were Paul Brown's bones in the orchard."

"Really?" Linda lifted her head, and her eyes became focused.

"Yes, and I've kind of buried the lede. The medical examiner says the cause of death was blunt force trauma to the head."

"No." Linda sat up straight, her voice gruff. She glanced down at the notebook. "They can't see this."

"I know. His words sound like motive, and he can't speak for himself." Jessica rested her chin on her fists. She had wondered if Linda, a former cop, would feel she had to turn the notebook in. It seemed like she'd prefer to protect Colby.

"Listen," Jessica said. "The deputy working on this, Lefty Griswald, told Robin she had to give him any evidence she had."

"Is that really his name?" Linda asked.

Jessica smiled. "Yeah, evidently. He's the cowboy type, black hat and boots along with his uniform. And I think he has the hots for my mom."

Linda took a long sip of coffee. "That's interesting. Does your mom have the hots back?"

Good question. One Jessica had asked herself. "I'm not sure, but it's a possibility."

"Well, regardless of any side romances, I think we must prove Colby's innocence. Even without this journal, he's probably already a suspect," Linda said.

"I agree. And I'd like to get the truth for Robin. She was really shaken up when Lefty told her about her dad. Can we start by going through what he said in the notebook?" Jessica asked.

The morose Linda whom Jessica had walked in on vanished, replaced by the quick-witted woman she knew. Linda picked up a piece of toast and took a healthy bite. Once she'd washed it down with more coffee, she opened the notebook and thumbed through its pages.

"I'm surprised Robin only found one journal." Linda thumbed past the drawings, including the one of her. "He almost always had a notebook with him, and I'm pretty sure this was his last one."

"Yeah. I was surprised there were only a few pages. He was quite the artist."

"He loved to draw." Linda turned to the first page with writing. She read it, then sighed. "All of this is true. Colby did hate his dad, and he hated the insurance business. He also didn't care about money the way his parents did, although when you grow up with money, I don't think you understand how vitally important it is."

"I've seen that in action," Jessica said. "When I worked in Juarez, I met a lot of very wealthy people my age who insisted they didn't need money while using daddy's credit card to pay for everything." Jessica hated the edge in her voice. She'd had to scramble so hard to afford clothing and transportation. So many times, she'd sat across the table from someone who had no idea that money just didn't show up whenever you needed it.

Linda flipped the page. She read Colby's words. "She'd never accept. Her future is brighter than me. I won't hold her back."

Jessica watched as a tear fell onto the page. Linda wiped it away with a finger.

"I would have said yes." Linda looked up at Jessica. "I was eighteen and it would have been stupid, but I loved him that much. I wanted to save him." Linda closed her eyes, pain etched across her face.

A long moment passed before her eyes opened. "Instead, he might have saved me. In his letter to me, he asked me not to be sad and to forgive him. He said we were both too young and dumb for it to work long term. He's probably right. By the time I left for college, his depression was already drawing me into its vortex. He's the one who pressed me to go to school. For a lot of years, I've wondered if that was a good decision. His letter released me from that guilt."

Goosebumps rose on Jessica's arms. Sometimes, good decisions didn't exist. Should you cut people out of your life? Should you let them back in despite the pain and anger it caused? Linda left her boyfriend to go to college at eighteen. Jessica had been sixteen when her parents left, and she'd quickly cut them from her life. Even now, at thirty, she wondered whether letting her mother back in had been the right thing to do. One never really knew the best path, you just took step after step along the chosen one. There were no do-overs, no sliding doors.

"Fortunately, the police won't care about that note," Linda said. "But this next one is a doozy."

"I remember that one. The 'I wish he was dead' isn't helpful, but the thought has probably crossed every teenager's mind. Do you know what he confronted his dad about? It seems like he thought his dad had an affair and had another child."

"I do remember this. Colby had always wondered where his dad went on the weekends. I think he ran into one of his dad's hunting buddies one weekend when his dad said he'd gone hunting. Colby said the guy hadn't been out with his dad in six months."

"Ouch," Jessica said. That would be a particularly sucky way to find out your dad was cheating.

"I've been thinking about this since we talked the other day, trying to remember the sequence of events. If I'm correct, several weeks before Mr. Brown disappeared, he and Barbara had a huge fight. I was there. She accused him of having an affair. That set Colby's hair on fire."

"They argued about it out in the open?" It seemed odd for a woman who cared about appearances to broadcast her husband's affair.

"They didn't know we were in the house. His mom was supposed to be at the tennis club and his dad at work. It was during the school day. Colby and I cut class to go to his house and hang out."

Jessica lifted her brows. Hanging out had a certain connotation.

Linda shrugged her shoulders. "It was spring semester senior year. There were far more interesting things to do than sit in class."

Jessica turned the conversation back to more depressing fare. "So that's why Colby thought his father cheated."

"He'd always suspected, but that conversation pretty much proved it for him. He started following his dad after that. That must be how he found out about the son. Not long after that, his dad disappeared."

Jessica sighed. "Colby makes a really good suspect."

"I know." Linda shook her head. "But it wasn't him. He would never have chosen to kill someone."

"But how do we prove that?" Jessica asked.

"I guess we've got to find the real killer."

# Chapter 14

The minute she returned to her truck, Jessica called Robin. She needed to see her, wanted to know whether Robin had read Colby's journal and decided her brother's fate. Soon, she pointed her truck in the direction of Robin's home.

Robin lived high on the mountain, atop one of the rocky ridges split by arroyos as the mountain spread its fingers toward the Rio Grande. During summer monsoons, the arroyos turned deadly, swirling with rushing water that annihilated anything in its path. Now, during the high desert winter, the land became achingly dry and the air crystal clear.

Jessica pulled into a circular drive in front of a stately Mediterranean-style home with cream-colored stucco and a red tiled roof. Even in the dead of winter, Robin had managed to coax lilac-tinged flowers from light green sage. Giant poinsettias framed the doorway, even though Christmas had long passed.

The door opened and Robin surged into Jessica's arms. Jessica would have backed out of the hug, but Robin clung so tightly she'd never get away. So she relaxed and wrapped her arms around the woman, her fingers pressing into the softest sweater she'd ever touched.

"Hey, it's going to be all right." The words spilled from Jessica before her brain kicked in, wondering what had made this woman so distraught.

"It's just all so tragic. Mom was right. I should never have dug into any of this. I made it all worse." Robin finally separated from Jessica but grabbed her hand to tug her into the house. "Please come in for a cup of coffee. Or I can make you some tea."

"Coffee's good." Jessica said, wondering how rude it would be to wrench her hand from Robin's grasp. It's not that she didn't like the woman, but Jessica didn't possess the touchy-feely gene that came with many women's sense of compassion. She decided against it, lest Robin resort to hugging her again.

The house soared with high ceilings and grand, sweeping rooms, but warm terracotta floors and butter yellow walls kept it warm and welcoming. Art splashed across every wall. A huge Mexican crow in a field of abstract color, a desert landscape in red and purple, and along one hallway, one of her mother's paintings that made the arid mountains look like shattered glass.

Large windows lit the bright kitchen. The immense views stretched across West El Paso. She could see across the valley into New Mexico, where the land arcing out of the valley became flat as a tabletop as it stretched west. Juarez's plum-colored mountains rose in the south, and in the middle of everything sat Mount Christo Rey. Overshadowed by taller mountains on either side, Christo Rey held two important artifacts, the statue of Christ at the top which drew pilgrims every Easter, and the obelisk stuck on one side where Texas, New Mexico, and Mexico met. The mountain used to symbolize the coming together of three disparate lands. Now, border walls and drug wars made it a no-man's-land instead of a place of unity.

"Here," Robin said, handing Jessica a mug of rich dark coffee and bringing her back from her wandering thoughts. "Please, have a seat."

Jessica pulled herself onto a barstool along one side of an island of honey-colored granite with veins of chestnut and gray. In constant movement on the other side of the island, Robin set out a plate of cookies and made herself a cup of tea. Jessica recognized the tension in her quick movements. Motion kept emotion at bay, but only temporarily.

"Robin, tell me what's going on."

Robin didn't stop. Not then. Instead, she pulled a barstool around the counter, so they faced each other. She set her tea on the counter, then returned for two small plates. Went back for napkins, and finally settled on the stool. Jessica watched her face crumble, although tears didn't fall.

"Deputy Griswald said he's pretty certain Colby killed Dad. I don't think Colby did it, and I knew him better than anyone." She wiped a single tear from her cheek. "At least I think I did."

"Why don't you believe Colby did it, and do you have any idea who did?"

"I've spent a lot of time recently, thinking about when Dad disappeared. That summer, we all thought we'd find him or that he'd come back. It took a few months for it to settle in that he was really gone. Colby and Mom slipped into deep depressions. By the time school started, I hardly saw either of them. They stayed locked in their bedrooms all day.

"You were only fifteen. How did you deal with that? You couldn't even drive." Jessica's parents had fled when she was sixteen. She'd at least been able to get herself to school. And Alma stayed with her at night.

"I arranged for my friend's mom to pick me up on their way to school. I told Mom when we needed food, and she had the grocery store deliver it. I think I ate mac and cheese every night for weeks. It's still my comfort food." Robin paused and took a long sip from her tea, seemingly lost in thought.

Jessica had spent so many years furious with her parents for the situation they'd put her in, thinking she was the only one who'd suffered such a tragedy. Yet what she went through didn't compare to this. Yes, her parents had left her, but they'd made sure she was safe. Alma became her guardian. Jaime the police officer moved in next door. She had money for food, clothing, and anything else she truly needed. She'd thought of herself as a badass for so many years, someone who'd become tough because of her trials. Yet here Robin sat in her welcoming home, able to hug freely and have a child. She seemed so comfortable in the world. Had all of Jessica's anger gotten her nothing?

Jessica shook her head. She had to stop the dangerous thoughts and get back to the here and now. "Colby," she said, the word coming out too loud. "He stayed in his room the whole time?"

"Well, he went out at night. Late, after he thought everyone was asleep. By the time school started, he stayed out more and more. I'm not sure mom even knew he wasn't coming home. They both disappeared into their own worlds. Colby was found in one of those old motels on Mesa Street. I'm glad they've been redeveloped now. I used to hate driving by there, imagining his last hours in some dingy hotel room. Alone."

On Robin's face, Jessica saw the deep sadness that came after a person had cried all the tears they had for someone. It left them parched, as dry as the desert with no water to wash the hurt away.

Jessica reached a tentative hand toward Robin. She squeezed her fingers gently. "I'm so sorry. That must have been terrible to go through." So much worse than anything Jessica had experienced.

"Yeah. His death was tragic. I always wished I'd known how to help him. I blamed myself at first. But eventually, I had to forgive myself. I was fifteen and struggling to take care of myself and Mom. His depression pulled him down like quicksand, and I couldn't get stuck there also."

Robin's words brought the quicksand to Jessica's feet. It would have been so easy to get trapped trying to help someone you loved. "How did your mom take his death?"

Robin cocked her head, her eyes seeming to pull at a memory. "Strangely, Colby's death brought her out of her depression. I mean, she was sad. Anguished. But she was present. I think she became afraid of losing me."

"Really?"

"Totally. She became supermom—up early every morning to make my breakfast and take me to school. She showed up for every activity I was involved in. Sometimes the attention became overbearing. We both started seeing a psychiatrist. He was the one who told me I had to forgive myself."

"I don't understand." All these people had done things to Robin. They should have been begging for her forgiveness. Although, except for Barbara, they were all dead.

"When people around you die, or disappear, or hurt you, your first reaction is to blame yourself. It's human nature. Once you work your way past that, then you can forgive them."

"What if they don't deserve it?" Jessica refused to wrap her head around Robin's way of thinking.

Robin's eyes glinted. "I thought it was my fault my mom stopped paying attention to me, that I wasn't enough for her to care about. Or maybe if I'd been a better person, a better daughter, none of the bad things would have happened. Once I set that burden down, I could see that she was just a person struggling to cope the best she could." A sly grin spread across her face. "I know you and your mother have similar issues."

A layer of steel formed around Jessica, bouncing the statement away. Robin had no idea what she and her mother had been through. Continued to deal with. "Let's talk about Colby."

Robin stared at her for a minute, then a slight shrug of her shoulders told Jessica she'd moved on. "Yes. Let's talk about Colby. The cowboy detective wants to frame him for my dad's murder. How do we stop that?"

"Did you read his journal? It was in the box you dropped off." If she had and Lefty got a hold of it, that might solidify his version of Colby's story.

"I started to, but once I saw the picture he drew of Linda, I just couldn't go on. He did have some good times in his life, but those last few months . . . " She dropped her head, and a tear fell onto the counter.

After a long pause, Jessica figured Robin couldn't continue. "There were some journal entries that showed how angry he was at your dad—before he disappeared. I'm not sure I'd turn those over to the authorities."

Robin slid off the stool and pulled a paper towel from the rack, dabbing it under her eyes. "Well, then it's a good thing you have them."

"That's what I thought." Jessica hoped Robin understood that she wouldn't be providing the journals to Lefty. Not spelling it out left them both with tacit deniability. "There's one more thing, and I'm not really sure how to bring it up."

Back on the stool, Robin leaned toward her. "Well, just shoot."

"Colby thought your father was having an affair. Actually, he thought your dad had a whole separate family."

Robin stilled. Her eyes lost their focus as if she rummaged back through her memories looking for something that fit. "My first reaction is that it's impossible, but the more I think about it, the more it fits with how much he was gone. There were lots of kids whose dads traveled for work, but mine always traveled on the weekends. Did Colby have any proof?"

"It's not clear. But I've also been checking your father's receipts. I found one-thousand-dollar monthly payments that seemed odd. I tracked them down to a guy who imports leather goods from Mexico, but when I tried to talk to him, he ran scared." The speculation about RG and that person's relationship to Paul didn't have definition yet. Mostly a feeling deep in Jessica's bones, it begged for more research.

"Do you think I have other brothers and sisters out there?" Suddenly at full attention, Robin sat ramrod straight. "Jessica. You have to find them."

Robin's response confused Jessica. She displayed no sadness or shame at her father's infidelity, just curiosity. Excitement, even.

"I think it's possible. If Lefty knew about it, it might give him someone else to think about instead of your brother. Although, how he intends to prove who is responsible for a forty-year-old wound is beyond me," Jessica said.

"Oh, who cares about any of that?" Robin's response surprised Jessica again. "I think I became an artist to deal with my loneliness after Colby died. If I have more family out there, I want to know."

"If your dad did have a second family, there's also your dad's mistress. I can't imagine your mom being happy about that."

Consternation crossed Robin's face, but her eyes still gleamed. "This is bigger than that. I've been starved for family. I wanted lots of kids, but it took years just to have one. Sometimes I feel like I've condemned him to a lonely future. But now, he might have cousins. Did you know he has zero cousins? Dick is an only child and after Colby died, well . . ."

If there are people out there whom I'm related to, I want to know about it. Please find them."

Jessica didn't like an unsolved mystery, but other circumstances stood in the way of resolving this one. "I'm pretty sure if your father did have a second family, that they're in Mexico."

"That would explain why I heard him speaking Spanish. You have to go down there and find them." Robin's excitement tipped to something more zealous.

Jessica remembered her promise to a drug lord's wife to never return to Juarez. The woman had saved Jessica from certain death on an earlier case. She'd learned some mysteries weren't worth solving. "I'm not sure I can do that."

"You have to. I'll increase your fee."

"It's not that." Although extra money would be nice. "I have certain restrictions about going to Mexico."

"Please, Jessica. Please. I really need this." Robin grabbed her hands, begging her for more.

"Listen. Let's both take a little time to think. We're not even sure these people exist, but if they do, it might not be the happy reunion you envision. And I need to do a little more research. If they're in Juarez, I definitely can't search for them. Even if they're not, it's a big risk for me." If ever there were a decision that needed more time and research, this was it.

Robin huffed out a frustrated little sigh. "Fine. I'll think about it and talk to my family. I'll call you at eight tomorrow morning with my answer. But be ready to pack your bags."

Somehow, the prospect of having additional family members had changed Robin. Before, she'd come across as confident but not assertive. Now, she seemed like a woman who wouldn't back down. Jessica wondered how Dick would respond to this new side of his wife.

And she wondered how Angus would react to her going to Mexico.

# Chapter 15

Jessica didn't drive home. Instead, she took Scenic Drive to the overlook. There, perched on the edge of the mountains, she stared across El Paso and into Juarez. Once, she'd crossed the border several times a week, meeting with clients, finding them the right industrial building or manufacturing partner. Over two years had passed since she last set foot in the city.

She missed the ballsy woman she'd been back then, when she thought she'd understood how to conquer danger. The intervening years taught her it couldn't be conquered, only survived.

Did she dare cross the border again? The thought of a wealthy megalomaniac telling her where she could and couldn't go grated. But she appreciated her life now far more than she had then, back before she'd opened her heart to love and forgiveness. Well, kind of forgiveness.

Robin's words about forgiveness and family echoed through her head. Her situation differed so immensely from Robin's. Of course you'd blame yourself if someone close to you committed suicide. Especially as a teenager.

But Jessica's parents had left. And she had been the one to finally visit them, make amends, giving them a second chance.

The view into Mexico grew dusky as the sun sank to her west. Her thoughts darkened, and her rebellious streak took hold and spread. She didn't owe anyone forgiveness. That had to be earned. And she wouldn't let threats keep her from doing her job. She'd avoid Juarez, but no one had told her to stay out of Mexico.

Jessica turned the key in the ignition. She drove west, toward home, toward the person she'd once been, a creature of the fluid border. The line separating the US from Mexico took many forms: river, barbed wire fence, and now, for parts of it anyway, the world's ugliest concrete and iron wall. It had always seemed a symbol of division, its lines drawn by far-away politicians who impeded the flow of goods, services, people, and cultures. They'd stop the wind from crossing the line, if they could. But despite their efforts, the border remained porous. It had to. American companies needed labor, and those coming north needed physical and economic safety.

Here, where generations of families grew up on both sides of the border, the wall seemed especially ridiculous. When politicians or a drug lord decided who should go where, Jessica would fight their authority and carve her own way through this desert land.

She drove toward downtown, the sun a yellow orb shining on everything beneath it. This earth would spin in and out of the sun's rays, oblivious to the humans trying to carve it into pieces. She had one life, and she'd throw the finger at anyone who tried to tell her how to use it.

———

That afternoon, she worked on the case from the office. She found the location of Rancho Gamboa just outside of Janos, Mexico. According to Google, it sat along a river a few hours south of the Columbus, New Mexico, border crossing. An hour due west of El Paso, the crossing in Columbus would keep her well away from Juarez.

A bit of her old fire came back. She didn't like danger for danger's sake, but that pull of excitement beckoned. In a slasher movie, she'd open the door to the basement and tread down the stairs first. She'd pit herself against the monster at the bottom because she'd learned survival meant quick action. Think something through too long, and you gave someone else the advantage.

She drove home excited to tell Angus about her plans. When she arrived, her mother's blue minivan waited in the driveway. Jessica's body used to recoil at such a surprise, their relationship could be the darkest of basements. This time, curiosity instead of dread swept through her. Maybe they could knit this thing back together.

She followed voices through the house and onto the back porch. Angus and Clarice sat on chairs watching Tela and the new dog play a dog version of tag.

"Have you renamed her yet?" Jessica asked. Angus jumped up and gave her a quick hug and kiss.

Her mom smiled at her and then turned back to the dogs. "I've named her Sheba."

"Like the cat food?" Jessica asked, incredulous.

Her mom's face fell, and she crossed her arms. "Sheba was a queen. You always ruin everything."

"Sorry," Jessica mumbled, eggshells crackling under her feet. "Sheba's a great name." The little dog didn't look anything like a queen, but Jessica truly hoped that's what her mom saw in her.

"Does anyone need a drink?" Jessica sure did. Her mom raised a half-full glass.

"I could use another," Angus said, tilting his longneck toward her. How long had her mother been here?

Jessica slipped into the kitchen and returned with two beers. The air filled with yips and growls as the dogs played. The backyard faced west, and she enjoyed the warmth from the last rays of the sun on her face, even as the air started to cool around her.

"So, what brings you out this way?" Jessica asked.

"I had to stock up at the pet store, and I thought I'd stop by and see how you two were doing. Is that okay?"

"Of course. You're welcome here anytime." Although a heads-up now and again would be nice.

"How's Robin's case going?" Clarice asked.

"It's getting interesting. I think there's a good chance Paul Brown had another family. I've got a lead I'm going to follow tomorrow. Linda gave me the day off."

"It's intriguing that Linda dated Robin's brother," Clarice said.

At the exact same time, Angus asked "Where are you going?"

"Mexico." Jessica's response hung in the air for long seconds.

"Jessica, you can't go to Mexico. Didn't you tell me the cartels would kill you if you went down there?" Angus's strained voice told her how hard he tried to stay in control.

"It wasn't the cartels. The wife of a businessman in Juarez warned me not to return to the city." She tried to play off the severity of the night she'd barely escaped, the demand that she not return if she wanted to live. "And don't worry, I'm not going anywhere near Juarez."

"Jessica." Angus's voice held every doubt he'd ever had about her.

"I'll drive out to Columbus and cross the border at Puerto Palomas. That's an hour away and not anywhere near Juarez. After that, it's a straight shot south for a couple of hours." She looked into Angus's eyes as she spoke, trying to let him know it would all be okay.

"I did not move all the way back to El Paso to have you getting yourself in trouble all the time." Clarice's voice trembled with indignance. "Heck, the last time I left, you went out in the desert and almost got yourself killed."

"But I didn't die. I didn't even get hurt. Besides, this isn't about you." Sometimes, her mother drove her crazy. She shouldn't have brought the Mexico trip up in front of Clarice. Only Angus mattered in this conversation.

"This is totally about me. If I hadn't convinced Robin to hire you, you wouldn't be in this situation. You need to understand that I was without my little girl for so many years, I can't have you taking risks like this. I need you around." Tears sprang to her mother's eyes.

Jessica took a deep breath, backing away from the rage that surfaced so quickly. The little girl her mother remembered changed long ago. Abandonment and experience had forged her into someone hard and sharp. She grew up on the streets and in the boardrooms of Juarez, escorting important documents or carving out million-dollar real estate deals. But the dangers for a white woman in Mexico didn't compare to the dangers of the poor and distressed crossing into the United States. Jessica would use the steel at her core to right wrongs, whether that meant chasing down the criminals killing immigrants or finding the lost.

"I'm a woman, Mom, and I have been for a long time."

"Of course. But please tell me you won't go to Mexico."

"This is a discussion between Angus and me. You are not a part of it. Thanks for stopping by, but I think it's time for you to head home." Jessica knew she was being rude by the hurt look on her mother's face. She feared looking at Angus's. But she'd reached her boundary with her mother.

Clarice called Sheba, then stomped out in the yard to pick her up. The dog clearly didn't know her new name. Even Tela looked at Jessica with disappointment as Clarice drove away. Jessica wouldn't let any of that get to her.

"Tamales?" Angus asked as he walked back into the house.

"Sounds great."

He pulled his mom's Tupperware out of the fridge and placed four of her homemade tamales onto a plate. A couple of minutes in the microwave, and they'd be steaming pockets of spicy goodness. Jessica pulled out a bagged salad and a container of cherry tomatoes.

They didn't talk until they finished dinner. Unfortunately, that meant increasing tension accompanied every fulfilling bite of food. Why had returning to Mexico become a need instead of a want?

She wanted to solve the mystery and, if possible, clear Colby's name. Robin hoping to braid a new strand of family into the current one intrigued her. Assuming the family existed, and she found them.

More importantly, returning to Mexico would give the finger to her fear. Whether driven by bravery or stupidity, confronting this phobia would give her back autonomy. As long as she survived.

"I understand that you are going to do this, whether I want you to or not." Angus's words interrupted her thoughts.

"Not necessarily, but I do think it's the right thing to do."

"Let's not play games. If I told you no, this would consume you until you found some reason to go down there." One eyebrow arched, as if challenging her, but his tone didn't leave much room for discussion.

She wanted to fight back, act as if desire equaled free will. But it didn't. She desired this—hungered to follow a clue into the desert and discover something that might change everything. She even craved the whiff of danger, it lifted her above the ordinary fray, injected her life with excitement.

Angus still stared at her, his brown eyes intense. A shiver went through her. He truly saw her, even the parts that didn't make sense. "I like it. I like the chase. I like walking through my fear to get at what's on the other side."

Giving voice to this part of her soul was like undressing the ugliest part of herself in front of him. Would he like what he saw? Would it turn him away? He swallowed and every cell in her body tingled. Who would want someone so far from normal? But he didn't move. His eyes didn't leave her.

The air between them thickened. She was going to take a chance, and he'd let her. He didn't know all the dangers she'd faced back then, but he'd seen the black SUVs that followed her. He had picked her up on that fateful night she'd survived. And he'd watch as she tempted fate again, not because he wanted her to, but because it was her nature. Desire thumped heavily through her veins in time with her heart. She wiped her lips with her napkin, took one last slug of beer.

She stood, needing action and suddenly hot in the cozy kitchen. She tugged at her sweater, then pulled it over her head. Her nipples went hard with only thin lace between them and the air, between them and his stare. He still hadn't moved, but hunger sparked in his eyes.

She removed each piece of her clothing with her vision locked on him. Her hands left traces of electricity on her skin as she unhooked her bra, slipped her fingers into her waistband to unbutton her jeans, and then slid her underwear down her thighs. Still, he stared.

She thought she'd explode just from his gaze, the fire there lighting her up from the inside. She wondered if her voice still worked, or if her throat had plumped closed with the passion swelling within her. "Pull your chair out from the table."

He shoved his chair back, propelling himself halfway into the kitchen. A chorus singing of freedom rang between her ears. He didn't want her to go, to put herself in danger again, but he wouldn't try to stop her. He'd let her be whoever she chose to be.

Jessica surged forward and straddled him, rough denim under her thighs and her breasts pressing against his soft cotton tee shirt. His eyes still locked onto hers, eager and defiant. She reached for his lips with hers, kissed him softly, then took his bottom lip in her teeth. He responded with a moan that traveled straight to her belly.

She kissed him again, pressed herself against him in a desperate bid to get closer than possible. Her hands pulled at his waistband, striving to get inside.

He stood, his hands grabbing her ass to keep her next to him. She marveled at his strength, lifting her five-foot-ten frame as if she weighed nothing. She thought he'd take her to the bedroom, but he lowered her gently until her feet touched the floor, then he spun her around and leaned her over the kitchen counter. She heard his belt unfasten, his jeans unzip, and almost came with desire.

Angus rarely let out the ferocious beast buried under a laid-back exterior. Every time she stepped toward danger, it must be a spur in his side. The promised drive into Mexico, the wanton disrobing, worked him into a frenzy, and she'd be the beneficiary of its unleashing.

He grabbed her wrists with one hand, pinning them against her back. He pressed himself against her, spreading her legs with his foot.

"Yes." Her voice came out husky before he had a chance to ask. Yes, yes, yes. He'd freed her to make her own mistakes, trapped her in a sexy game, and she wanted all of it.

# Chapter 16

The highway stretched before Jessica, a bullet slicing through the creosote and sand. Out here, the sky formed a giant dome, sometimes pockmarked with clouds, but today a sapphire sky reached toward infinity.

A few conical peaks rose to her right, the Potrillo Mountains. She'd visited the ancient volcanoes with her parents as a child. They hadn't hiked long that day. When her dad told the unfortunate story of a friend of his who'd seen a colony of hundreds of rattlesnakes in a culvert of the mountains, her mother had demanded they leave.

After they turned the truck around, it got stuck in deep sand, and they'd had to hike miles back to the road she traveled now, all under the hot skies of summer. Clarice often claimed Jessica had much in common with her father. Perhaps the penchant for bad decisions was hereditary.

Not that returning to Mexico was a bad decision. She'd seen few cars on the highway, a couple of trucks, several border patrol vehicles, and a sedan stuffed with people. No threatening SUVs with blacked out windows. That had been years ago.

Jessica drove an hour west along the Mexico/New Mexico border without encountering a single human structure but for barbed wire fences. Gravel roads occasionally crossed the two-lane highway and sometimes a rutted path wandered out into the desert, winding among mounds of sand.

Finally, she passed two houses seemingly stranded at the edge of nowhere, then the road turned left and spilled into town. Forget stop lights, Columbus looked like a one stop sign town. She idled at the four-way stop a moment, a permanently closed history museum to her left and a green roadway sign to her right, with an arrow pointing south toward Mexico. She turned north into town instead, wanting to fill her tank before the two-hour drive.

Once she'd topped off the truck, she drove down Broadway, seemingly the town's main street. Cute western buildings from a prior century lined the road, many of them painted in cheery blues and yellows. Only three cars sat in ample street parking. She'd read that fourteen hundred people lived in Columbus and wondered where they all were. She found another stop sign. And a post office.

She headed back toward the border and stopped at a restaurant with a drive-thru advertising green-chile cheeseburgers. "Town seems pretty empty," she said to the teenaged girl at the window. "Is something going on?"

"There's never anything going on around here." The girl passed Jessica her change and a bag heavy with food.

This time she turned her truck toward Mexico. She ate as she drove, trying to stay close to the fifty-five mile per hour speed limit. The extra hot green chiles made her eyes water, while the crispy fries sated her burning lips. She appreciated the distraction as much as the food as she traveled the final three miles to the Mexican border.

A few low-slung businesses lined the last quarter mile, mostly customs brokers and related businesses. She passed a giant cross to her right, as if she should expect a religious experience. Nerves had her almost wishing for absolution. But she'd seen nothing to alarm her the entire trip. No black SUVs, no men with guns. The logical side of her brain told her she had nothing to fear, but the ancient lizard part of her psyche screamed at her to beware. The final sign had an arrow pointing straight ahead: *Mexico Traffic Only No Turn Around*.

She drove forward under a long white canopy and was waved into Mexico without even lowering her window.

The town of Puerto Palomas began just steps from the border and bustled with all the energy Columbus lacked. Vehicles thronged streets lined with buildings in every hue of the rainbow. Overlapping signs called out pharmacies and medical and dental clinics. They catered to Americans who couldn't afford health care in their own country.

As she drove deeper into town she found the bars, restaurants, and hotels. She imagined wild nights of tequila, ranchero music, and bar fights. In a way, the desert outpost reminded her of an oasis, a gathering place that probably drew revelers from hundreds of miles away.

Auto shops and tire stores told Jessica the town would end soon. The empty desert brought comfort. As in the US part of her trip, the two-lane road slashed through open space. It had been built several meters above the desert floor, and the view extended for miles. She saw nothing to fear.

Slowly, the desert changed from sand flats to rocky crags zigzagging into the distance. Arroyos became gorges, and rugged hills began encroaching on the road. If the desert she'd driven through on her way to Columbus evoked beach sand, this quickly turned to badlands.

Despite the harshness of her surroundings, as the miles dragged on, they smoothed over the rough edges in her mind, wearing down fear and anxiety with each spin of the wheels. She was doing a job. She was supposed to be here. Nothing more.

By the time she turned off the highway, the desert had changed again to undulating rock hills carved by stony creek beds lined with scrawny trees and bushes that hinted at water, even if it couldn't be seen. The highway had become no more than a narrow two-lane strip of pavement with no shoulders. Occasionally a gravel path led off the road with no sign marking it. Jessica turned onto one of these now, forced to rely on GPS in the absence of street signs. The gravel road seemed slightly redder than the surrounding landscape, and it followed a shallow creek as it curved around a hill and down into a depression.

The view opened up as she rounded the hill, and she slammed on the brakes. A pecan orchard spread in front of her. While smaller than the orchards in New Mexico, she couldn't mistake the dark trees majestically stretching toward each other to form a canopy. It had to be a sign.

The road swept around the orchard then made its way back toward the creek. Several adobe buildings came into view and cattle grazed behind a barbed wire fence. Jessica drove slowly, looking for an entrance and planning her next steps.

A main cluster of buildings surrounded a courtyard and seemed to be the heart of the ranch. She parked next to a copper-colored sedan with rounded bumpers that had to be from the 1980s. She didn't see Abel's blue truck. Her stomach sank. Perhaps this wasn't the right place.

A young woman exited one of the buildings and stood at the edge of the courtyard looking at her. Jessica opened her door.

"¿Aquí es el Rancho Gamboa?" Jessica asked as she approached the woman. The woman's skirt and long black hair fluttered in the breeze. She couldn't be more than twenty.

"Sí." The woman's soft voice held a question.

"Yo soy Jessica Watts. ¿Está Sr. Abel?"

"My uncle is not here." The woman spoke in perfect English with barely an accent.

Jessica relaxed. She'd found the right place. It might not matter if Abel were here. In fact, she might get further without him. "Do you know when he'll be back? I drove from El Paso."

"He went to Casas Grandes to pick up some pottery. He should be back in about an hour. You're welcome to wait inside." The woman gestured to one of the adobe buildings, then turned and led the way.

Jessica followed, her senses on alert. Would she find Paul Brown's second family here? Heck, if the skeleton hadn't already been identified, she might even wonder if he'd hidden here for all these years. Hard to imagine. His fancy house on Rim Road might only be a few hundred miles away, but it differed immensely from this dusty farm isolated in the Mexican desert.

She paused at the threshold of the building. The woman she'd spoken with held open a solid wooden door. Jessica stepped from bright sun to blinding darkness and waited for her eyes to adjust. Colorful woven rugs covered terra cotta floors. Dark wooden furniture offset creamy walls.

"You arrived during a tamalada," the woman said, ushering Jessica into the kitchen. This room, brightly lit by windows on either side, smelled of ground corn, stewing meat, and chiles. Two women manned the stove while two others sat at a rectangular table in the center of the kitchen piled with corn husks and masa.

"Ella es Jessica Watts. Busca a Tío Abel." The woman Jessica had followed introduced her and said she was looking for Uncle Abel.

So, the young woman was Abel's niece. The women at the table could easily be her sisters or cousins.

"Welcome," said a silver-haired woman tending the stove. "Abel should be back fairly soon. We are happy to have you wait here."

"Thank you." Jessica had so many questions she wanted to jump into, but experience had taught her that pleasantries and going slowly would get her further in this culture.

"May I get you something to drink?" asked the older woman. She had a grandmotherly look about her, and if Jessica had to guess, she'd bet her daughter stirred an enormous pot on the stove.

The older woman pulled a cobalt-colored glass from an open shelf. "We have Coke, orange Fanta, and mineral water."

It astounded Jessica how well everyone spoke English. This far off the tourist track, locals typically spoke only Spanish. "Thank you for your hospitality. I'd love a Coke."

The woman uncapped a thick glass bottle, and Jessica smiled. She loved Mexican Coke, the kind made with real sugar instead of corn syrup. The flavor surpassed anything manufactured in the US.

Jessica glanced around the room. Two younger women, perhaps in their twenties, sat at the table and formed an assembly line. One spread masa, cornmeal mixed with lard, onto corn husks, and the other filled them with meat stewed in a red sauce before wrapping them into individual tamales.

The silver-haired woman set Jessica's drink on the table and motioned for her to sit. "I am Mayra, and this is my daughter Irma." She gestured to the woman at the stove who nodded at Jessica. "And these are my granddaughters Julia, Gloria, and Araceli."

Araceli, who had led Jessica into the home, took her place at the table and started folding tamales. Jessica sat at an open seat and took a sip of Coke. The bubbles tickled her throat while the cold, sweet liquid revived her from the long drive.

"May I help?" Jessica asked, taking a corn husk and spreading it open onto the plate in front of her.

"You know how to make tamales?" Araceli asked.

"Only the assembly part. My husband's family makes them every Christmas." Jessica grabbed a paddle sticking out of the masa and scooped a generous portion of the yellow paste onto the open husk. She spread it across the top half of the husk just thick enough to cover the ridges.

"Very good." Mayra praised her handiwork.

Jessica handed the masa and husk off to the granddaughter in charge of filling it with meat and sauce. She spread another husk in front of her, repeating the action. The motion of spreading the paste kept her hands busy, and she settled into the repetitive movement.

Mayra returned to the stove, stirring and tasting. She asked her daughter to add more salt to the meat, then came back to the table to survey the assembly. The granddaughters stole glances at Jessica but kept quiet. "Your husband's family makes tamales. Are they Mexican?" Mayra asked.

"Yes, Mexican-American. His parents are from El Paso. Olivia and Miguel Delgado."

Mayra cocked her head as if thinking. "I do not know them, although I have not been to El Paso in many years."

Jessica couldn't help wondering if she'd been back since Paul Brown's death. She needed a key to open that conversation.

"Are you doing business with Abel?" Mayra asked.

The whole room seemed to turn its attention to Jessica. "No, not really. I have some questions about Rancho Gamboa. I'm working for a woman named Robin Brown. She hired me to find information about her father." The warm room grew stifling with pressure. She shouldn't have been so blunt, but Abel might not talk to her at all, and she came here for information.

Mayra stilled, her brown eyes filled with questions. "What is it you want to know?"

Jessica looked around the room, every eye focused on her. At the stove, Irma's hazel eyes bore through her. Araceli had the same eyes, golden-green in the center and darkening to brown at the edges. The other women stared back with dark brown eyes. "I found some information that made me think . . ." She couldn't go on. Was she supposed to accuse this woman of having an affair with a married man? Her face seared with embarrassment, and she reached for the Coke.

Mayra exhaled, and a light inside her went out. She suddenly looked old and frail. She took the seat at the head of the table and rested her head in her hands. Irma came over and placed a hand on her mother's back as if to comfort her. Then she nodded her head at the other women, who returned to the tamales. Jessica did as well.

Eventually, Mayra raised her head. She seemed to have conquered whatever emotion had brought her down, and pride now glinted from her eyes. "Paul Brown was the father of my three children. I loved him very much, but I was young and too trusting. I have taught my children and hopefully my grandchildren better." She reached for a masa-lined husk and added meat and sauce. Her fingers expertly rolled the tamale.

Jessica had arrived seeking the truth, but hadn't thought about the shame that would bring. She studied the other faces in the room. Only compassion crossed their features. Love surrounded Mayra. Jessica could almost see it anchoring one woman to another.

"I think you should leave." Irma directed the comment at Jessica. She didn't sound angry, just tired.

"It is okay, daughter. I knew this day would come." Mayra's brown eyes penetrated Jessica. "What do they want?"

"Robin just wants to know the truth about her family. She never knew what happened to her father. Until now." Jessica had one remaining bomb and deployed it into the room. "Paul Brown's body was found on his pecan farm."

"Aye!" Mayra's hand flew to her chest, and her eyes filled with tears. "I always wondered what happened to him. I followed the story in the papers. When he disappeared, I knew something terrible had occurred. He would never abandon us. He loved all his children."

She didn't heave or sob. Silent tears rolled down her cheeks, but she held her chin high and pressed her shoulders back. Jessica could see both the devastation and pride that roiled through her.

"I'm sorry to bring you this news." So many questions ran through Jessica's head. When did you last see him? Who knows about his family in Mexico? Did he leave you any sort of nest egg? How did you raise your children? She bit her lip to keep the words inside.

"Irma, we need to tell Abel y Susana." Mayra glanced at her daughter.

"Si, Mamá." Irma squeezed her mother's shoulder.

"Irma, Susana, and Abel are Pablo's children," Mayra said, using the Spanish word for Paul. "They need to know their father didn't abandon them."

Irma knelt beside her mother. "You are what matters. You raised us. You built this family. You have always been the only thing we needed."

Jessica could see the love on Irma's face, could feel the force of it in the room. Had she ever loved her own mother so selflessly?

"Lo siento. I am so sorry you never had a real father who lived with you." Mayra stroked her daughter's cheek. "But you were born of a great love. And I'd make the same mistakes again because it gave me you and my family." She looked around the room, taking a long second to stare lovingly at each granddaughter.

When her eyes landed on Jessica, she seemed almost surprised to see a stranger in the room. "Thank you for bringing this news." A question crossed her face. "Do they know how he died?"

Jessica paused, knowing she would again blow up the warmth in the room with her next statement. "They think he was murdered."

# Chapter 17

The young women gasped at the revelation of a potential murder. But Irma and Mayra stilled, as if the grave news hadn't surprised them. Jessica immediately wanted to probe deeper, but she'd already upset this family so much.

"That is a tragedy," Irma said. "Is there a particular reason you wanted to speak with Abel?"

"I tried to talk to him in El Paso, but he ran away from me. Robin, Paul's daughter, wants to know more about her father. No one there knew about his second family. Well, his son suspected it, but he died years ago."

Irma and her mother shared a glance. Irma turned back to Jessica. "His wife knew about us."

The shock flowed through Jessica like an icy wave. Of course Barbara knew. Sitting high above El Paso in her fancy house, she probably hated the fact that Paul had a second family. Jessica would be furious if that ever happened to her, but for someone trying to impress the community, it would be devastating. A thought flickered through the back of Jessica's mind. But no, surely, she wouldn't have gone that far. Barbara might hold the ice queen title, but murder was a different dimension of evil.

Suddenly, the door flew open, spilling light into the dark living area. "Hola, mamá. Qué rico huele aquí." Abel stepped into the kitchen.

Jessica steeled herself. He might think the food in the kitchen smelled great now, but finding her in his home would likely sour it for him.

His eyes swept the room and landed on her. Shock crossed his features, and a red anger rose on his cheeks. "You. Why are you here?"

"I tried to talk to you in El Paso, but you ran away. I'm here at the request of Paul Brown's daughter."

His eyes went first to his sister, who shook her head. "Leave us."

Jessica thought he'd directed the comment at her, but he nodded to the younger women at the table. They scurried out a back door.

"I don't know why you are here tormenting my family." Abel's voice came out in almost a growl. "But you need to leave us alone and never come back."

"Abel, Mamá told her," Irma said.

Abel sighed heavily with more than a trace of anger in his breath. "Do not tell the woman you work for anything about us. Paul Brown wouldn't acknowledge us when we needed him, and we want nothing to do with him or his despicable family now. We are good people. Leave us alone."

"I can't lie to my client," Jessica said.

Abel had made a good point. This family didn't deserve to be pulled into a situation created by the man who deserted them, but he had left everyone in his life. And now it looked like that hadn't been his fault.

"Robin is just trying to find out more about her dad," Jessica said. "She didn't know he had a second family. For years, she wondered what happened to him, what drove him away. I just told your mother that they found his body in the pecan orchard."

"So what? He's been gone for years. I'm glad he's dead." Abel towered over her, his voice suddenly threatening.

"What you don't know," Jessica stood, unwilling to feel small and threatened, "is that he was murdered. Blunt force trauma to the head. The sheriff is trying to pin it on his son Colby."

"Ah. The poor little white boy with lots of money and opportunity. The one who chose drugs and laziness instead of hard work. The one who was given everything. It sounds like a story right out of the Bible. Only the prodigal son killed himself instead of returning home. He probably did kill his father." Abel's hazel eyes flashed, and his hate toward Colby came off him in waves.

Jessica understood. He'd been abandoned by his father. So had she. But she'd had opportunities, a place to live, high school then college, friends who helped along the way. Her father hadn't left her south of the border with no way out. She understood his hate, let it mingle with her own betrayal.

"I'm sorry. I did not come here to hurt you or your family. My experience is nothing like yours, but I know what it's like to be abandoned by your parents."

"My mother never abandoned me." He went to his mother's side and placed his hand on her shoulder. Irma stood beside him, both of them fiercely protective.

Jessica looked into the depths of Mayra's eyes. They shone with pride and love, and maybe just a little fear.

"I am sorry if I've upset you by coming here. I was trying to help a daughter who wanted to understand her father. I did not mean to cause any trouble." At least she hoped she didn't. Her desire to solve the puzzle of Paul's death didn't give her the right to burden others.

"It is good you came," Mayra said before looking up at her children. "She is your sister," she whispered.

"No." Abel's voice sliced through the air. "We must have nothing to do with that family. It is too dangerous."

Dangerous? That wasn't the word Jessica had expected. She hadn't figured out the source of Abel's fear, but it radiated through the room.

"Can I leave my card in case you change your mind? I think Robin might like to meet you. I'd like to interview you about the time surrounding Paul's death. Robin doesn't think her brother killed him, and she'd like to clear his name."

"That boy is already rotting in hell for his crimes. We don't know that he didn't kill his father."

"Abel!" His mother's voice was sharp. "Do not talk of the dead that way. He was your brother."

"Paul Brown was not a father to me, and those people are not my siblings."

"He was your father. You know that. He loved you for sixteen years. Until he disappeared. Do not forget that."

"Mother, it is you who forgets. You forget how he told us he would no longer acknowledge us, no longer provide for us. He wasn't a man. He was a scared child. I renounce him as my father. I am the one who built what we have here, after he stole my dreams. So many promises he broke."

Jessica watched the pain cross Abel's face. She glanced at Mayra and saw nothing but sadness in her eyes.

"He promised he would move us to the US," Abel said. "He said he would live with us. He vowed to pay for my college, so I studied, and the University of Texas accepted me. Then he took it all away. We were not important enough for him. And it all fell to me."

He shook his head, then looked directly at Mayra. "I grew your father's business. I brought in money. I helped support you and my sisters and their children. I had to become a man when I was still a child, and I tell you, we will have nothing to do with Paul Brown or his family." He heaved a sigh as if the words had both stolen his energy and given him strength. "You need to leave."

Jessica slipped a business card out of her wallet and left it on the table, looking at him with defiance. "Thank you for your hospitality," she said, nodding at Mayra and Irma and ignoring Abel. Then she left the house.

Walking out of the dark house was like walking out of a movie theater into bright sunshine. Jessica struggled to parse story from reality. Abel displayed his fury, but fear lurked in the house as well. As she drove away, Abel's blue truck and the adobe shrank in her rear view mirror, some relief coming with the fading threat.

Back on the highway, her mind zipped in a hundred directions. Fully ensnared in the web of this mystery, she wondered if Abel had killed his father. His pain and anger at losing out on his future cut through all other emotions. But would that alone drive someone to kill? Surely some of the story remained hidden.

Another line of thought followed Mayra and the family who clearly loved her. The sordid words of mistress and affair in no way defined the woman she'd met. They'd had so much taken away from them, a father, and likely any money and connections he'd provided. Yet they were rich.

They lived in a beautiful, if isolated, valley surrounded by pecan groves. Their home was warm and filled with love. And the tamales smelled delicious.

She needed to talk to Robin, a woman who had lost the same father, if not the money and opportunities. Instead of Mayra, Robin had grown up with the cold and uppity Barbara as a parent. Not to mention Robin's husband. Yet the woman seemed filled with love, especially when she talked about her son.

How did women like Mayra and Robin create contentment, even happiness, out of loss and betrayal? Jessica sure hadn't learned that trick. She'd lost her parents, temporarily. But now her father was gone for good, and she mostly tolerated her mother. She claimed Angus as her family, but was that enough? And how did one get from here to there? The miles slid beneath the truck's tires as she contemplated the mystery she had to solve and the future she drove into.

———

As soon as she crossed the border and turned east toward El Paso, Jessica called Robin. She hadn't figured out a tactful way to share that she'd found her father's lover along with Robin's half-siblings and their children. Nevertheless, the information burned a hole in her as it tried to escape.

Robin answered the phone on the first ring, as if she knew Jessica had important information to share.

"Have you learned anything?" Robin asked. "That sheriff called and warned me that a reporter from the *El Paso Times* had pestered him about the story and might publish something about Colby murdering my father. That's ridiculous, and they can't prove it. What are we going to do?"

Jessica hesitated. No one knew what happened to Paul Brown all those years ago. He could have fallen and hit his head on a rock. Speculation about Colby seemed unfair, but bringing in a whole other family might cause the sheriff to shine his quick light in that direction.

But Robin deserved to know.

"You know how Colby thought your dad had an affair and another family?" Jessica threw the words into the silence Robin left.

"Yes," Robin said after a pause.

"Well, I found them. They're in Mexico, and I just visited them."

"Them? Tell me more."

"The woman . . ." Jessica stopped, not wanting to apply the words affair and mistress to the strong woman she'd met. "She has three children, two daughters and a son, and at least some of them have children. I didn't get specifics. They, well at least the son, have mixed feelings about your father."

"I have siblings?" Robin seemed to have bypassed the whole part about mixed feelings.

"Well, half-siblings, I guess."

"And my kid has cousins? He'll be so excited. He always wanted cousins."

Jessica hoped Robin's expectations about family had mellowed. Obviously not. "I think you need to take this slow. I'm not sure they're as excited about their growing family."

Jessica waited for a response that never came. She called Robin's name, then looked at her phone. No service. Nothing but her thoughts and the empty desert ahead.

---

Jessica pulled into her driveway, relieved to be off the road and needing to pee. She scrambled up the steps and flung the door open as soon as the lock turned. Tela whined and bounced, wanting Jessica to stop and play instead of heading to the back of the house.

As soon as she left the bathroom, she dropped to her knees and rubbed the dog. Almost impossible to pet, the furry creature jumped away and zoomed around the room.

"I don't know why Angus left you inside." Jessica walked to the back door and opened it, and the dog sped out and raced down the fence line. Jessica closed the door. She'd play with her once she'd burned off a little energy. In the meantime, she could clean the trash out of her truck.

She gasped as she walked into the front room. Dick Saunders hulked just inside the doorway.

Terror raced through Jessica, paralyzing her. The last time she'd had intruders in her house they'd threatened to kill her dog, then kidnapped her and took her to Juarez. With a little help, she'd escaped that time. This time Jessica was alone.

"What the hell have you done?" Dick's voice raked across her like coals, but in their heat, she found her voice.

"Get the fuck out of my house."

He approached instead. Each step toward her, he seemed to grow larger. He probably only had three or four inches on her five-foot-ten height, but he had to weigh almost double what she did, and some muscle accompanied the middle-aged gut. He probably prided himself on working out at the gym.

Jessica backed up a step toward the kitchen. Could she make it to the knife block before he made it to her? She wished she had El Diablo, her taser flashlight, but it lived in the glove box of her truck. Jaime Castro, her cop friend, had encouraged her to get a gun, but she hadn't listened. If she got out of this mess, that would be first on her agenda.

"Why are you trying to ruin my family?" Rage came through the words and became visible in the deep flush creeping up his neck.

"What the fuck are you talking about?"

"You told Robin she had a family in Mexico. You found them. I'm her family." His bullying voice rose to a yell.

Jessica took another step back toward the open kitchen. "She does have family in Mexico, you sick fuck. I can't solve your marriage problems."

"I don't have marriage problems. I have a problem with you. Those people, they're going to want money. I've built a reputation here, and I don't need beggars from Mexico trying to ruin that."

What an asshole. "I'm pretty sure they don't want anything to do with you. You need to leave before I call the cops." Of course, she'd left her phone in her truck, and she'd have to get past him to get it.

"I own the cops."

The ego of rich guys like Dick really pissed her off. Comfortable with her own anger, she relaxed. "Trust me, you don't."

Dick stopped advancing, and Jessica realized he'd come here without a plan. Touching her in any way really would ruin his reputation, unless of course, he planned to kill her and hide the body. But insurance agents probably didn't kill people.

"I can ruin you." He probably believed his hollow threat, but his sneer now seemed more like a playground bully than a real danger.

"Look around. I'm not the one living in a mansion near the country club." Not that she'd trade her twelve-hundred square foot home for anything. "And as for my reputation, I'm Joe Watts's daughter. I think he's already taken care of that." Who knew having a criminal for a father would ever work in her favor?

She could almost see him deflate and decided to play her advantage. "Speaking of reputations, what's your connection to Jeremy Wright and the group that kidnapped the Guatemalan girls and killed their relatives?"

Suddenly, the threat was back. "I don't know what the hell you're talking about, but I'd advise you to stay away from that."

"Why? I know you were involved with bringing Jeremy here. How deep does that connection go? Those girls deserve justice."

He stared at her a long time without saying anything. Jessica couldn't tell whether he'd attack or flee next. She straightened, trying to make herself imposing.

"You're nothing but a piece of trash. If you want to end up like others who died in the desert, keep pursuing those guys. It will certainly solve my problem. If you're smart, you'll stay away from them and my family." He gave her one more nasty look, then turned and left.

Jessica slumped against the countertop. How could someone as bubbly as Robin be married to such a rage machine? Still, he'd given her a lead. She didn't know how closely he connected with the evil men in the desert, but he knew about them.

She walked to the truck and watched his Mercedes drive away. The car's exhaust left a trail of evil in the air. She'd fight it, but not today. Not when it had come to her doorstep and entered her home.

Jessica got her things from the truck. Locked it. Locked the front door. Called the dog in from the back and locked that door also. The windows in the living room which expanded her view into the front yard and neighborhood beyond had turned from welcoming to threatening. She took Tela into the bedroom and hugged the dog tightly.

She'd fight her way through this fear hangover and find a way to slay the evil and protect the innocent. But she needed to be better prepared. If she went after them, they'd come after her.

# Chapter 18

Jessica reached out to Jaime for recommendations and then signed up for a basic shooting academy. Unfortunately, the first opening wasn't available for several weeks. But even signing up for the class made her feel stronger. She wouldn't be threatened in her own home again.

Once she'd learned how to shoot, she'd see about getting her mom training as well. The terrier-chihuahua mix she'd picked up at the animal shelter wouldn't protect her against men like Saunders. She didn't think the man had anything against her mother, but just his connection to her mom's home made the hairs on Jessica's arms rise.

Making a plan solidified the ground beneath her feet. She'd beaten evil in the past through a combination of bravado and luck. Now she'd add preparation to that mix.

As her fear seeped away, her curiosity returned. She wanted the truth about Paul Brown's murder. So many people had reasons to be angry with him. He had betrayed his wife. His son knew about the betrayal and hated his father. Now she knew Paul had an entire second family, including another son who held his fury at his father close to his heart even decades later. Who else had a man like that swindled or pissed off? Had a hunting buddy pulled a Dick Cheney on him and hit him in the head? Was it a business deal gone bad? His ex-partner seemed to dislike him, and that guy really got screwed over.

After Dick Saunders's performance today, Jessica would readily believe he had killed his father-in-law to take over his business, but Dick and Robin didn't meet until years later. Who among this cast of characters had caused his death? Or did Paul realize the chaos he'd caused and how many people he loved hated him? She'd consider suicide if he'd had a gunshot wound, but he probably didn't whack himself in the head hard enough to die.

The phone rang. Robin. Jessica answered and heard crying. Had Dick hurt her?

"I've screwed everything up," Robin said.

"Are you okay? Do you need to get out of your house?" Jessica asked.

"What? No, I've already left. I'm on my way to see you."

No. She couldn't come here. Jessica hadn't started her shooting lessons, didn't own a gun. She needed to prepare for Dick's return, and if he followed his wife today, she wasn't ready.

"Wait. You shouldn't be driving. Are you near a park or somewhere else we can meet?"

"I'm driving down Thunderbird. You've got to help me make things right."

"Let's meet at De Leon Park, near the playground. I'll be there in ten minutes."

Jessica hung up, grabbed her keys, and whistled for Tela. She didn't know how Dick Saunders had driven his wife into such a frenzy, but she'd figure it out and go after him. How could someone like Robin end up with a man like that? Jessica must have had that thought a thousand times.

The stoplights went her way, and she made it to the park in seven minutes. Robin had already arrived and sat at one of the blue metal picnic tables. She and Robin had the park to themselves, so Jessica let Tela off her leash to run around and explore.

Jessica took a seat opposite Robin. The woman's tears had dried, but her red-rimmed eyes and puffy skin showed her distress.

"Are you okay? Did anyone follow you here?" Jessica asked.

A confused look passed over Robin's face. "Yes, I'm fine. I just really screwed up."

"Where is your husband?"

Robin tilted her head, obviously baffled by the question. "I don't know. He's probably at work. Why?"

Jessica wasn't sure how much to share with Robin. Maybe she'd let the conversation play out before sharing the man's threatening visit. "I was just concerned when you called crying."

"Concerned about Dick? Oh, he'd never hurt me. I know he can be a little rude sometimes, but he's all bluster."

This woman clearly didn't know the man she'd been married to for decades. "If it's not that, then what's wrong?" Jessica asked.

"Lefty called again." A sob escaped, and the tears returned. "He talked to a reporter. They're planning on running a front-page story in the *El Paso Times* insinuating that my brother killed my dad. He said they didn't have any other suspects, and the story fit. Lefty said he couldn't charge my brother with anything since he was dead, but this is almost worse. Colby doesn't have the chance to prove himself innocent."

"Why the hell is that guy so intent on blaming someone for Paul's death?"

"He said it was important to close the case."

"Huh. He'll probably get a commendation or something positive put in his personnel file. That's a ridiculous reason to move so fast. There are a lot of people who might have killed your father."

"I know. That's where I screwed up. I told him you found my dad's other family."

"What! You know he'll go after them." No, no, no. How could she have done that? Who knows what Lefty would do with that information? His quick trigger in the blame game wouldn't bode well for Mayra's family. Jessica couldn't help shaking her head at Robin. She wished she'd never taken this case, never had the opportunity to hurt a family who'd already lost so much.

"I know. I panicked. I didn't want Colby's name dragged through the papers again. I can't take it, and I don't think my mom can either."

"How's she going to take learning about your dad's affair and his multiple children with another woman?" While Mayra said she knew about the affair, Jessica guessed Barbara would never admit it.

Robin flat out wailed at Jessica's comment, as if the thought hadn't occurred to her. Tela, who'd returned to the picnic table, howled in agreement. Jessica sat silent through the banshee storm, trying to figure out their next move.

They'd have to warn Mayra and her family about what was coming. Why hadn't Jessica asked for a phone number from one of them? Would she have to drive back out there?

She hushed and leashed Tela first. Robin had stopped wailing but sobbed heavily, her head resting on the table. Jessica reached out and placed a hand on her shoulder. "Robin. You've got to pull yourself together. We have to start dealing with this now."

Robin looked up, her face soaked and her nose bubbling with snot. She rubbed her eyes, smearing mascara across her cheeks. Jessica just shook her head.

Then, Robin heaved a vast sigh and took a mini pack of tissues from her Louis Vuitton handbag. She blew her nose with one tissue, then wiped her face with another. Finally, she took a small vial of moisturizer from her bag and spread it across her face, wiping the last few smudges of mascara away. Without the makeup, and with the eyes of a sad, lost child, Robin looked years younger.

"You're right," she finally said. "I'm ready. What do we need to do?"

"First, don't take any more calls from Lefty. At least not until we've contacted everyone who needs to know this is coming."

"Okay. You're right. But I need to tell my son he has cousins."

"Before that, let's find a way to contact Mayra and her family. Lefty might consider them suspects, and we should warn them about this. Especially since he's talking to that reporter."

"Do you think they're suspects?"

Jessica didn't have an immediate answer. Abel remained furious at his father, but she couldn't say he was any angrier than Colby had been. "I think it's way too early to tell. Just like your brother, Abel was angry with Paul. It seems like your dad had decided to cut them off, although I'm not sure about that. We need to talk to them again."

"I really want to talk to them," Robin said.

"Well, we should make sure they want to talk to you. Also, I don't know how to get in touch with them except to drive out there. Although maybe that guy at the saddle store would give me Abel's number."

"You mean Conrad White? I know him."

"Really?" Could Jessica be that lucky?

"Of course. He imports art from Mexico, and I'm an art dealer." Robin whipped out her cell phone. "Let me call him. Whose number do we need?"

"Abel Gamboa."

Robin's face glowed with a warm smile as she spoke with Conrad. This woman's ability to turn the waterworks on and off amazed Jessica.

"He's got the number in his office, and he'll call me with it tomorrow morning. I'd love to call him myself, but I think it's best if you talk to him first.

"Thanks. The first thing you need to do is talk to your mom. I can't imagine she'll take this well."

"She's going to be furious. Would you come with me?"

Jessica couldn't imagine anything worse. Uptight and socially conscious Barbara Brown would have to watch the perfect world she'd built crumble. Again. Except this time, instead of being the victim, the poor widow whose husband disappeared, she'd be the woman whose husband cheated on her. As much as Jessica disliked Barbara, she felt terrible for what she'd go through.

El Paso society could turn on a person. Her mom's Junior League friends had dropped her the second they'd learned about her father's arrest. Hell, the kids at Jessica's school had shunned her, even though she was sixteen and clearly had nothing to do with her father's actions. Only Angus had stayed by her side. Robin would have to be that person for Barbara.

Robin looked at Jessica with pleading eyes, waiting for an answer. Jessica would help her through this. After all, Robin hadn't caused Paul's deceit. And she was a good person. She'd found her mother a place to live.

"Yes. I'll go with you. I need to talk to my mother as well. I think she and Lefty are becoming friends, and I want to warn her about him."

"Mothers," Robin said, shaking her head. "I've tried to be a much better one than mine, and I think I've succeeded. My son is great. Make sure you do the same when you have kids."

"That's probably not in the cards for me." Jessica's knee-jerk response to the kids' question seemed off today. She'd lived her life by the motto that kids with bad mothers should not have their own children. Best to stop the cycle before anyone else got hurt. Robin probably was a good mother. That opened up possibilities Jessica had never considered. Maybe the past didn't have to repeat itself.

Robin started to say something, then stopped, seeming to swallow her words. "Meet me at my mom's tomorrow morning, say eight o'clock?" she finally asked.

"Sure." Hopefully the meeting would go better than last time, although given the subject, probably not.

They walked to their vehicles, and Jessica wrapped her arms around herself in the growing chill of the desert evening. Tela dragged behind her, seemingly out of energy as well. Jessica should have brought up Dick's visit, but Robin already had so much to worry about.

Soon, she'd warn Robin about her husband. Soon, she'd warn Mayra and Abel about the coming storm. Soon, she'd untangle the mystery of what happened to Paul Brown, and then she could focus on the killers in the desert.

But tonight, she would sleep curled up in Angus's strong arms and rest up for the coming battles.

# Chapter 19

Robin had already parked her car in the circular drive when Jessica arrived at Barbara's house. She exited the Mercedes as soon as Jessica pulled up.

"Thanks for coming today. This isn't going to be easy," Robin said. Understatement of the year.

They walked to the front door, and Robin used her key to open it. "Mom, I'm here." Her voice rang through the house.

A slight woman with dark skin and an apron greeted them in the foyer. "Hola, Miss Robin. Su mamá esta en su vestidor."

"Gracias, Lupe. I forgot you were here today."

Robin turned to Jessica. "My mom's in her dressing room. Come on back."

Jessica nodded to Lupe and gave her a quick smile, then followed Robin down the hallway. This had to be a mistake. Surely, they could find a way to solve this mystery without bringing down the world of an old lady, even a mean one.

Robin knocked on the door before opening it. "Mom, it's me. I'm here with Jessica Watts."

Jessica followed her into the room. Barbara sat at the makeup table surrounded by oversized glowing lightbulbs. Jessica caught her cold stare, and the silver lipstick tube poised at her lips. Barbara's eyes returned to the mirror, and she finished applying the shimmery mauve lipstick without saying anything.

Robin stood near her mother, hands at her sides like a little girl waiting for a reprimand as Barbara capped her lipstick and blotted with a tissue.

She turned to face them as she rose. "I thought I told you not to bring her back to my house."

Barbara's eyes remained on Robin, dismissing Jessica like a piece of trash. Maybe this wouldn't be so hard after all. Jessica could play the bitch as well. But she wouldn't mean it. Her heart ached for this rude, unhappy woman.

"We need to talk, and Jessica has some information to share."

The mother-daughter standoff lasted long seconds. Finally, Barbara sniffed. "Fine." She planted herself on one of the rose-colored velvet sofas.

Robin sat on the opposite one and patted the seat beside her as she glanced at Jessica. Jessica's feet didn't want to move, and she dreaded making herself comfortable in such an uncomfortable situation. She forced herself forward.

She sank into the plush fabric and considered a polite "hello" or "nice to see you again" but kept mum. Seconds of awkward silence passed.

"Mom, Jessica has learned some information. This is going to be very hard to hear, but you need to know. Dad had an affair, and he had another family."

If Jessica hadn't been staring at Barbara, she might not have noticed how the woman stiffened, as if her spine had become steel not bone. Her light blue eyes narrowed just a bit, as if in prelude to the storm brewing within.

"That is a lie," Barbara said, her words sharp.

"I'm afraid it's not. I've met them," Jessica said. Although, she had no proof, except that Abel looked remarkably like his father, down to the hazel eyes.

Barbara's cutting gaze moved from Jessica back to her daughter. "Why are you trying to ruin me? I told you to leave all this alone. There have been rumors about that Mexican whore for years, but none of it is true."

"Colby knew. It was in his journal," Robin said. "There's more. The man investigating dad's death knows, and we're worried he'll think Dad's other son is a suspect. Also, he's talking to someone at the *El Paso Times*."

"No," Barbara wailed. "I've done so much to keep this family name out of the gutter. What's wrong with you? Don't you see how this affects you and your family as well? It'd be better if they thought Colby killed your father than to let this out."

"How can you say that?" Robin's shocked voice bounced against the walls of the small room.

Jessica remained stuck on the phrase "Mexican whore" that Barbara had used. Robin hadn't mentioned Mexico, meaning Barbara knew more than she let on. What else did she know?

"Your brother was on drugs, and he hated your father. Maybe he did kill him."

"You can't believe that. Please tell me you don't believe that." Robin's voice had quieted, but it quavered with passion.

Barbara sighed. "No. I don't believe he killed your father. But Colby is dead. Your father is dead. Why drag everyone else through the trash for something that happened so long ago?"

"Because you want to know the truth." Jessica couldn't keep her mouth shut. It wasn't fair to Colby to pin this on him, even if only memories of him remained.

"The truth is overrated." Barbara's eyes returned to Jessica, but the fight had gone out of them. "I'm sure you'd have preferred that they hadn't caught your father and put him on trial."

"Actually, I'm glad that happened. He broke the law. He needed to be prosecuted."

"But it ruined your life. It ruined your mother's life. She used to be such a vibrant woman." Barbara's voice dripped with pity.

"She still is. And my life is going quite well." What a bitch, projecting her issues onto Jessica and her mom. "You're the one who doesn't seem happy."

The minute the words left her lips, she wished she could take them back. Cruelty wouldn't change Barbara's attitude, and it had no place in the professional job Robin had hired her to do. On cue, Robin looked at her with wide eyes.

"I'm sorry. I shouldn't have said that," Jessica said.

"No," Robin said. "You're right. I want the truth. And I want to get to know the rest of my family." She turned her gaze back to her mother.

"They are not your family." Barbara practically spat the words. "They'll just want your money, just like they always have."

"How much do you know about this?" Jessica asked.

Barbara stood. "I'm going to my room now. You've both ruined my day, maybe the rest of my life. Please show yourselves out."

Barbara stood, smoothed her plaid skirt, and tottered slightly on her high heels as she left the room. Jessica heard the slam of a door, then click of a lock further down the hallway.

Jessica stood. "I better go."

"Wait. I need you to find out who killed my father. You're right. The truth is the only thing that matters."

Jessica nodded, even though she doubted the statement. People's feelings mattered. But arresting the wrong person mattered most of all, and now she'd have to deal with a deputy determined to find a suspect.

She also, of course, had a job to do. Linda would want to know that Colby was right—there was another family. Unfortunately, despite Robin's plea, Jessica was no closer to finding Paul Brown's killer.

# Chapter 20

Linda parked herself in front of Jessica's desk the moment she arrived. Jessica shared the news about the family in Mexico first. Linda's prosecutorial mind went straight to whether Abel might be guilty.

"He's furious with his father the same way Colby was," Jessica said. "But nothing about meeting him and his family made me think he's a murderer, and we have zero evidence. But that sure doesn't mean the sheriff won't try to arrest him. He was willing to throw Colby under the bus. Who knows how he'll treat the illegitimate Mexican son. Unfortunately, Robin told him about the second family."

Linda commiserated with Jessica over the bad publicity Mayra's family might face but didn't have any sympathy for Barbara. "That woman deserves whatever she gets."

"Probably. Both she and Dick Saunders think Paul's Mexican family will come after them for money. They don't seem to realize we went after them. If they wanted money, they could have come after the family years ago."

Jessica glanced out the window just in time to see Lefty Griswald pull his deputy vehicle in front of the office, right behind her truck.

"Shit. That's the New Mexico sheriff. I've got to split."

"Why?" Linda asked, turning to lock the front door.

"He's dying to pin this case on someone. First Colby, and now he'll want information on Abel Gamboa. By the way, Barbara thinks everyone should just let Colby take the fall for his father's death so all the gossip will die down. If this guy finds out about Colby's notebook, who knows what will happen?" Jessica slipped her wallet and car keys out of her backpack.

"Barbara's a bitch. Slip out the back and I'll stall the sheriff's deputy." Linda headed back toward her office while Jessica ran for the back door. She sprinted across the packed brown dirt of the backyard, thinking again they should do something with the space.

The gate in the chain link fence squealed as she opened it, but she closed it again despite the noise. An open gate would give away her escape route. Grateful for the alley, she slowed to a trot while she figured out where to go. She slid her phone out of her pocket and glanced at the time. Five after nine.

Suddenly, the phone buzzed in her hand. Lefty. She turned it off and kept walking. When she reached San Antonio Street, she slowed to a quick walk, trying to blend in with the lawyers and jurists heading to the El Paso Courthouse.

Half a block past the courthouse, she found her refuge and swung open the door to the Tap, her favorite downtown bar which opened at nine in the morning every day but Sunday. Fortunately, her favorite bartender Irina already manned the long bar top.

"Good morning," Jessica said, turning to glance out the window. The dark interior meant no one could see in without opening the door, but Jessica had a clear view of the street. "I'm really glad you've got the morning shift today."

"That makes one of us." Irina reached into a bowl of limes and set several on a cutting board. "Why are you here so early?"

"Some pendejo deputy wants information from me about a family in Mexico. He needs to do his own investigation." She hoped calling the deputy a jackass in Spanish would earn her a few points with Irina. Jessica glanced at her, and Irina nodded, her iridescent eyeshadow glinting in the scant light.

"You want anything to drink?" Irina asked, starting to slice limes.

Jessica seriously considered a shot of tequila. This day already felt like it had lasted twelve hours. "Just a coffee if you've got it."

A few minutes later, Irina set a steaming mug on the bar. "Isn't it illegal to withhold information from the authorities?"

"Not usually, at least not to local officers. But it's easier just to avoid them." Not exactly a law school answer, or one she should be proud of. She glanced back out the window in time to see the New Mexico Sheriff's vehicle rolling slowly down the street.

"Shit." Jessica ducked.

"Come behind the bar."

"Can't I just escape through the back?"

"Trust me. You think you're the first person who's hidden in this bar? We probably save a marriage a month by hiding spouses here. Although that's not the sign of a healthy marriage."

Jessica peeked out the window again. Lefty was backing the vehicle into a parallel parking space. Jessica scuttled down the length of the long bar and slid behind it.

"There," Irina said, pointing to the lone space under the bar top with nothing in it.

Jessica crouched in the tiny space, not wanting to sit on the floor. The shadow of the counter above bathed her in darkness in an already dim space. The aroma of stale beer surrounded her. "It smells back here."

"Welcome to my world." Irina's Doc Martens stopped right in front of Jessica, and a hand towel appeared before her face. "Sit. He's coming in, and this may be a while."

Jessica dropped onto the proffered towel and tried to make herself as small and quiet as possible. She'd be more comfortable on the run, but she trusted Irinia to end the game of cat and mouse.

The space grew momentarily brighter as the front door opened. Fear of being discovered prickled her skin.

"Good morning. Have you seen Jessica Watts this morning? Her boss told me she comes here for an early drink sometimes. Disturbing habit. She probably needs to get into a program."

Had Linda sold her out? Why else would she have sent him here? Maybe she wanted Colby's name cleared at any price and thought the info about Abel would do that. The thought turned Jessica's stomach. She hadn't worked for Linda long, but she trusted her, looked up to her.

"Jessica?" Irina asked. "What does she look like?"

"About five foot ten, black hair, blue eyes. Probably around thirty."

"Haven't seen anyone like that today."

"Are you sure?" Lefty asked.

Jessica couldn't imagine the glare Irina must have given him. She didn't put up with much bullshit. She couldn't, working in a place where half the customers wanted to drown their sorrows and the other half searched for a good time.

"Do you mind if I look around a little?"

"Go ahead."

Fuck. He was going to find her. Then what would she do? She tried not to breathe as footsteps passed within inches of her on the far side of the bar.

"Mind if I go in the back?"

"Suit yourself, but don't scare María, the cook."

His footsteps faded, and Jessica imagined him going into the kitchen, a place she'd never been. It must be tiny, given the footprint of the building. She thought she heard voices in the background but wasn't sure. Soon she heard steps again, then doors opening and closing. He was checking the bathrooms against the back wall. Those rooms she knew. The bar remained the only place left to check. He'd find her.

As he walked to the front of the bar, his steps seemed to stop inches from her hiding place. Probably only a thin sheet of plywood separated them.

"Here's my card," he said. "Please have Jessica call me the next time you see her."

"Whatever," Irina said, sounding bored.

Jessica stayed put, the seconds dragging into minutes. The rhythmic slicing of limes and a refrigerator turning off then on played to a background of silence. Finally, she couldn't take it anymore. "Is he gone? Is it safe to come out?"

"Oh, yeah. He drove away a while ago."

"Why didn't you tell me?" Jessica dragged herself from the cramped space, then stretched out her back and legs.

Irina just winked at her. Probably payback for disrupting her morning.

Jessica made her way around the bar and dropped a twenty in the tip jar. "Also, I need a beer after all that." She'd considered a fresh coffee, but this day drove her to harder fare. Besides, she didn't want to leave the safety of the bar just yet.

She sat in silence, checking her phone while Irina stocked olives and maraschino cherries into open containers next to the limes. Her phone buzzed in her hand. This morning just wouldn't quit giving.

"Hey, Robin. What's up?" she said into the phone.

"I want to thank you for everything you've done to help me. I'm more determined than ever to meet my Mexican family. Also, Conrad got back to me. I've got a phone number for Abel Gamboa. Where are you? Maybe we can call him together."

Just a few sentences, and Robin had already made the day more complex. She thought of these people as family, but Abel certainly wouldn't see it that way. Especially when he found out his new sister sicced the cops on him. Not to mention "calling him together" sounded like an ambush.

"I'm at the Tap having a beer."

Robin waited long seconds to reply, probably wondering what had driven Jessica to drink before ten in the morning. "I'll be right there," she finally said.

"Awesome." The phone had already gone dead.

———

Twenty minutes later, Robin walked in. Lefty hadn't returned, but two men in their forties had arrived and ordered tequila shots and coffee. Fortunately, they'd settled at the other end of the bar, as Jessica had no desire to talk. Not that Robin wasn't about to quash that dream.

"I didn't know you drank Corona?" Robin said as she climbed onto the barstool next to Jessica.

"It seemed like more of a morning beer than Tecate."

That got a chuckle out of Irina. "What would you like?"

Robin looked perplexed for a minute. "I'll have the same. I don't usually drink beer, you know, the carbs."

Jessica pressed her lips together to stifle a grin. Irina just shook her head, then glanced at Jessica. "You want another?"

"Sure. Why not?" No reason not to lubricate this day straight into hell.

"Let's call Abel." Robin practically bounced on the stool, all glittery eyes and perfectly coiffed hair.

Her excitement about calling her "brother" made Jessica's stomach rumble, and not in a good way. "Hold on there. Remember when I told you Abel had strong reservations about your father—like he hated him."

"Yeah, but Dad is dead now. We know that for sure. Hating him won't do any good."

"It's not exactly going to change his life for the better. The damage your dad did has festered for almost forty years. Abel would have had a completely different life if your dad had claimed him as his son and given him the opportunities he gave you."

Robin started to respond, then seemed to think better of it. When Irina set her beer down, she took a long sip. Then she coughed as if she'd drunk poison instead of weak beer. "That tastes awful."

"It grows on you," Jessica said.

"Can I have a white wine?" she asked, waiving at Irina. Then she turned back to Jessica. "I understand he's upset. A lot of people are upset with my dad right now. I think my mom is heartbroken."

"Robin," Jessica interrupted. "Your mom seemed far more angry than heartbroken. Plus, she already knew about the affair. We didn't tell her the family was Mexican. But she knew that. Not only does Abel have the right to be upset at his father abandoning his mother and their three children, Lefty is sure to make him a suspect in this case."

"If he didn't do anything to hurt my dad, then that won't be an issue."

"What world are you living in? Lefty already tried to pin this on your brother. He's sure as hell going to finger a Mexican man." Had she not read the news over the past few years? So many people of color had been falsely arrested, beaten, even killed because of overactive law enforcement. The US legal system endangered Abel, it would not protect him.

The energy drained from Robin. She reached for her wine. Jessica saw a tear leak down her face. "I really want to meet the rest of my family."

Jessica understood how tricky the family ties could be. "Listen. I need to talk to Abel and warn him about Lefty. He came to the office looking for me today, and I'm sure he wanted to ask me about Abel. Let's give the family an open invitation to contact you, although they may want to wait until this case dies down."

"Invitation." Robin perked up again. "We can invite them to the gala. All of them."

Jessica didn't understand how Robin could think about a party at a time like this. But the more she thought about it, the more the idea resonated. "I think that's a good idea because it involves the whole family, not just Abel. You may have better luck with the rest of them, and they seem to be wonderful women." Plus, if Jessica invited them and they decided not to come, she'd still done her job.

"Please. Tell me more. I want to know about each one of them."

Jessica recounted the generosity of Mayra, the protectiveness of Irma, and how fully the granddaughters participated in the tamalada. She spoke of the adobe structures built around a courtyard, all of it nestled in a pecan tree filled valley. As she talked, she convinced herself Robin was right. These families needed the opportunity to get to know each other and to build something new in the future. She doubted Barbara or Dick would see it that way, but Robin deserved this chance.

"Give me the number and I'll try to call Abel," Jessica said.

Robin pulled out her phone and searched under her contacts until she found the listing for Abel Gamboa. "I really wanted to call him, but I knew I needed your help."

Jessica entered the numbers into her own device and called. She heard the long beeps of an international call. On the third ring, someone picked up.

"Hola," a woman said on the other end.

"Hola. Habla Jessica Watts." She was about to ask who it was after introducing herself, when the woman spoke again.

"Jessica. It's Araceli. It's good to hear from you."

"Oh. I thought this was Abel's phone, but I'm really glad it's you."

"This is Abel's phone, but he's not available right now. Do you need to talk to him? I was going to call you later today and apologize. Abel's behavior upset my grandmother, and she asked me to tell you we are sorry."

"No worries. Seeing me at the kitchen table surprised him. It's no big deal. I have to tell you something. Paul Brown's daughter, Robin, would really like to meet you all. She considers you to be family."

"But I thought the Browns wanted nothing to do with us."

"The mom, Barbara, she was Paul's wife. She is not very happy about this. But her daughter Robin feels like part of her family is missing."

Robin grabbed Jessica's arm and nodded as a tear made its way down her cheek. She held her hand out as if she wanted to take the phone.

"There's something else," Jessica said into the phone as she shook her head at Robin. "They are still trying to find out who murdered Paul Brown. There is a New Mexico sheriff's deputy named Lefty Griswald who has made this his personal crusade. I am worried that he'll come after Abel."

"Abel? Why?" The concern in Araceli's voice ratcheted up.

Then Jessica heard a different voice in the background. "¿Que pasa? ¿Quien es? Dame el teléfono."

Of course Abel wanted to know what was going on and who was on his phone. Araceli must have covered the phone with her hand or tried to hide it, because Jessica only heard distant muttering for a few moments. Then an angry huff came through the phone.

"Why are you calling me? I told you to stay away." Abel's voice slammed into her.

"I can't. I have information you need to hear." Jessica hoped he wouldn't hang up.

He didn't respond immediately, probably debating how to finally get rid of her. "What is it?" he finally asked.

"The deputy investigating Paul Brown's death knows about you and your family." Jessica delivered the blow, striking Abel and Robin with the words. Robin looked sick, and Jessica hoped she wouldn't lose her wine.

"Ah. Thanks for sharing that information with him. I knew we couldn't trust you. I suppose he thinks I killed my father."

An urge drove Jessica to tell the truth, but it wouldn't heal the family relationship if he knew Robin had told the deputy, so she stayed silent about that. "I'm not exactly sure what he thinks, but he's trying to find me and I'm avoiding him."

"Why?" Abel asked.

"Because this cold case has become a big deal to him, and I think he's a little too quick to accuse people." Abel didn't respond, so Jessica continued. "May I speak with your mother?"

"No." The line went dead.

Robin looked on the verge of bawling again, especially after Jessica told her he hung up. Jessica couldn't take any more family emotions today. She pulled out her wallet to pay the bill.

"I've got it," Robin said with a sniffle.

Before she left, Jessica thanked Irina. The woman had helped her, no questions asked. Jessica wouldn't forget the kindness. Irina acted and dressed tough, but she was pure gold.

As she walked back to the office in the bright El Paso sun, Jessica thought about all the ways one could blow up a family. Did they ever come back together? She'd once tried to find a missing woman, an heiress to one of the wealthier families across the border in Juarez, Mexico. That ended up being a family fiasco with no hope of recovery. She had tried for years to keep her own family apart after her parents blew it up. Even though they had reunited, Jessica preferred her friends to her mom. She kind of hated herself for that, but the rocky past blocked the way to a full recovery.

An ocean of hurt and betrayal, not to mention an unsolved murder case lay between Robin and the family relationships she desired. But a woman that plucky wouldn't stop trying, not unless her husband or mother found a way to stop her.

If Jessica had that strong of a devotion to family, perhaps she could fix things with her mom. But she'd spent much of her life learning to hate the woman, and it seemed impossible to reverse that training now.

And she had plenty of reasons not to. Her mom dating Lefty Griswald, if that's what was going on, chief among them. Buying an inappropriate dog, despite its cuteness. Defending Dick Saunders. Despite these justifications, something bigger and deeper blocked her ability to forgive.

She sighed when she reached the office. She'd opened the door to a million tasks that needed taking care of, and she could leave thoughts of family behind. But she still had to worry about Lefty returning. She'd peered around every corner as she'd walked the few blocks back, worried she'd find him lurking just out of sight. He seemed to have given up, for now.

She needed to set this case aside, at least for a few days, and let things calm down. Maybe Abel would reconsider, or she could find a way to invite Mayra to Robin's party. Maybe it was just too soon for any of that. Relationships took a while to heal.

# Chapter 21

Jessica marched straight into Linda's office. She had one thing to deal with before she returned to her daily tasks. Only one person could have told Deputy Griswald where to find her.

"Glad to have you back," Linda said as Jessica stood in the doorway.

"Did you send the deputy to the Tap?"

"I suggested it," Linda said. Something on Jessica's face must have given away her ire. "Oh, no. Tell me you didn't go there."

"Of course I went there. Where else was I supposed to go?"

"I had no idea you'd choose to go to a bar at nine in the morning." She cocked her head for a minute. "Although now that I think about it, I might have chosen the same."

"Are you sure you didn't send him after me so he'd look at Abel Gamboa as a suspect, not Colby?" Jessica wished the words back as soon as they left her lips. She did worry that Linda's feelings about her first love tinged how she saw this case, but she shouldn't have voiced them. Not without some kind of proof.

"I can't believe you just accused me of this. Have you been drinking?"

"Well, I was in a bar." Jessica had no idea how to salvage this. Her words dug her ever deeper into a chasm she couldn't escape. She loved this job more than any she'd ever had, and her big mouth had just put it in jeopardy. But still, she didn't know who to believe in this case. So many people disliked Paul Brown, including the woman in front of her. Sometimes it seemed like any of half a dozen people could have killed him. If only she could explain that instead of letting the hurt, belligerent side of her take over.

"You need to take the rest of the day off." Linda's face had grown severe, and she looked every one of her sixty years.

"Fine." Jessica turned in a huff, and two steps later wanted to sink to her knees in regret. Why did she always make her life so hard?

She trod across the warm terra cotta floor to her desk lit by the morning sun. When she picked up her backpack, she saw the list of items she'd planned for the day written on a yellow legal pad. Leaving was the last thing she wanted to do. Her fingers ran over the rich wood of the desk, hoping she'd return soon.

She sat in her truck, berating herself for ever taking the job with Robin, for hurting the woman who'd given her a chance when she'd screwed up her first legal job. Now this one might slip away. Finally, she texted Linda.

*I'm sorry. Please don't fire me.*

No response. She turned the key in the ignition and drove away.

At least Tela would comfort her. Her dog never knew that Jessica created most of her own problems. She only understood emotions and had a loving response for each one.

When she walked in the house, both confusion and joy lit Tela's face. But Angus had left for the day, and even with the dog, the lonely walls of the house closed in on her.

"Let's ,go see Mom," Jessica said, and Tela responded with a tail wag and a bark.

---

Jessica could see her mother through the window when she pulled up to her cottage. Clarice waved at her, paintbrush in her hand. Sheba bounced like a ball, appearing and disappearing in the window near her mom.

By the time Jessica and Tela had exited the truck, her mom stood at the open door and Sheba beelined toward them, barking incessantly. The two dogs took off, chasing each other around the nearby trees.

"This is an unexpected surprise," her mother said, wrapping Jessica in a hug.

Jessica actually hugged her back, grateful for the caring gesture. She tried to quell her overdramatic thoughts, but the day had just been so shitty.

"Let me show you what I'm painting," her mom said when she finally let go. She grabbed Jessica's hand and practically pulled her into the cottage.

The furniture once near the window now crowded the rest of the room. A drop cloth covered the tile beneath the glass, which let in light filtered by the trees. A large canvas sat on an easel, half of it painted and half with only sketch marks. The painting still had her mother's shattered glass style, but lavender mountains rose to meet a cotton candy sky. Where once her mother's paintings evoked a tragic midnight, this one showed the dawn.

"It's beautiful. It's so different." Jessica had always seen herself mirrored in her mother's bleak images. This painting showed the effervescence of Clarice's change since moving from Fort Davis to El Paso. Tinges of darkness remained where violet blurred to slate or pink briefly tinged blood red, but overall, the painting reflected hope. Jessica didn't find herself in it at all.

"I thought I needed to try something new." Her mom sighed deeply as she touched the edge of the canvas. "It was hard losing your father, letting go of that part of my life. I'm trying to paint my future."

Jessica bowed her head and fought back tears, overcome with grief for her father and awe for this woman who kept reinventing herself. At whatever cost.

"What brings you out here in the middle of a workday? And would you like something to drink? I picked up a couple of pecan sticky buns that would be great with a freshly brewed pot of tea." Clarice moved toward the kitchen. "By the way, you smell like a brewery."

"Thanks," Jessica said, about to launch into how she'd already had a hard day and didn't need her mom's judgement. But then her eyes saw the painting, her mother's hope for a brightness to come. "A sticky bun and tea sound wonderful."

Jessica trailed Clarice to the other side of the large room and took her place on a stool. "I guess this house is working out for you, if you're painting and all."

"I love it here. And I'm no longer worried about intruders now that I have Sheba."

"Mom, she's not built to stop an intruder."

"No, but she'll warn me."

And then what, Jessica wondered. She should ask her mom to join her firearms class. Nix that. Given their volatile relationship, they probably shouldn't be in the same room with loaded weapons.

Jessica heard the crunching of gravel under tires and turned to look out the picture windows. "No, no, no. I've spent all day avoiding this guy. I never should have come here." Jessica spun around. "You don't have a back door, do you?"

"It's just Lefty. Why would you want to avoid him?"

"Mom, everyone but you wants to avoid this guy. He's a little too vested in finding Paul Brown's killer."

"But it's his case. Of course he's invested in it."

Jessica sighed. Her mother's comment rang true, but Lefty seemed to want easy solutions. And Brown had mucked up his life enough that any number of people might have killed him.

"I'm out of here," Jessica said. "Tela, let's go."

Jessica opened the door before Lefty had a chance to knock. "Nice to see you, Deputy Griswald. Enjoy your visit with my mother."

"Not so fast." Lefty's bulk filled the doorway, and he made no move to enter the house. "I've been looking for you all day, and I need a few minutes of your time. Good afternoon, ma'am," he said, turning to Clarice.

"It's nice to see you, Lefty. Would you like some hot tea?" A sour look crossed Lefty's face. "Or perhaps you'd like me to brew you some coffee?"

"Coffee sounds wonderful."

Jessica fumed through the conversation. Of course he'd make her mom brew a whole pot of coffee. Typical of guys like this. "I'm sorry, I've got to leave now and don't have time to talk."

"I highly recommend you make time." Lefty still hadn't budged from the doorway.

"Are you planning on arresting me?"

"Jessica!" Clarice yelped. "Stop that right now. Let's all sit down and have a chat."

Christ, did her mother think she was four? Still, Jessica backed away from the door. Lefty walked in and closed it behind him.

"Care to join me in the kitchen?" Lefty said.

Jessica crossed her arms in defiance but sauntered back toward her mother. She might as well get this over with.

Lefty pulled out a barstool and made himself comfortable. "It's nice to see you, Clarice."

Jessica wanted to puke, especially when she saw the happy way her mother gazed at him. Even Sheba wiggled at his feet, seemingly impressed with the deputy. At least Tela stayed by her side.

"Please sit," Lefty said, nodding at the adjacent stool.

"No thank you. I'd prefer to stand."

"Suit yourself. What can you tell me about the son Paul Brown has in Mexico?"

"You know, I haven't done any DNA testing." Jessica had no reason to share information with him.

"What?" Her mother's eyes grew big. "Why didn't you tell me?"

"It's not really my story to tell," Jessica said.

"He's a person of interest in a murder investigation. You need to share any information you have on him with me. That includes his address and phone number."

"Why? So you can accuse someone else of killing Paul Brown without actually doing any detective work?"

"Young lady, I won't have you interfering with an official investigation. You might consider yourself to be some kind of amateur detective, but this case actually needs to be solved."

"Why?" She'd started to wonder if leaving this case unsolved would be better for everyone involved.

"Because there's a murderer on the loose."

Jessica ignored her mother's sharp intake of breath. "For all we know, the person who killed him forty years ago has already met their own demise. And given what I've learned of Paul Brown, it wouldn't surprise me if he bashed himself in the head with a rock."

"Shovel is more likely." Lefty dead-panned the answer.

Clarice gasped, and a chill went down Jessica's spine. The gleam in Lefty's eye showed he enjoyed the surprise.

"How do you know that?"

"The skull was flattened in a way that had no sharp edges and hit a broad area of the left side of his forehead. At least, according to the coroner. It would be difficult to hit yourself in the head with a shovel hard enough to cause death." Lefty gave Jessica a long stare. "Now, let's talk about Mr. Brown's Mexican kids."

"There are a lot of people who had the opportunity to kill him. Have you talked to his hunting buddies or any of the guys he had investments with? Heck, even his business partner didn't seem to like him much. Why are you concentrating on the kids?"

"He had two teenage boys, both on the verge of adulthood. Stories about brotherly jealousy and violence go back through history, from Marvel's Thor and Loki to Shakespeare's King Lear and his illegitimate brother Edmund to the Bible's Cain and Abel. Sons of that age want their father's approval."

It shocked Jessica that this cowboy looking deputy seemed to be well read. Better read than she. "You didn't strike me as a literary kind of guy."

"Jessica," Clarice said, Disappointment laced the word. Jessica wished her mother would support her just once.

"So, based on your reading of the classics and a few recent movies, you are certain that one of Paul Brown's sons murdered him forty years ago. That seems a little biased to me." She'd already disappointed her mom. Why not push further?

"I think both are likely suspects, but for all I know, his son in Mexico has an alibi. I won't know until I can question him. And I need you to tell me how to contact him."

"And if he does have an alibi, you'll go back to accusing Colby, who can't answer for himself? What about Mrs. Brown, or Robin? They could wield a shovel."

"They wouldn't have had the strength or the height to cause that wound." Lefty shook his head. "For all of your accusations about bias, you don't want to look at the most viable suspects. Why is that?"

Jessica didn't have an immediate response to the question. For all she knew, Colby had killed his father. His own writings certainly gave him motive. Yet her gut told her to believe Linda and Robin. And Abel. He had motive and residual anger. That anger could be key. If he had killed his father, wouldn't his anger have morphed into fear of being caught? Especially after so many years? She shook the thoughts away. Bias or not, one truth remained. "You don't have enough evidence to be certain one of his sons killed him."

"I'm pretty good at getting confessions out of people. That's why I need to know where to find Gamboa."

Jessica had watched plenty of true crime on TV, and she knew her mom had also. "Confessions get forced all the time."

"Are you refusing to cooperate with me?" Lefty's voice sliced through the air.

"Yes. I am." She pushed false pride into her voice. Part of her wanted to cooperate and work with him to solve the crime, but a larger part of her didn't trust him. Maybe her experience with the El Paso sheriffs made her wary. They'd arrested her and been on the wrong side of right in her dealings with the corrupt preacher. She'd trusted herself then, and she did now. Even so, she couldn't get past the feeling they'd missed something in this case. Almost too many people had issues with Paul Brown.

Lefty stood. "I hope you change your mind. Here's my card."

He walked across the room and opened the door, then turned around. "I don't know if you're looking for a payday or some kind of glory, but that's not what solving cases and law enforcement are about."

"The only thing I want is the truth." She met his stare with defiance.

"Clarice, I'm sorry I can't stay for coffee, and I hope to see you soon." He tipped his black cowboy hat, then closed the door.

"Jessica. Why do you have to be like that?" Lefty hadn't even reached his car before her mother started berating her. "He wants to find the truth, and you won't even help him."

Jessica shook her head, disappointment flowing off of her in waves. "What do you see in him? Are you already looking for a replacement for Dad?" She knew the words would sting. What in her made her want to hurt this woman? Retaliation for the way she'd been hurt so long ago? Perhaps. She thought she'd be beyond this by now, but her mom still brought out her most petty, childish instincts. Maybe they'd damaged their relationship beyond repair. Maybe Jessica was too damaged to forgive.

She looked at her mother and saw the pain she'd caused reflected back at her. Her rational brain understood that her mom just wanted to recover a normal life. She'd been banished to the wilderness, just like Cain. Jessica chuckled. And where did that leave Abel?

"I'm glad you find this funny. I don't know why you are behaving this way, but it's completely embarrassing. Your father would be so disappointed." Heated anger sparked the words.

"Yeah, because he always stood for the truth and justice."

"He did."

"He was arrested and prosecuted for breaking the law."

"He was just trying to protect the people who worked for him."

Jessica stared at her mom, who would always forgive her father despite everything he'd done to them. To Jessica. An ugly part of her wanted to rise up, to slap her mother. The hurt child inside her forever wanted to punish someone, to pinch back for every unkind word and look she'd had to endure.

"You're just like him," her mother said, her punishment arriving first.

Jessica stood, whistled for Tela, and walked out the door. Time to set new boundaries with her mother. They were, after all, just another form of punishment.

# Chapter 22

Jessica growled once she'd stepped outside and closed the door. Tela cocked her head and cast a confused glance at her. Frustration nagged at her in so many ways. She couldn't seem to improve her relationship with her mother. She couldn't make Lefty less pompous and more curious about who might really have murdered Paul Brown. And she'd utterly failed at solving the case on her own. Every day seemed to bring a new suspect.

Exasperation swirled in her, and she didn't want to confine it to her truck or worse—take it back home and spring it on Angus. Instead, she started walking. She stomped down an aisle of tall trees, their bare branches looming above her. A breeze swirled dead leaves at her feet. Tela thought it a game and chased after the leaves, running ahead of her through the trees.

Of course she ended up back at the crime scene. Or gravesite, however one wanted to look at it. Seeing the caution tape and a hole in the ground did nothing to relieve her vexation. She walked on, curious whether she strode over other bones from other murders through the ages.

Morbid thoughts for a cold afternoon, what could be better? She tried attacking one problem at a time. Her mother. Jessica kicked at a fallen branch, and a burst of wind whipped it toward her face. She flailed an arm up to protect herself and managed to get the branch stuck in her hair. She shook her hair to the side and pulled the mucky wood from the once-clean black strands. She wiped her cheek where she thought it had landed, and the back of her hand came back streaked with mud and a little blood.

Damn it. Why wouldn't anything go her way? Just thinking about her mother caused disaster, or at least caused the elements to attack her. Clarice just wanted a new life, a second chance. Given the new painting, she was succeeding. So why couldn't they get along?

Jessica dropped the slim, foot-long branch. Tela grabbed it and ran, turning around a few yards away as if she wanted to be chased. At least it wasn't a bone this time.

Jessica put the thoughts of her mother behind her. She couldn't do anything about that. It was what it was. The same with Lefty. She wouldn't be able to change him. She sure hoped her mom wouldn't get involved enough to try. It's not that she didn't want her mom to find love again someday, she deserved that. Everyone did. But surely Clarice could do better than Lefty. Not that Jessica cared, after all, it's not like her mom was around when she chose Angus. Or when she went through those many years of pushing Angus away and sleeping with a string of guys she knew for only one night.

It hurt to look back on that woman who'd numbed herself from the hurts of the world with booze and sex. She'd thought it hadn't mattered. If she could fill that greedy hole in her with vices, at least she'd be full. But it hadn't worked like that. The temporary high just left her wanting more. More destruction, more danger. It was as if she took out her revenge on her parents on her own body. Is that what she'd done?

She shook her head. It wasn't like that. She'd had fun. She still liked the call of danger, but now she kept the sex to Angus—way more fulfilling than anyone else. She kept the danger to solving cases and helping people.

Maybe she'd grown up. Except when her thoughts circled back to her mom. What made relationships with parents so difficult? Is that what happened with Abel? Had his anger festered for years the way hers had? Jessica had never wanted to kill her parents, she just wanted to abandon them the way they'd abandoned her. Like for like. Hurt for hurt.

Paul had taken away Abel's future, or at least that's the way it would have felt to a seventeen-year-old. And what about Colby? Paul had condemned him to a future he didn't want. How did either boy forgive their father? And when you're a teen, you think it's all your fault. You're not as good as your dad's other son. You're not good enough to make your parents proud. You're not good enough to make them stay.

Abel directed his rage toward a dead father. None of it blew toward Mayra, at least none that Jessica had seen. Colby had taken the fury out on himself. That hurt both parents, assuming he didn't know his father was dead. Assuming his mother even had a heart.

Jessica had no doubt Barbara could kill someone. That woman hated embarrassment. If she'd throw her own child under the bus because of convenience and not wanting an ancient story in the press, she certainly might have killed Paul for causing her shame. But using a shovel in a pecan grove seemed far-fetched.

Perhaps she hired someone to kill him. Of course, Jessica would love to pin the crime on Dick, but Barbara hadn't known him then.

Paul's partner might have been a candidate, but he certainly hadn't benefited from Paul's death. Maybe she should talk to him again. He'd mentioned the dead man's questionable business dealings, a common motive for murder.

She avoided fingering Mayra. She couldn't picture the beloved grandmother as a young woman having an affair with a married American. How had she even found him? She lived so far from civilization. The more she learned about this case, the more questions she had.

Jessica heard a deep rumble, and a gust of wind shook a few remaining leaves from the trees. When she looked up, the shards of sky visible through the branches had turned graphite gray. Had that really been thunder?

Most of El Paso's desert's sparse rain fell in July and August, bringing welcome relief from scorching temperatures. Now she pulled her jacket tight, the January winds bringing in ominous weather. She spun around. She'd purposefully headed in a different direction from where Tela had discovered Paul Brown's body.

Having walked down one row of trees, getting back should be easy, except that Tela had taken off in a crosswise direction. If that dog went back to the crime scene and started digging again, she'd be in big trouble.

Jessica turned where she'd last seen Tela, calling her name. Soon she heard barking. "Tela," she shouted into the wind. The barking increased, but the dog didn't return.

Tramping through the orchard, Jessica thought she heard human voices alongside her unruly dog. Maybe Lefty had returned to the crime scene after leaving her mother's. She sped up to a jog. An engine started.

Jessica reached her dog and realized she'd arrived back where Tela had found the body. She looked down the alley of trees and glimpsed a bright blue truck speeding away, not the black and white of the sheriff.

Blue truck. Could it really have been Abel? How would he have possibly known to come here? Unless he'd been here before, like the night Paul Brown died.

She studied the ground. The chaos of footprints left no clues.

Jessica pulled her phone from her pocket. By now, Abel had likely reached pavement and a smooth road back to Mexico. She found his name in her recent calls, listened to the phone ring, then go to voice-mail.

"Abel, this is Jessica Watts. I just saw you drive away from the Browns' pecan grove. We need to talk."

What if he was the killer? Would he kill again to keep things quiet? "Tela, come." Jessica started jogging toward her mom's cottage as soon as she issued the command. Her mind raced. Pickup trucks sat in damn near every driveway in this region, plenty of them blue. But Jessica rarely believed in coincidences.

Abel might be the killer, and if he'd killed once, he might kill again. She had to reach her mother.

# Chapter 23

Jessica heaved a sigh of relief when just her white pickup and her mother's van came into view. She'd dreaded seeing the blue truck there.

She swung open the door which her mother hadn't bothered to lock after Jessica left. As she burst into the room, Sheba barked in a frenzy, and Clarice dropped her mug and spun toward the door.

"What on earth?" Her mom looked terrified.

"I'm sorry to scare you, but you should have locked the door. You need to stay with me tonight." Adrenaline still sped through Jessica's blood. Sheba had quieted, and she and Tela sniffed each other.

Clarice bent and retrieved the mug, now separated from its handle. "This was my favorite." She turned and dumped it in the trash before cleaning up the mess.

"I'm sorry. I was just scared someone would hurt you." Jessica crossed the room to help. "I'll get this. You go pack something to take to my place tonight."

"Honey, I'm fine here. Why are you acting like this?"

Jessica stilled. She wanted to tell her mom the truth, but hunches weren't facts. "I was walking in the orchard, and Tela ran off to the crime scene. She started barking, but by the time I got there, all I saw was a truck driving off."

"Oh, it was probably Lefty. He might have been hanging around until you were gone. You weren't exactly nice to him."

"The truck was blue. Abel Gamboa's truck is blue."

"Oh. Do you think it was him?" Shock hit Clarice's blue eyes.

Jessica could see her putting the pieces together. Only one explanation made sense.

"If he knew where the body was, that means he did it. You have to tell Lefty." Clarice stared Jessica down.

"Fine. Will you stay with Angus and me tonight?"

"I think I'm fine out here. What would he want with me?"

Probably nothing, but why take that chance? "Mom, please. It's not like Sheba can protect you."

"I'm an adult, and I get to make my own decisions."

Her mom sounded more like a petulant child than an adult at the moment. Jessica remembered saying almost the same thing to her mother when she was sixteen. She had insisted she could take care of herself. Now, she'd never know if she would have been better off with her parents or on her own. Life may present you with choices, but in the end, you only walked one path.

"I know you're an adult, but it would make me feel better if you stayed with us. Just for tonight." And tomorrow, she'd get her mother a bigger dog.

Clarice didn't remove her hands from her hips. Jessica couldn't tell what emotions ran through her mother, but she didn't look happy.

"This conversation sounds eerily familiar," Clarice said. "I let you have your choice, back then. It was probably my biggest mistake."

"I made a good life for myself."

"From what I've heard, that's questionable. You're doing fine now, but you have to admit you had a lot of hard years. I should have come back. I should have tried harder. I'm really sorry about that." Her mom's taut posture melted, and she wrapped Jessica in a hug.

Jessica stayed rigid. So many feelings twisted through her. Regret that she'd refused to take her mother's calls or open her letters. Betrayal that her parents ever thought they should leave their daughter. She still wanted to hang on to that righteous sixteen-year-old full of anger at the people who had ruined her life. They hadn't cared enough to stay, even though staying put her in danger. Funny how they'd wanted to protect her from criminals, and she'd ended up crossing paths with them again and again and barely surviving. But she had survived. A ray of pride cut through the regret and betrayal, and she grabbed hold of the woman she'd become.

"Mom." Jessica extricated herself from the hug. "Please, this is for your safety. Can we put the past behind us, at least for now? I don't want to spend all night worrying about whether you're in danger out here."

"Of course."

And it was over. All of the angst from the conversation, Jessica bore alone. Her mother had capitulated without an argument, something Jessica had probably never done.

Just like that, a smile returned to Clarice's face. "I'll be right back with a packed bag. You call Lefty."

Her mom marched toward the bedroom, and Jessica drew her phone out. She still didn't want to believe it ended this way. Paul Brown had wronged Abel and his family. But if he had murdered his father, he should be in jail. Shouldn't he?

She pulled out her phone and stared at the screen, hoping some new information would reveal itself. She wavered between calling Lefty and reaching out to Abel again to see if he had a different explanation.

She pressed the numbers and lifted the phone to her ear.

---

Jessica's phone rang at midnight, pulling her out of a deep sleep. She grabbed it from her nightstand and mumbled hello.

"Hello? Jessica, it's Mayra."

Jessica sat up straight, bringing the comforter with her and causing Angus to grumble. She slipped out of bed and headed toward the kitchen before worrying about waking her mother. The guest room flanked the small home's kitchen and living area.

"Just a minute," she whispered into the phone before closing herself in the bathroom. Finally, she leaned against the counter and tried to gather her thoughts. "Is everything all right?"

"No. Abel is really upset. He doesn't know I'm calling. A reporter from El Paso called him today and wanted to talk about his father."

Could this get any worse? A flare of anger lit in Jessica. Either Lefty or Robin must have called the reporter. Either way, bigger issues faced Abel.

"Mayra, I think I saw him today. I saw his truck where Paul Brown's body was found. I have to tell the sheriff." She'd tried to already, kind of. She'd left a message for Lefty on his office landline instead of calling his cell phone. Although she had no reason, she'd struggled with the decision to call him. She had clung to some hope that it wasn't Abel's truck.

"We were there." Mayra's words cemented Jessica's guilt. She should have done the right thing.

"We used to visit Paul at the pecan grove. He first took us there the day after he bought it, on Abel's sixth birthday. He said someday he'd build a house there, and we would all live there as a family."

Mayra's words ripped Jessica's heart out. She'd thought of past Abel as a teenager, an angry young man—something she understood. Now she comprehended all the years he'd been a child, believing in his parents and longing for his promised family. And all that time his father had another family who thought he'd loved them exclusively. She wanted to go back in time and kill Paul Brown herself.

"I believed Pablo." Pain coursed through Mayra's voice. "I was so stupid back then. I thought he loved us too. If it had just been me, his love would have left me scarred, but whole. Instead, I let him steal the innocence from my children. They'll never have faith in people the way I did. Abel never married. He's never been able to trust."

"And that made him kill his father." Jessica didn't know whether her words to Mayra were question or statement. As much as it hurt Jessica to bring it up, Abel had balanced the mental anguish with physical injury.

"No! He never would have done that. I promise you that." Mayra's shrill voice echoed through the phone and off the bathroom walls.

"But last night, he knew exactly where the body was. There is only one way he could have known."

"Abuela, que pasa?" Jessica heard another voice, one farther away. Mayra's exclamation must have woken others.

"Jessica, I have to go." Mayra's voice had lowered to a whisper. "I swear on my life and all that is holy that Abel did not kill his father."

The call ended. Jessica shivered, her bare feet freezing on the cold tile. Now what? She'd wait for Lefty's call in the morning. Give him Abel's phone number if he didn't have it already. None of this seemed fair.

She typed a message to Robin. "Call me in the morning. We need to talk."

# Chapter 24

The next time her phone rang, Jessica grabbed it, punched the button to turn it off, and slid it under her pillow. She needed to turn the damn thing off at night.

She tried to bury herself under the covers and snuggle against Angus's warm body, but the early gray light of morning already filtered through the curtains. Curious, she pulled out her phone. The clock read six thirty-five, and the call had been from Robin. When she'd asked her to call in the morning, she thought the woman would wait until a reasonable hour.

A whimper drew her away from the phone. Tela rested her head on the bed, staring at her with one blue and one green eye. She licked her chops and whimpered again.

"It's not time to eat yet," she told the dog. "It's only six thirty."

"I know." Angus's sleepy voice caught her off guard.

Jessica pulled herself out of bed. Since she'd already woken everyone up, she might as well get the day going. Her mom strode into the kitchen while Jessica started the coffee. When Clarice asked about her plans for the day, she said she needed to get to the office early. She didn't want to speculate about any of the pieces she'd set in motion, at least not with her mom.

---

By the time Jessica made it into the office, her agitation had hit an all-time high. Despite Linda not returning her text yesterday. Jessica assumed she still had a job. And she needed Linda. Everything about this case seemed so unfair. Fortunately, Robin hadn't called again, and Lefty must not have found her message yet. She threw her phone on her desk and marched straight into Linda's office.

"I need help," she said, dropping into a chair in front of Linda's desk. She explained seeing the truck at the crime scene, her call to Lefty, and Mayra's midnight call to her. "The fact that he showed up at the exact spot where Paul Brown died points to Abel, but this whole case is infuriating. The guilty party is Paul Brown, yet he ended up dead."

"Seeing a truck at a crime scene isn't evidence. The only real evidence is a bashed-in skull. Any DNA from the scene is certainly degraded, so from a legal standpoint the case will be hard to prove. I think your deputy will try for a confession."

"It still doesn't make it right." Jessica fumed in her seat. Her strong emotions embarrassed her. How could she fight for her clients as an attorney if she couldn't see past her own sense of justice?

"Nothing that happens today will make Paul Brown a good guy. He lied and cheated, betraying two families in the process. That doesn't excuse murder, but you need to stay objective. Abel visiting the orchard doesn't seal his guilt. You need to learn the truth about what happened. Having known the guy, I still think there's any number of people who may have killed him."

"So, like you've told me before, just take it one step at a time and see where the clues lead." Jessica took a deep breath, willing herself to listen to Linda's wisdom.

"Exactly." Linda shuffled a few papers on her desk.

"Thanks. Also, I'm really sorry about yesterday. I shouldn't have lost my temper. I want to work here and hope I still have a job." She looked into Linda's eyes, praying her own showed she meant her words.

"Well, you do make good coffee. Speaking of which, I'd really like some." Linda gave her a smile.

A good portion of Jessica's tension melted away. "Coming right up."

"Before you go, there's something I have to tell you. The girls have been moved to a detention center in Pecos."

Another blow. Between the lack of sleep and all the tension, Jessica almost broke down in tears. But that wouldn't help Mari or Angela. She inhaled, accepting the news and vowing, again, to solve the crimes they'd witnessed.

She'd texted Robin after learning about the girls' transfer, determined to uncover the connections her husband had to the men in the desert. Also, honestly, because something in her chest didn't want Abel to suffer, again, for his father's indiscretions. She started by asking if Robin had given Lefty or the reporter Abel's number. She swore she hadn't.

Jessica asked if they could meet. Robin said she'd be at her mom's all morning and invited Jessica over.

"Are you sure that's a good idea?" Jessica asked.

Robin explained it was the only time she had that day. Jessica left the office as soon as she'd made Linda's coffee and taken care of a few urgent, work-related tasks.

Frustration consumed Jessica as she drove to Barbara's house. She hadn't made progress on who killed the girls' family as they crossed into the US. And now the girls lived two hundred miles from El Paso. They needed answers. She hadn't studied in days, and she had tests coming up and papers due. If she flunked out of law school, then what the hell would she do with her career? She hadn't gotten her mother the right dog. She hadn't wrapped up this stupid case that had nothing to do with justice.

Her phone rang. Lefty. He'd just have to wait a few more minutes. Jessica's old truck didn't have a fancy Bluetooth connection that would allow her to talk and drive at the same time. Of course, avoiding him felt better than explaining why she'd procrastinated telling him about the blue truck she'd seen.

By the time she pulled into Barbara's circular drive, all the things Jessica hadn't done threatened to explode her into a million pieces. She took a deep breath and held it, struggling to contain the angst and anger.

She shuddered as she released the breath. All she could do was move forward.

Jessica grabbed her phone as she opened the truck's door and saw the message notification. She'd call Lefty back later.

Robin swung the door open seconds after Jessica rang the bell. "Come on in. We're having breakfast and I've set you a place."

Jessica followed her, thankfully not to that bizarre rose-colored dressing room, but into the kitchen. A bay window collected morning light, illuminating Barbara's perfectly coiffed silver hair as she sat at a small table picking out grapefruit sections with a tiny silver spoon.

"Good morning, Lupe," Jessica said to the maid who now stood behind the largest stove Jessica had ever seen. All for one little old lady. She nodded at Barbara who barely acknowledged her presence.

"Come sit over here." Robin gestured toward the sunlit table. "I picked up croissants on my way over this morning, and the grapefruit is delicious. Lupe can make you an egg if you'd like."

What was this, Downton Abbey? The poor woman probably had to do all sorts of tasks outside her job description. She sat, trying to tamp down on surly Jessica who'd arrived ready to hunt bear. Maybe she did need to eat.

Robin made small talk while Jessica stuffed her mouth. The croissant had a million flaky, buttery layers, and each bite of deliciousness settled her. Barbara finished her grapefruit and signaled to Lupe to take it away. Jessica, Robin, and her mother looked at each other in silence.

Jessica started. "I've got several things I need to talk to you about. I was at the pecan grove last night and saw a blue truck near the place where your dad was found." It didn't seem right to call it a crime scene in front of Robin.

"Does it belong to that Mexican?" Barbara's nasty voice cut in.

Jessica inhaled, trying to keep from calling the woman a bitch. "I didn't see who was driving it. Robin, perhaps we should take this conversation somewhere else."

"It's about time we pin Paul's murder on someone." Barbara pushed herself out of her chair. "I'm going to my rooms."

Pin the murder on someone? Who talks like that? Jessica took a good look at Barbara as she stood staring daggers into her daughter. "Ma'am, do you know something about Paul's death that you haven't told us?"

Barbara turned her icy gaze to Jessica. "I told you to leave this alone. Nothing good will come of digging this up. The past should have remained buried. But I'm fine with that Mexican going to jail. Better that they look at him than my family."

"Do not refer to him as 'that Mexican.' He's my brother." Robin's voice sliced toward her mother like a sword, felling her as she collapsed back into the chair. Maybe Robin did have a little of the old lady in her after all.

"Colby was your brother." The words came out sharp and defiant, but Barbara's posture had deflated. Every year of her age showed in the lines on her face. Makeup cracked in the folds of her cheeks and the lipstick remaining on the outer edge of her lips seemed garish instead of sophisticated.

"He was. And so is Abel. Mother, I know this hurts, but Dad had a whole other family, and I want to get to know them."

"But what if he killed your father?" Barbara had resorted to pleading, something Jessica doubted she'd done much.

"What if Colby did? What if a business associate did? Why are you so eager to accuse the first person to come along? Don't you want to know what really happened to Daddy?"

Long seconds of silence stretched across the table. Robin leaned forward, vibrant and strong, seeming to steal whatever energy Barbara had left. Jessica stayed quiet, watching the battle play out before her.

"So much happened back then, and I don't want to know." Barbara's voice, now slight, could barely be heard across the table. "I don't want to know about him cheating on me almost the entire time we were married. It's shameful. He deserved what he got."

"Momma, it may be shameful, but it's not your fault. You can't carry that burden."

While Robin's thoughts went to family, Jessica couldn't get over Barbara thinking her husband got what he deserved. That was motive. A

Barbara forty years younger would have been a force to behold. What would that type of shame lead a person to do? Except Lefty said the blow came from a taller person. Unless Paul had been on the ground. Or she could have paid someone to kill him.

"Did you have anything to do with Paul's death?" Jessica asked. She caught Robin swiveling toward her from the corner of her eye but kept her gaze on Barbara. The older woman's forehead tightened, and her eyes narrowed, but she didn't immediately respond.

"Of course not," she finally said, then heaved herself from her chair and left the kitchen.

The room seemed to hold its breath, then Lupe turned on the faucet and ran a dirty plate through the water. The noise broke the spell of Barbara's departure.

Robin rose and gestured to Jessica. "Let's go talk."

Jessica feared Robin would go after her mother, but she turned the other direction and headed down a short hallway to a back door. They stepped out on a lush grass carpet, an expensive luxury in El Paso. Normally, people with lawns grew Bermuda grass that went fallow and straw-like in the winter, but Jessica stepped across actual green grass. Tall trees arched over the lawn, and she could imagine the oasis they formed in the summer when the now-bare branches filled with leaves. A slate patio with furniture and an outdoor kitchen lay to her left, but Robin marched straight across the grass.

At the edge of the property, a low wall separated manicured landscaping from harsh desert. A wide, flat arroyo stretched thirty feet below them before rising up the far bank. Houses stared back at them from the other side. Jessica recognized one home, now painted dark blue, where a friend once lived. She'd played spin the bottle there with a group of friends, feeling edgy and all grown up. She must have been fourteen then, with no idea what the future had in store.

Robin sat on the wall and swung her legs to the arroyo side. It was the action of a girl, not the middle-aged woman in wool slacks and quilted jacket before her now. Jessica joined her, looking down on the dry land beneath them. Yuccas reached their spikes toward a low-slung gray sky.

Yesterday's storm hadn't materialized, but dark clouds plump with rain or snow still hugged El Paso's mountains.

"I don't know what's wrong with her," Robin said. A mockingbird chattered on a nearby branch.

Jessica waited. Neither the bird nor Robin had said anything worth a response. Jessica could see beige paths through cactus and brush probably used by deer and coyotes. She wished for a superpower that would allow her to jump the thirty feet down and wend her way up the arroyo to the mountains, leaving this fancy house and all its secrets behind.

"It almost sounded like she was involved in Daddy's death."

A chill went through Jessica, some combination of the cold wall upon which she sat and the threat of the clouds above. She crossed her arms to try to hold on to her warmth.

"I don't even know what to think anymore. Two days ago, everyone thought Colby had killed him. Yesterday, you found Abel's truck there. Today, Mom sounds guilty. What will tomorrow bring?" For once, Robin didn't sound on the verge of tears when speaking of her father's death. Instead, her voice seemed rough, as if the search for her father had worn away her edges and sanded down her brightness.

"Maybe we should get them all in a room together and let them fight it out. Except Colby, of course." Jessica wondered what would have happened if Colby and Abel had met face-to-face. Would they have hated each other? What about Robin and her two half-sisters?

"I want them to come to the party."

"Yeah, we could get them all drunk and loosen some tongues." Terrible idea.

"There are people in my family who will want to sweep this under the rug, pretend like it never happened. I want my welcome to show everyone how serious I am about bringing them into the family."

Jessica nodded, wondering if Barbara or Dick would be first to the broom. That reminded Jessica about Robin's earlier promise.

"Thanks for offering to make Casa Sagrada the beneficiary of the party donation. The girls I was working with have been transferred to

Pecos. You and your husband knew Jeremy Wright, who had them for a while. I'd like to know more about the people Jeremy knew in El Paso. I need your help with this."

Robin turned toward Jessica. "Can you get Abel and the rest of his family to my party? Is the border a problem?" Robin's tone told Jessica this was a negotiation.

"They likely have Border Crossing Cards, but I doubt I can get them here. Why would they come here for a party? Lefty is as eager to go after Abel as he was to accuse your brother of killing your father. Plus, now the reporters are after him."

"What if he did kill him? Don't we need to know the truth?"

"So, you just want everyone to show up like some TV drama, start screaming, maybe throwing things, and then someone will slip and reveal the truth? I don't think that's how real life works."

"I want to see them. I want to get to know them. I need to start somewhere."

"You'll start something all right." Jessica shook her head at Robin's naiveté. The woman hadn't accounted for the power dynamic. She was safe and white, ensconced in her own community. She wanted these relatively poor Mexicans to waltz into her fancy party and bare their souls. They didn't stand a chance against US opinion and the American justice system. They'd be eaten alive.

"Look. I can help you get the names you need. I'll talk to Dick. But you need to help me too. I am determined to find out who killed my father, and I will get to know my new family."

"And if one of them is responsible for your father's death? This does not sound like a good plan."

"Well, I'm fucking tired of people judging my plans." The sentence came out twisted, as if the size of the giant curse word made all the other words bend around it.

"Cuss much?"

"Damn it, Jessica. I'm being serious. You have to help me. We're so close, I can feel it. We'll find out who murdered my dad, and then I can get to know my siblings."

"Sure. You can wrap it up neat as a bow. What if it's one of your siblings? What if it's your mom? What if we don't find the answer? I appreciate that this has caused a lot of trauma for you." Jessica waved her toward the freshly edged lawn, pristine patio furniture, and enormous house. This woman didn't know trauma. She may have lost her father, but her wealth and privilege had bought her peace and safety. Those didn't exist for Abel and his family. All of Paul Brown's wealth had gone to his daughter. Jessica straightened. She'd promised to work for those who needed help. The woman in front of her would be fine no matter what happened. But Jessica needed her to help the others. She wavered.

Robin jumped into the opening she'd left. "I don't expect you to understand why I want to meet them so badly. I was sad after I lost my dad. Devastated. But after I lost Colby? The world went dark. My mom dragged me to therapists, forced me to go to school. I used to hide under my bed in the mornings, and she'd reach down and pull me out by my arm, an ankle, even my hair once. I hated her for a long time after that." Robin crossed her arms, mirroring Jessica's position. Both women had so much hurt to hold inside.

"I'm sorry," Jessica started, "but . . ."

"Wait. I turned all my anger, all my hurt, on her. I started going to school again, just to get away from her. I signed up for every sport and club that met before or after school so I wouldn't have to be home with her. When I was home, I was in my room. Or out here. It's always too hot or too cold for her outside. I had to wait six long years to get to college, and every day my hate grew, poisoning our relationship."

Jessica dropped her head. That same poison had been her elixir. She'd hated her mother for leaving her, and that hate grew each and every year until she almost drowned in it.

"When I met Dick," Robin continued, "he told me I'd regret it if I didn't forgive her. I brought him back to El Paso and told her to her face I forgave her. She said nothing, just looked at me like I was broken." Robin laughed, the noise sharp in the cold air. "In that moment, I realized she wasn't the one I had to forgive. My mom is a frigid woman, and nothing is going to change that. I wanted a full and open heart, and she didn't stand in the way of that. I did."

Robin's words had turned to Greek, unable to penetrate Jessica's understanding. Far beyond frigid, Robin's mom was a stone-cold bitch. Pulling her from under the bed by her hair? No one should forgive that shit.

"I had to forgive myself for hating my father for disappearing. I had to forgive myself for my anger at Colby's betrayal. I hated him too for a while, even though I knew he hurt so bad he preferred death to life. I had to forgive myself for wishing my mother weren't the one to survive and for wishing she was someone different. I was just a kid. I did the best I could at the time."

"Yeah." Her words made Jessica uncomfortable. Robin's Pollyana world didn't encompass her, perhaps because Robin had never supported herself. She went from her mom's house to college to being supported by Dick. Jessica had clawed her way through early adulthood. Hell, she was still doing it.

Besides, Jessica had more important things to worry about. "You think you can really find out how many people in your husband's circle were involved with Jeremy Wright?"

Robin smirked and shook her head. "You are just determined to fight the world forever, aren't you?"

Whatever that meant. Fighting was living, breathing. The idea coalesced into an explanation. "A couple of years ago, I promised to do everything in my power to fight for justice for those who don't have it—especially for women who've had their voices blocked and their power taken away. That's worth fighting for. Every day." Her willingness to fight gave her pride in herself, one of the scant places she found that particular emotion.

Robin's eyes locked her in a steady gaze. "I can get the information from Dick. Can you get the Gamboa clan to show up at my party?"

"I can invite them, but I can't force them to come. There are some hard feelings there. They lost their dad too, but they also lost the future he'd promised them. I'm not sure if you've thought about that part of it."

Robin looked out to the desert. "Believe me, Dick won't let me forget that part of the story. He's sure they want money to make up for any hardship. Do you know the particulars?"

"I think your dad promised Abel he'd pay for college in the US. They all speak perfect English, even the grandkids. They also thought they'd get to live with him at the pecan grove."

"Oh." Anguish threaded through Robin's voice and a single tear slid down her cheek. "How many did you meet?"

"Mayra, her daughter, Irma, and three granddaughters. And, of course, Abel."

Robin reached out to touch Jessica, her palm warm and soft against Jessica's wrist. "They are my family. Please help me connect with them." The longing in Robin's voice caught Jessica off guard.

The sadness of lost families wrapped itself around Jessica. "I think we've got ourselves a deal."

# Chapter 25

That afternoon, Jessica sat at her desk, her chest tight with everything she had to accomplish. She talked to Lefty about seeing the truck at the pecan grove that could be Abel's. She left a message on Abel's phone about the party, practically begging the family to attend the party. The two calls seemed absurd when compared with each other, but she'd keep her client happy and let the Gamboas decide the next step.

Work consumed the rest of her day, but she caught up. She pulled a heavy textbook from her bag and cracked it open to reveal the many chapters she had to read before she could start on the paper due next week. Plus, she wanted to go to the pound and get an actual guard dog for her mother.

She glanced at the clock. Four twelve. She'd study for forty-five minutes, then go to the animal shelter. Tonight, she'd lock herself away from Angus and her mom and make time to catch up with schoolwork.

The door rattled and Linda walked in. Jessica hoped to give her a quick update on the day's business, but Linda took a seat in one of the chairs in front of her desk.

"I'm glad to see you studying," Linda said. "How did things work out with Robin this morning?" She relaxed into the chair as if she had all the time in the world to chat.

"Honestly, I have no idea who killed Paul Brown, but I'm not done with the case. Also, I promise I'm getting all my work here done. I've confirmed all of your meetings for tomorrow, and the upcoming court schedule is on your desk along with the Brady contract." After her outburst yesterday, Jessica wanted to prove her worth.

"I'm not worried about that. You're doing a great job here. I just want to make sure you pass all your classes and get your degree. Another attorney would be a fine addition to this office."

Although Jessica wanted to play it cool, she couldn't help but smile. She'd love to work here beside Linda, taking on real cases and showing up in court to defend her clients. "I'd like that. Although, I do have to study more. Robin's case has been more time consuming than I expected. She wants me to get them to show up at her party this week, but I only have Abel's phone number, and I'm pretty sure I'm the last person he'll want to talk to."

"She wants them at her party? Why then, of all the times in the world she could choose to meet them?"

"I think Robin wants the meeting to be a public affair so her mom can't hide it. I swear, the way Barbara acted this morning, I almost think she had something to do with Paul's death. She really doesn't want the past uncovered and doesn't care who takes the fall for his death as long as people quit looking into it."

"Huh." Linda's brow furrowed. "She had a pretty good reason to be furious with him. Damn near everyone did. That man was not a good person. Hell, I'd probably kill him again if I had the opportunity."

"Again?" What the hell was Linda saying?

"Well, you know—seeing that he's already dead." Linda's eyebrows rose in surprise. "I didn't kill him. It's just a figure of speech. There have been a lot of people I've been closer to killing than Paul Brown. But that doesn't mean I'm sorry he's dead."

Jessica took a breath. The stress of this day plucked every last nerve. Of course Linda wanted the man dead, that might have saved Colby. Her curiosity got the better of her. "Do you think Colby wouldn't have killed himself if his father hadn't died?"

The sigh that emanated from Linda seemed to shake the woman to her core. "Actually, he might have tried to kill himself sooner. His father made him feel tiny, and Colby hated the options his father had given him: go to college, and then join the company or enlist in the Army."

"What a dick. Colby should have just gone out on his own."

"He wouldn't have made it. He was an addict." The words sat between them, a damper on the conversation. But then Linda perked up. "I'm glad you took on this case. It's helped me realize things like that. Colby became an addict, and that wasn't my fault. He was also seriously depressed. For years, I'd blamed myself for that because I'd left him and gone to college. But even if my leaving contributed to his depression, it didn't cause it, and my staying wouldn't have healed him. When you're eighteen, you think the world and everyone in it revolves around your decisions. It doesn't, and you shouldn't carry that burden around with you. It can make you bitter."

"I don't think you're bitter."

"Ask my three ex-husbands if I'm bitter." Linda's grin lit her face.

Man, Jessica loved this woman. She was as broken as Jessica in some ways, but she was out there fighting, making a difference in the world.

"Back to studying," Linda said.

Jessica glanced at the clock. Almost five. "Actually, I'm going to cut out a few minutes early today. I need to get my mom a dog that can actually protect her." She needed chunks of time to attack the law textbooks, not a few minutes.

"Sounds good." Linda stood and headed back to her office.

Jessica had just slid her chair underneath the desk when her cell phone rang. She didn't recognize the number but answered anyway.

"Hello, Jessica. It's Araceli."

———

Jessica left the office, phone stuck to her ear. Even through the low-slung clouds, the sun had warmed the truck's cabin, forming a cozy cocoon. This surprise phone call needed privacy.

"I'm calling on behalf of my grandmother. She's here with me on speakerphone. Abel has disappeared."

"What do you mean? Where has he gone?" *And why are you calling me?*

"The sheriff called here." Mayra's voice sounded far away and soaked in tragedy. "The officer wanted to question him about Paul's murder. He didn't do it, but they'll never believe him. It's just like it was back then. The legitimate son, the white one, is exonerated, given everything. No matter what, Abel always has to pay for the sins of his father."

"Did he agree to meet with the officer? Is that why he's gone?" Jessica doubted that. He'd more likely gone to ground. He'd be impossible to find in Mexico, or at least too expensive for a relatively small sheriff's department to find. Not to solve a forty-year-old crime.

"No. We talked about what he should do. He is innocent, I promise you that. But then the reporter from the *El Paso Times* called again. Did you tell them about us?"

"No. Never. I wouldn't do that." A fury rose in Jessica for every unfair thing that had happened to Mayra and her family. "I let the sheriff know that I saw a truck the same color as Abel's at the pecan grove last night. I'm sorry if that causes any problems, but that was my duty. If it helps, I feel rotten about it. I'd give anything to know who the actual killer is."

A long silence passed. Jessica's guilt grew with each second. She should never have taken this case so far from her desire to help the downtrodden. Robin had plenty of money to make her problems go away.

But Jessica had seen the desire in Robin's eyes. The craving to know what happened to her father so long ago, the longing to know the siblings she'd never met. But what if her need destroyed the other side? Mayra almost certainly relied on Abel for income.

A heavy breath came through the phone, pulling Jessica back into the moment.

"Abel left his phone here. That's why we know he's trying to disappear," Araceli said. "He received another call a few minutes ago. She said her name was Robin, and I hung up on her. That's Paul's daughter, isn't it?"

Jessica heaved a sigh as the soup of this case thickened again. "Yes. I left a message on Abel's phone about this. She wants to invite your family to a party because she wants to meet all of you. She has a romantic vision of a long-lost family." The family she didn't have—siblings who didn't kill themselves, a mother full of comfort instead of coldness.

"A party?" Araceli asked with curiosity and maybe even excitement.

"Yes. She's an art dealer and hosts a big gala every year. Her son is going to be there." *Your cousin.* Jessica tried to send the unspoken thought through the wireless connection.

"Jessica, this is Mayra. I want to prove Abel is innocent."

"Mayra, if Abel didn't kill Paul, then who do you think did?" And why was Abel at the crime scene yesterday?

"I would like to ask Barbara who killed him." Mayra's pointed words held none of the earlier sadness.

"Well, she'll be at Robin's party. Why don't you come?" Jessica feared saying the words, worried she'd break this gossamer thread of connection. The possibility of having them all in a room, possibly uncovering the truth, shone like hope in a bottle.

Lightning flashed across the sky, sending a jagged beam toward El Paso's mountain ridge. A low rumble quickly followed, growing into a clap of thunder.

"Holy crap, we're about to get a storm." Jessica warned herself as much as spoke into the phone. It didn't matter. The line had gone dead. Jessica texted the details of the party. She'd done what she could.

She started the truck as fat raindrops splattered against the windshield. Somehow, the warmth had dissipated from the truck, and Jessica turned the heat on high. She had to keep moving forward, one step at a time, through the storm. Perhaps when she came out the other side, the killer would become clear. Until then, she had a dog to find.

———

Jessica pulled up to the animal shelter. The fat, lazy drops of the storm's beginning had morphed into sheets of rain. She'd have to make a dash for the door. Few desert dwellers carried, or even owned, raincoats and umbrellas.

She jumped out of the truck and ran to the door, pressing the speaker button as freezing rain pelted her. The temperature must have dropped twenty degrees in the last thirty minutes.

She gave her name, and they buzzed her in. Once in the heated office, she pulled wet hair off her face. She couldn't do much about the drops that darkened her turquoise blouse.

"Hey, you were here the other day," said the young woman behind the desk. "You were with your mom."

"I sure was. Mom loves the dog she got, but she also needs a guard dog."

"Is she here?" The woman peered around Jessica as if expecting Clarice to materialize.

"She couldn't make it today." Not that she'd been invited. If Jessica left this decision to her mother, she'd probably go home with Sheba's twin and still not have a dog to protect her. "Will you show me the big dogs again?"

The second the dogs saw them, the barking started. Jessica had remembered a large black dog and a shepherd toward the front of the kennels, but she didn't see them this time. When she asked, she learned they'd been adopted.

About halfway down the row, Jessica stopped. An enormous tan dog with white toes and a black mouth stared at her with hope in its eyes. When Jessica paused, the dog's throat rumbled, then she let loose with a giant clap of a bark.

"She's so beautiful," Jessica said, noticing the short, dark gold fur and long curved tail. "What is she?"

"She's a Cur mix."

Jessica hadn't heard of the breed before. The dog watched them, silent, despite the chaos erupting around them. Jessica needed to find a protector, so she rose onto her toes, lifted her arms in a high vee and roared at the dog. Immediately, the dog let loose with a series of loud barks and squatted, bouncing from side to side as if ready to pounce.

Jessica relaxed. The dog quit barking and stood calmly. The woman showing her the dogs gave her a side-glance, as if she wondered about

Jessica's sanity. Next, Jessica dropped to her knees. Jessica glimpsed the white of the dog's eyes at the maneuver, but she didn't bark. Jessica lowered her head, submissive, and reached a palm toward the animal. The beast took a tentative step forward and then another before stretching forward to sniff Jessica's outstretched hand. Finally, she pressed her large head into Jessica's palm.

"Hi," Jessica said, looking into the dog's eyes. She stroked the top of the animal's head and scratched her neck behind her ears. The dog had a black snout, black ears, and black outlining its golden eyes like thickly applied makeup.

"She's sweet when you're not scaring her," said the shelter attendant.

"She is. And she's really big." Solid muscle passed under Jessica's hands.

"Eighty pounds."

"What's her name?" Jessica asked.

"Hera. She was a Greek goddess, the protector of women."

"I'll take her."

Jessica arrived home, new dog in tow. The entire trip, Hera had sat beside her, her new harness hooked to the seat, and surveyed the scenery without barking or even moving much other than her head. As good as the dog behaved, she worried about bringing her home to Tela and Sheba. Meeting Sheba hadn't fazed Tela. She clearly saw her as a pint-sized playmate.

In the driveway, she texted Angus to grab a hold of Tela and keep her in the living room. Jessica had a firm grip on Hera's collar as she swung the front door open. Tela barked up a storm, and Hera tensed. The second Sheba rounded the corner and glimpsed the huge dog in the doorway, she let out a little yelp and ran behind Clarice, who sat at the kitchen table. Jessica knew the little twerp couldn't handle guard dog duties.

Tela let out a whine and pulled against Angus, who held her tight against his leg. "Who are you, beautiful?" he asked.

Jessica stepped into the house, making soothing noises to all the dogs. Hera remained silent, but Jessica felt her quiver. She hoped the dog would remain calm. Jessica needed this to work.

"Oh, my gosh," Clarice said. "You got another dog."

Jessica walked a few steps closer to her mom. Sheba growled from behind Clarice's ankles.

"This is Hera," Jessica said. "She's an excellent guard dog with a ferocious bark. I got her for you."

"You picked out a dog for me?" Indignation shot through Clarice's words.

"Mom, you need a dog who can protect you. Look what happened last time." She nodded toward Sheba. "She's cute and all, but I'm worried about you staying at the grove all alone. This dog will protect you."

As if she understood the conversation, Hera took a tentative step towards Clarice. A growl rumbled in Sheba's chest, but it didn't stop Hera, who ambled up to Clarice and sat in front of her. Dog and woman surveyed each other, Clarice clearly the more skeptical of the two. Hera sighed, then laid her large head on Clarice's knee.

Jessica expected Sheba to erupt in a frenzy of barking. Instead, she reached her nose toward the new dog and sniffed. Clarice scooped Sheba into her lap, and the two dogs sniffed each other. Then, Sheba licked Hera's snout. Clarice exhaled, all the fight gone. She patted Hera's head, and the dog scooted even closer.

*Smartest dog on the planet.* Jessica had never witnessed such a perfect performance. She moved toward Angus, gave him a kiss, then bent to Tela. "Don't you go ruining this."

The dogs met, then Tela took them on a tour of the house. Soon, Hera lay curled at Clarice's feet while Sheba and Tela chased each other around the kitchen.

"You did good, but don't ever do anything like that again." Clarice's eyes pierced her daughter. "I am an adult, and I get to choose my own pets."

"She's more than a pet. She has a job to do." Clarice might not realize what she needed in a dog, but Jessica sure did.

# Chapter 26

Jessica stepped onto the back porch later that night, letting the dogs out one last time. She shivered despite her flannel pj's and parka. Even the dogs seemed unhappy with the weather, gently placing their feet on the cold, wet grass and staying close to the house. The rain had stopped, but the temperature continued to drop. Morning would probably see the roads slick with ice.

Jessica pulled her phone from her jacket, wishing she'd worn gloves. She called Robin to update her on her conversation with Mayra, although it still seemed like a terrible idea to have invited her to the party. Robin, however, seemed happy at the possibility of Mayra showing up.

"Did you learn anything from Dick about Jeremy Wright's connections?" Jessica's hands shook as she asked the question. The cold seeped further into her as if not just the weather but the topic caused a chill. When she exhaled, her breath exited her in a visible cloud of steam.

"He wasn't too happy when I asked him about it. For some reason, you've hit on a sensitive topic. I didn't get anything out of him today, but I will." Robin's voice had dropped to a whisper, and Jessica wondered if she worried about Dick overhearing her. How safe was it to live with a man like that?

"One more thing," Jessica said. "Abel has disappeared. I probably should have led with that."

"What do you mean, disappeared?"

"His mom called me because she didn't know where he was."

"That sounds like a guilty move," Robin said.

Jessica couldn't disagree. "Well, I'll see you at the party. It should be an interesting night." Probably the understatement of the year.

Several days later, Jessica stood outside the historic Cortez Building in downtown El Paso. Twilight had dampened the wind some, although low clouds still hung over the city. The building faced San Jacinto Plaza, the city's central square, and the warm glow from the park's lighting bounced off the clouds and illuminated the area in a halo.

Unfortunately, no heat emanated from the light. Normally when the sun set in El Paso, temperatures dropped. Today, the sun hadn't ventured out at all. It made for a rare cold and damp day.

Jessica stomped up and down the sidewalk, trying to keep the blood flowing to her feet in their inappropriate, glittery, strappy sandals. She'd promised Angus she'd meet him outside before the party and, given who might or might not show up, putting off the drama for a few more minutes seemed like a good idea. The wide entrance of the hotel bore plaques at either end, one from the National Historic Registry and the other from the Texas Historical Commission. She looked up at the tawny brick building with its decorative cast trim. According to the bronze seals, the building was originally a hotel. She'd only known it as an office building with a few shops and restaurants on the ground floor. She'd never visited the second-floor art gallery or the insurance offices on the higher floors.

She shivered and pulled her wool coat more tightly around her. At least she had picked up a pair of fleece-lined gloves when she'd shopped for shoes on her lunch break. Angus would love this dress. She glanced down at the emerald velvet shimmering from the edge of her coat to her painted toes. Its high neck kept her warm against the chill and looked quite demure. But when he took her coat off, he'd learn the dress had no back from the clasp at her neck to just below her waist. Little sparks of happiness kept her warm as she anticipated that moment.

Finally, he swung around the corner, a big grin lighting his face the moment he saw her. Seeing him made everything brighter. She'd had a good day. Work had been light, which allowed her to catch up on schoolwork. She hadn't heard anything from anyone about Robin's case, and her mom had called to tell her how much she loved Hera.

"You are gorgeous." Angus planted a kiss on her lips and wrapped his arms around her in a hug so big it lifted her off her toes.

"So are you." She looked him up and down. He wore a black suit with subtle lavender pinstripes. He'd cut his hair to collar length and grown a trim beard to go with it. He looked like an adult, with mere glimpses of the kindergarten through college best friend shining through. She'd stepped into the future without even knowing it.

"Come on, handsome. Let's go inside." She pulled him toward the door, trying to cover the rush of pride flowing through her. Angus always had potential, but the last two years he'd spent growing his own business had changed him. She'd often taken his presence in her life for granted, but as she'd struggled with internal demons and external monsters, he'd grown solid, becoming a constant she could rely on.

They stepped through the leaded glass doors into a wonderland. Now she knew why this building, so plain compared to the many beautiful ones downtown, had earned its historical markers. Warm coffee-colored tiles paved the floors. Ornate painted woodwork decorated white walls, and heavy dark-wooden lintels held up a painted and carved ceiling. Even the elevators, with their carved dragons and brass doors inlaid with stained glass, glowed with beauty.

"I feel like I've stepped into a Spanish castle from a far and magical past." She spun around, taking in deco chandeliers and plush furniture. She led him toward a staircase in the center of the room. "I think we go up here."

Half a dozen people surrounded a coat check station on the second floor. Jessica glanced toward a room on her left where the buzzing of people filled the air. She glimpsed a grand ballroom sporting a variety of paintings hung on tall, crème-colored walls.

She looked back at Angus. "Take my coat?" It slid easily off her bare shoulders. She heard his breath hitch and tried to contain her grin by planting her teeth into her bottom lip as she turned toward him.

"I don't . . . you look . . ." Angus struggled for words. "Damn, you are so hot. I'm so lucky."

"Like it?" she asked.

"Love it. Love you. Is it new?" The desire in his eyes washed through her, leaving her breathless.

"I've worn it once before. To a fancy real estate party long ago. I'm glad you like it." She licked her lips, wanted to unclasp the dress and let it slide to the floor. If only they were alone.

"You're not wearing a bra." His eyes had gone round and definitely didn't meet hers.

Jessica shook her head. So much for thinking he'd grown up.

"Okay, perv. Put our coats away and let's join the party." She spun toward the ballroom door, feeling his eyes on her bare back. Impressing Agus like that almost made her giddy with confidence, and desire.

She sauntered into the ballroom. It had the same carved wood beauty as the rest of the building, and a wall of windows looked over the square. On the remaining walls she noticed several of her mom's paintings, not the new softer-colored ones, but the vibrant, jagged paintings that tried to tear your heart in two. Colorful abstract pieces by some other artist hung nearby. Along one wall, sheetrock jutted into the ballroom, forming cubbies and providing more space for art. These held round-bodied Latinas painted in bright pinks and greens and blues. The mix-mash of styles made the room a chaotic rush of color.

"Jessica, I'm so glad you're here." Robin waved to her from several feet away, finally giving Jessica's eyes a place to rest. Dick stood beside her, glowering when he heard her name.

Fuck him. She'd get the goods on him eventually. She checked over her shoulder just as Angus entered the room. She reached for his hand and drew him toward Robin.

"It's lovely to be here. Thank you for having us," Jessica said, air kissing Robin's cheek. "Hi, Dick. Nice to see you again. You remember my husband, Angus."

Dick barely acknowledged Jessica but reached for Angus's hand and gave it a vigorous shake. "Welcome."

Jessica turned back to Robin but made sure her voice reached Dick as well. "Thank you so much for having Casa Sagrada as the designated charity for this event. I'm sure the money you raise will help many immigrants in our region."

Bright spots of cherry lit Robin's cheeks as she warily glanced at her husband. "Of course. I'm glad we could help them. Let me show you where your mother is." Robin grasped Jessica's hand and practically dragged her through the ballroom.

"I haven't had the chance to talk to him again, so please don't ask." Robin sounded on the verge of anger. Or maybe her husband's clear distaste for the charity made her stressed. Jessica didn't care, she'd get to him one way or another.

They rounded a wall holding an autumnal painting featuring deer and mountains and almost ran smack into Clarice. Behind her, Jessica saw a huge painting, probably five feet by five feet. Jessica recognized the slashes of mountain rising up like a cathedral organ, jagged and hued purple and smoke. Las Cruces, New Mexico, sat at the base of these mountains, and Jessica had seen their spires in the distance from the cottage's windows.

"Mom. That painting is spectacular." In the most haunting way imaginable. Even cast in paint, the mountains seemed to be growing taller, coming for her.

"Thank you." Clarice reached for her hand and gave it a squeeze. "I didn't think it was quite ready to show, but Robin insisted on exhibiting it tonight." Her mom almost seemed shy talking about her work.

"It's fabulous. I wouldn't be surprised if it sells tonight. Now, I've got to go greet our other guests." Robin whirled away in a swirl of black taffeta.

Clarice looked wonderful. Someone had professionally styled her hair and applied makeup, far more than she usually wore. Her floor-length navy dress had lines of sequins that grew thicker as they fell toward the carpet. The lovely, if severe, dress fit well, but her mother wore it like it bound her in all the wrong places.

"Nice dress," Jessica said, throwing a question into her voice.

Clarice's hands ran down the fabric as if smoothing it. "Thank you. Robin let me borrow it."

That explained it. Clarice, at least the woman from Jessica's memories, preferred flowing dresses and soft colors. The dark and shimmery dress she wore tonight screamed politician's wife, not artist.

"I love you, Mom." The words surprised Jessica, and she saw the shock mirrored on Clarice's face.

"Oh, I love you too, honey." Clarice squeezed Jessica in an awkward embrace.

Jessica pulled away as soon as possible. She searched for Angus and found him behind her, the grin on his face telling her he knew she'd surprised herself.

"Let's go get a drink." She started to pull Angus away. "Would you like us to bring you anything?"

"No, thanks. Go have fun." Clarice waved them off. As Jessica glanced back, she had the eerie feeling the painted mountains might swallow her mother. If she'd already had a drink, she'd wonder whether someone had slipped something into it.

They located the bar and took their places at the back of the line. Angus put an arm around her. "It's cute how much you love your mom."

"Shut up," she snapped.

His throaty giggle caught her off guard. She shot him an angry glance.

"Admit it. You love her. You may even like her."

"Stop tormenting me." She shook her head, then focused on the narrow shoulders and graying hair of the man in front of her. She hated exploring her feelings about her mother. Clarice had abandoned her. She'd told herself that for so many years. But lately, another thought accompanied that one. She'd abandoned her mother. They'd both caused insurmountable damage. Building on the scars of that damage had become the only way forward. Tough path. Tough women.

The line moved forward. The man in front of her stepped back to let someone pass through the line, gently bumping Jessica in the process.

"I'm sorry, ma'am." He turned to face her.

"Sheriff Burns." Cold recognition sunk through her. This man had ordered his deputies to arrest her. His men refused to investigate when she'd heard a girl cry from a locked building. He'd had some kind of relationship with the demented pastor who'd taken the girls, and probably the men in the desert who'd killed their families. For all she knew, he lay at the heart of the problem. "Nice to meet you."

"Do I know you?" he asked. He cocked his head and examined her as if looking for something familiar.

"Jessica Watts." She didn't offer him her hand. "And this is my husband, Angus Delgado."

"Nice to meet you, sir." Angus, of course, did shake the man's hand. He was polite like that.

Burns had barely taken his eyes off her. "You're Joe Watts's kid, aren't you?"

Ah. The line assholes always led with. Your father was a criminal. What does that make you? She nodded.

"Didn't you get into some trouble with our office a couple of months ago?" he asked.

Jessica took a moment to figure out how to respond. She stared at his shiny chrome forehead gleaming in the overhead lights. His eyes squinted small and rat-like, black under their heavy lids.

"It's a shame what happened to those girls out in the desert. Is your department making any progress on those crimes?" She refused to back down from his gaze. She wanted answers.

"Well, I hear they moved on somewhere else, and we're all sorry about what happened with that preacher." His voice held no emotion, just a politician reporting the so-called facts to an unknowing constituent.

"I hear you were pretty close with Pastor Wright. I know several people saw you having lunch with him. And the crimes I'm talking about are what happened to the family members the girls crossed the border with." The ugliness of the situation lit a fire in her veins that she struggled to control.

"Lady." The sheriff almost spit the word, although his voice remained low enough that no one else could hear. "You need to be very careful about your language. It almost sounds like you're insinuating I was involved in this."

"Are you? That would explain why your deputies didn't investigate when I told them I'd heard a voice in a locked building at the ranch." Jessica felt Angus stiffen beside her.

The sheriff smiled and crossed his arms. "I have no idea what you're talking about. Nothing like that was in the report. The report said you trespassed on the property of a man who found you threatening."

"Do you find me threatening?" She shouldn't toy with a man this powerful, but Jessica did lots of things she shouldn't do. And he was law enforcement. He should be on her side, looking for the truth and meting out justice.

He chuckled, although nothing in his demeanor suggested humor. "You Wattses aren't known for making good decisions." Then, he turned his back to them.

Angus grabbed her upper arm. "What the fuck?" he mouthed.

She shrugged as they moved closer to the bar. She'd explain later. She would not let men like Dick Saunders and Lee Burns get the better of her. She would fight injustice, regardless of where it lay.

Burns stepped up to the bar, then turned back to them. "May I buy you a drink?"

She wanted to tell him no, that they didn't want anything bought with his dirty money. But she also didn't want to look weak or afraid.

"Sure." She stepped to the well-stocked bar. "Do you have pineapple juice?"

"We do," the bartender said.

"I'll have a Matador." She sparkled with glee as she turned to Burns. Jessica rarely drank the tequila, pineapple, and lime concoction. But Matador meant killer, something he wouldn't miss. "Angus, what would you like?"

Burns stared at her, fire behind those rodent eyes. She gave her best sugary Texas smile.

Angus looked caught in a trap. He stepped warily to the bar. "I'll have a Shiner. Thanks."

"Thank you for the drinks." Jessica stared directly into Burns's eyes. He happened to be her height, and in heels, she had a few inches on him. She enjoyed looking down on him. "See you around."

"Fuck, Jessica," Angus said, after leading her halfway across the ballroom. "I think you just made the sheriff hate you. Whatever happened to using honey instead of vinegar to get what you want?"

She laughed. "I don't think there's an ounce of honey or anything sweet in me. That guy needs to know I'm coming for him."

"No. He doesn't. He has hundreds of officers who work for him, and you've painted a target on your back."

Angus was probably right, but life had scraped up Jessica too many times for her to care. She wanted her enemies out in the open where she could see them. But how did she take the next step, the one that went from veiled threats to concrete action?

A woman walked in the door wearing a perfectly cut tuxedo jacket with a hot pink pocket square and floor-length black skirt. Linda. Amazing how the universe answered your questions sometimes. Once, she'd wondered whether Linda had covered up for Colby or even had something to do with Paul Brown's death. In the end, she didn't really give a shit. This woman could help her find answers.

# Chapter 27

Linda knifed through the crowd like a shark cutting through water. She gave head nods and clasped hands with people along the way, barely slowing her stride. Then she walked straight up to Sheriff Burns. They briefly embraced, and she said something that made him smile.

Their close familiarity cut through Jessica like a machete. Linda knew all about her issues with the sheriff. Jessica had made sure to tell her before she took the job in case Linda didn't want an employee crosswise with one of the region's main law enforcement agencies. Jessica had shared her theories about the sheriff's role in what happened with the girls' families. Hell, she'd asked Linda to take on the girls' case.

Just when she'd decided to trust her boss, Jessica became mired in doubt. Again. Every part of her wanted to go on a wrecking ball attack. Angus laid a warm palm against her bare back.

"Hey. It's going to be okay. Don't jump to conclusions. I know how much you like her, and she has no idea you just had a run-in with the sheriff. Besides, I think you won that round."

Jessica leaned into him, taking a small moment away from the fight. She relaxed. She couldn't stop the swirling thoughts, but she'd take one step at a time until she had answers.

She sipped her drink. Pineapple tasted out of place on a winter's night, but that wouldn't stop her. "I'd have preferred a shot."

"I know. You just couldn't pass up the opportunity to call the local sheriff a killer." Angus gave her a squeeze.

"Well, when you put it like that, it sounds bad." She watched the wiry man still conversing with her boss.

"It's been a bad year for you and sheriffs," Angus said. "I get the feeling you're not a fan of that Lefty guy."

"Yeah. He's not so bad, just super eager to pin an old murder on someone. Plus, he might be dating my mom."

"Wait, you didn't tell me your mom was dating that guy."

Clarice stood on the opposite side of the ballroom, speaking with a dark blond man with his back to Jessica. "You know, she deserves happiness. If she wants to date Lefty, I guess that's fine." Although surely there were better options out there. Her mom put a hand on the man's shoulder, and Jessica could almost feel the light squeeze. Maybe he'd made an offer on one of her paintings.

The man turned and seeing his face punched Jessica in the gut. Tomás Garcia, a ghost from the past. She almost spit out her drink. She'd worked for him before, but after the last time, she'd never trust him again. How many vipers had Robin invited to this soiree?

Tomás saw her and tipped his drink in her direction. Fuck.

"Let's go see what's through that doorway." Jessica practically dragged Angus toward an open double door near the front of the ballroom.

They stepped into another ornate room with carved ceilings and more art on the walls. This room held colorful, whimsical paintings: a half-cartoon longhorn trotting through an orange field, a broad-shouldered man in a cowboy hat staring into a night sky filled with pink doves, a cowgirl, a coyote, and a horse napping on a blanket of flowers. Plush sofas formed seating areas around low tables. Another bar sat at one end of the room, and no one waited for a drink. They'd stepped through a magical wardrobe into Jessica's ideal party.

"Drinks," Jessica said, heading for the bar. She ordered a tequila and a beer.

"Are we Ubering, or should I stay sober?"

"Drink up, my friend. It's not often we're invited to fancy parties."

"Yeah, well if you're going to dress like that, I'm happy to attend." He reached for her hip, then ran his hand across plush velvet until he reached the bare skin at the small of her back.

The warmth of the tequila flowed through Jessica as she downed the shot. Accompanied by Angus's fiery touch, she wanted to blow this party and take her lover home.

Angus pulled his hand away. "Fuck. I hate this guy."

Jessica turned to see Tomás striding toward them.

"You're certainly someone I hoped to never see again," Jessica said as he approached. She'd had her run-ins with the rich kid from Juarez over the years. First fighting a drug dealer he'd introduced her to at one of his Juarez night clubs, and then when he'd threatened to kill her as she tried to help a woman escape his clutches.

"It's lovely to see you too," he quipped. "Jessica, I need your help."

Revulsion ran through her. "I will never help you again. Remember, I know what a bastard you are."

"Please, just hear me out. I'm married. I have a child." The energy seemed to drag out of him as his shoulders sagged and he hung his head. "I was horrible before, truly horrible. I'm sorry. My situation then seemed desperate, but I am a new man now."

"Sure." Jessica wanted to slap him. Or worse.

"She said she didn't want to talk to you." Angus wrapped an arm around her and turned toward the door.

Normally Jessica hated overprotective bullshit, but she wanted to escape. How dare Tomás approach her? She'd almost been killed because of him. A sliver of ice slid down her spine as they left the once-joyful room.

They stepped back into the now-crowded ballroom. The lights had dimmed, and waiters circulated with trays of canapes. Jessica wanted to leave, to be done with social traps and awkward moments. Instead, Linda approached her, a glass of champagne in one hand.

"Jessica, great to see you. You look fantastic."

"Thanks." She had no reason to delay another painful conversation. "I saw you talking to Sheriff Burns. You two seem to know each other pretty well."

"We're about the same age. He was a new deputy when I joined the police department. When I became an attorney, I often worked with him on cases."

"Are you friends? I'm sorry to interrogate you, but you know he arrested me on the Jeremy Wright case, and I was right on that one. Plus, I'm concerned about his involvement with what happened to the Guatemalan girls." Jessica didn't want to find a new job. But if Linda couldn't be unbiased about the sheriff, she couldn't be trusted.

"I know all of that. We're colleagues. In the distant past, we were a little more than that. But I think it's smart to keep him close. I'm on your side."

Jessica wished Linda's words brought a sense of relief, but the night had gone too strange. What bogeyman would jump out next? Still, she smiled at her boss as a peace offering.

"*There's* someone I want to avoid," said Linda.

Jessica turned. Barbara had entered the ballroom wearing an ocean-blue floor length organza gown that she'd probably last worn in 1978. She strode toward her daughter, spine stiff, like a queen visiting her subjects.

"You and me both. That woman hates me." Jessica shuddered at yet another person she'd prefer not to see.

"What is it with this party?" Angus asked. "You promised this would be fun."

"Yeah. It looks like I lied." Jessica took a heady swig of beer. "Thankfully, the bars are stocked." Jessica spied her mom out of the corner of her eye. She should introduce Linda to her, although the room didn't need any more drama.

Sharp voices turned her toward the ballroom entrance. Barbara's voice carried across the room. "Why?" She pointed at Jessica.

"Oh, fuck. I really should have stayed home." Too late now. Robin waved her over.

"You're going to need another drink soon." Angus took her hand and started toward Robin.

"Hell, let's all go," Linda said. "This should be fun."

Jessica could think of many labels for the evening. Fun didn't make the list.

Barbara had lowered her voice, but as they closed in, her harsh whisper became clear. "You've got to let this go. Can't you see how ridiculous it is to bring your private laundry into a social event? People will talk." Barbara looked angry and desperate. Dick glowered, nodding, behind her.

"I'm no longer taking your advice. I've missed out on years of family. Never again. In fact, I invited them here tonight."

Barbara looked horrified, but Dick grabbed his wife's arm. "What?" he growled.

Robin flinched and looked at where his meaty hand grasped her. She tried pulling away. Jessica, Angus, and Linda all stepped forward.

"Hey, let her go," Jessica said.

"What are *you* doing here?" Barbara directed her question at Linda, her horror at the situation transformed to disgust.

"Barbara. How nice to see you." Linda clearly felt the opposite. Jessica wouldn't have been surprised to see her eyes roll.

Barbara turned to her daughter. "You have lost your mind. I'm leaving."

She spun around in a blue flourish, but it was too late. Mayra and Araceli stood at the door.

The tension in the room turned up to eleven. Jessica pictured the leaded glass windows blowing out over the park like in a movie. Fortunately, the din of the party remained, the drama playing out unnoticed by most.

Araceli looked different from when she'd greeted Jessica at the ranch in Mexico. Tonight, she wore a sparkly dress that showed her curves and her sophisticated hair and makeup would have fit into a New York nightclub.

Mayra moved out from behind her granddaughter. Free from embellishment, her amber dress dropped from an empire waist to just above her ankles. The simple design highlighted the gorgeous fabric. Its glow lit Mayra's face like a warm candle.

Both sides waited, expectant. Jessica realized Robin had never seen these women and might not know who they were. She stepped forward.

"Mayra, it's nice to see you again." Jessica heard a sharp intake of breath behind her and imagined Barbara's apoplectic face. "Let me introduce you to our hosts."

"Oh, my gosh," Robin said, materializing at Jessica's side. "It's so nice to have you here. Thank you for coming."

"You are Paul's daughter." Mayra reached for Robin's hand and looked her over, a smile on her face.

Robin beamed in the gentle light of Mayra's gaze. Jessica could picture a life where Mayra had been Robin's mother, loving instead of cold like Barbara.

"You have your father's smile. Please, let me introduce you to your niece. This is Araceli."

Robin greeted the young woman with a broad smile and a warm hug, joy dancing across her features. Jessica chanced a glance back and saw Dick striding away from them toward the bar. Barbara stood still as a statue, half-hidden behind Angus and with an agonized expression. She looked like she'd been struck by lightning. Jessica doubted her silence would last.

"I can't wait for you to meet my son." Robin bubbled with delight.

But Jessica feared what would come next. This family might eventually get their happily ever after, or at least some semblance of it, but the story had just begun.

As if on cue, Barbara emerged from behind Angus. "You are not welcome here." Her voice was ice.

Robin turned to her mother, spine straight. "Yes, Mother. She is. This is my gallery. My party."

"I remember you from that night." Mayra's voice remained soft, but Jessica heard echoes of the years of unfairness pressed into a loaded spring.

"What are you talking about?" Barbara took a half step back.

"The last night we saw Paul. I saw you in the truck. The vehicle you were in almost hit us at the turn into the pecan grove."

A long silence stretched between the women, allowing the din of the party back into the space. The hairs on Jessica's arms rose. They must be talking about the night of Paul's death. They were there.

"You're mistaken," Barbara said. "And it was a mistake for you to come here. You're nothing but a whore and a liar. Paul loved his family. He wouldn't have slept with someone like you."

Jessica wanted to slap the ugly words back into Barbara's mouth. She'd seen how much Abel looked like his father.

Somehow, Mayra remained serene. "I know he hurt you. He hurt both of us. I didn't know he was married until I was already pregnant. For that, I am sorry."

"You lie." Barbara's voice boomed into the room. People turned to look.

"No. He lied. But I was a stupid girl who believed the fictional tale he wove. That he was single. Then, that he would leave you. That he would take care of us." Mayra paused, appeared on the verge of breaking down. Instead, she glanced at her granddaughter and Robin, seeming to gather strength from them before facing Barbara again. "But that was so many years ago. We've both raised our families. It is time to bury the past."

Barbara trembled, a movement likely fueled by either sadness or rage. "I will not be a part of this." She lifted her head like a haughty, ancient princess, and stomped past Mayra and her daughter, ocean-blue chiffon trailing in her wake.

# Chapter 28

Everyone seemed content to watch Barbara leave. Jessica had to stop her. She hoped that with emotions running this high, she could get Barbara and Mayra to recall what happened that night.

"Wait!" Jessica yelled. Barbara had already passed through the ballroom doors. These women were there that night. They knew what happened to Paul. She trotted after Barbara, who'd already reached the ballroom door.

Jessica had gained on the older woman, but barely. Her unfamiliar heels slowed her down while Barbara scampered away in them like a master. She passed the check-in table and kept going. "Barbara. Wait."

Barbara had veered toward the elevators' closed doors. When she heard Jessica, she glanced back, then swung into the ladies' room instead. Jessica followed.

She hadn't signed up for chasing people into restrooms, but she wouldn't let this opportunity pass her by. A stall door slammed shut as she entered the ladies' lounge. This room had a sitting area with two sofas and several benches along a mirrored wall. She loved the opulent bathrooms of old hotels, as if women would sit in here and chat with their friends before joining their dates at a ballroom dance.

Jessica stood at the intersection of carpet and tile between the lounge and the toilets. "Barbara. I know you're in here. We need to talk."

Nothing. She tried again. "I'm not going anywhere. Even if I have to wait here all night."

Still no response. But the door to the lounge opened, and Linda herded Robin, Mayra, and Araceli into the room. Jessica briefly glimpsed Angus on the far side of the door.

"Where is she?" Robin asked.

"Using the facilities. Can we sit and have a chat?" Jessica gestured toward the sofas.

Jessica pulled a bench over to Mayra. "Earlier, you talked about seeing Barbara at the orchard. Was that the night Paul disappeared?"

Mayra looked down at her hands clasped in her lap. "That was the last time I saw him."

"You met him at the orchard? Do you remember what day of the week it was?"

"Friday night."

Araceli sat beside Mayra and took her hand. Linda and Robin faced her, silent.

"Please. Tell us what happened that night." Jessica hoped the truth would finally come out.

"I went to see him. I had to talk to him."

Jessica waited her out and hoped the others would as well. Mayra raised her eyes to Jessica, and the pain she saw there made her want to stop the questions. But she couldn't. They needed the truth. Jessica nodded for Mayra to continue.

"He said he couldn't see me anymore. Not that night. Before. The last time he visited us in Mexico. Eighteen years we were together and suddenly he tells me it's over." She shook her head, then looked at Araceli. "I'm sorry."

"Abuela. You have nothing to be sorry for," Araceli said.

"But you were supposed to have a different life. Abel should have gone to college. He was so smart. Pablo promised he'd pay for his tuition. But he lied. When he visited that last time, he said he couldn't support us anymore. He said to never contact him again. He gave me a thousand dollars and then left. That wasn't enough to pay for a smart boy's dreams or my beautiful daughters' futures."

"What an ass." Linda whispered the words, but everyone heard them.

"I couldn't let him get away with it. We had three children together. I thought if I saw him again, I could convince him to at least put Abel through college. But he wouldn't take my calls. So, I came to El Paso."

Jessica saw the fierceness a younger Mayra would have had, heard it in her voice. Crimes of passion caused so many murders, but in this case, if she'd killed him, the dream of a son going to college would have certainly died too.

Jessica heard steps behind her. The water turned on. Moments later, Barbara stepped into the lounge.

"I knew about you," Barbara said. "He paid you every single month. He took money away from his legitimate children to pay for his whore. It had to stop."

"I thought you were behind it." Resignation laced Mayra's voice as she stared at Barbara.

"What happened that night when you met him?" Jessica asked. This couldn't devolve into a fight, at least not yet.

"I begged him to support his children, to put Abel through college. He said he was sorry, but he had to choose." Mayra's spine remained stiff, and she held her head high, but a lone tear rolled down her cheek.

Jessica couldn't imagine what it cost to hold that kind of pain inside, to be the one not chosen. The shame knifed through her, twisting when it reached her gut. Hadn't she also been the one not chosen? Shame blossomed in her like a desert weed fed by anger instead of sun and rain, just the way it had all those years ago. Jessica just might have killed Paul if she'd been in Mayra's place—the same as she'd wanted to punish her parents. And did, for many years.

"When I saw he wouldn't change his mind, I left. I left my pride and my dignity under those trees. But I didn't leave my heart there. Paul had given me my children, and even if he didn't recognize it, I knew they were my greatest gifts."

Jessica wanted to bow down before this woman who had chosen love instead of hate. The most difficult decisions brought the greatest rewards. Jessica sensed sadness in Mayra, but not the bitterness that sucked you dry year after year until nothing but a husk and strained relationships remained. Like Barbara. Like herself.

"You killed him." Barbara's calm statement hit like a bomb.

"No! Never. I couldn't have. I wouldn't have. I loved him." Mayra clutched her chest.

All faces turned to Barbara. "You were right. I was there that night. I found him. He'd been battered."

"Mom. How could you? You saw him that night? You were there?" Robin's incredulous voice entered the fray.

Jessica understood Robin's confusion. It made no sense for Barbara to keep Paul's murder quiet, especially if she could place his mistress at the scene.

"It's not true. We . . . I . . ." Mayra stopped and took a breath. Jessica could see her putting herself back together.

"I did hit him," Mayra said. "I punched him because I was so angry. Fathers shouldn't leave their children with nothing. But he was fine when I left."

The math didn't work. At maybe five-four in height and a buck twenty in weight, Jessica doubted Mayra could have delivered a killer punch to the six-foot-tall Paul.

"Where did you hit him?" Jessica asked, catching a flash of fear on Mayra's face.

"In the head. On the mejilla." Mayra wrung her hands and looked at her granddaughter.

"Cheek," Araceli said.

Suddenly, a woman who spoke almost perfect English couldn't remember the word for cheek? It didn't make sense.

"Describe the scene when you arrived and found Paul." Linda directed the command at Barbara.

"He was on the ground. His eye was swollen shut. Someone had knocked the hell out of him. I think we should call that sheriff. We just heard a confession."

"Was he dead when you found him?" Jessica asked. It still didn't add up. Maybe Mayra was a killer, but both their stories couldn't be true.

"I don't know. I didn't touch him."

"Why didn't you call the police? Why have you never told me this?" Robin sounded on the edge of panic.

"Wait." Jessica had to find the real truth. "You two saw each other as Mayra left and Barbara entered the grove. Did either of you notice any other people or vehicles out there?"

"She was the only one," Barbara said.

"I did not kill him. You could have killed him after I left. That's why you didn't tell the police."

Barbara wavered and grabbed the door frame to support herself. Jessica could almost see her brain working.

"I didn't tell the police or anyone else. How could I have admitted that my husband had an affair, for years? That he'd had other children. It would have ruined us."

"Would it have?" Robin asked, voice harsh. "Would it really have been worse than not knowing what happened to your father for all these years? Would it have been worse than letting the media accuse your own son of killing his father and probably hastening his own death? You thought your reputation was worth that much?" Robin's cheeks had gone vermillion, and she practically snarled at her mother.

"I did it to protect you."

"I don't believe that for a second. You're the one obsessed with this family's reputation."

"I told you not to dredge this up." Barbara sounded panicked.

"That's my father they found in that field, and whether you loved him or not, I did. I don't care who he slept with. He didn't leave me." Robin's words sank like an anchor through Jessica. The ache of abandonment never left lonely children.

"I don't think Mayra could have killed him." Linda detonated the comment into the room. "She's too small. Especially for a blow to the head."

"Barbara probably couldn't have either." Jessica looked at the two women, similar in stature, with Barbara probably a good five years older than Mayra. Not that it would have mattered forty years ago with both women in their prime. But they'd placed each other at the site close enough together that it couldn't have been anyone else.

"Maybe it was your son," Barbara said. "He definitely had the strength to kill Paul."

"He wasn't there." Mayra's words came out harsh, and she stared at Barbara with a fiery gaze. "I was alone. Were you?"

The tension between the two women crackled. They seemed to size each other up, each ready to pounce. Jessica didn't know who to take in a fight. Barbara made up for her age disadvantage with sheer meanness, although Mayra had shown a fierceness tonight Jessica hadn't seen before. It had to be tough to bring up three kids without a father, and without nearly the resources at Barbara's fingertips.

"I was also alone." The words came out slow, as if each sound was a separate decision. "Of course I was alone. I wouldn't have wanted anyone to know I was searching for my cheating husband."

"Oh, Mom." Robin sighed as she let the words escape.

"And on that distasteful note, I've had quite enough of tonight. I'm going home." Barbara turned and walked out the door. This time, no one followed.

"I'm afraid we must go also. This has been a mistake." Mayra stood. "I wanted to meet you, to glimpse the other side of Paul's life. But your mother is right. Some things should stay buried."

Robin surged up from the sofa. "No. Please stay. You haven't seen the gallery yet, and I'd love for you to meet my husband and son. Please. I beg you to stay."

"I don't know," Mayra said, aging before Jessica's eyes. Tonight's battle had taken a lot out of her.

"I apologize for my mother, and I really appreciate your coming here. Please, stay just for a few minutes. I would love to have a relationship with you."

Mayra nodded, and Araceli took her hand and led her out while Robin held the door. Only Linda and Jessica remained in the lounge.

"I feel like I'm missing something," Linda said.

"I agree. I'm not sure they're telling the truth, but I can't figure out why."

"Well, there's no reason to stay in the ladies' room." Linda rose then offered a hand to Jessica.

Angus waited outside. "What the hell happened in there?"

"There was kind of a confession that they both were at the pecan grove the night Paul was killed. They both deny killing him, but something doesn't add up."

"Have you had enough of this party? I'm ready to go as soon as you are." He ran a warm hand down the length of her back, leaving an electric trail that had her skin tingling.

"Soon. I'd love to talk to the granddaughter for a minute, then we can say our goodbyes to Mom and Robin. Then home." She planted a soft kiss on his cheek, a promise for later.

They reentered the ballroom, and Jessica noticed Mayra's amber dress near her mother's part of the exhibit. She quickened her step and arrived just as Robin introduced Mayra and the others to Clarice.

"Hi, Mom," Jessica blurted, inserting herself into the conversation. Clarice gave her such a warm smile at the exuberant greeting that it almost broke Jessica's heart. As Clarice showed them each painting, Jessica herded Araceli away from the others.

"I'm so glad you came tonight," Jessica said. "I didn't think you would."

"I feel so guilty," Araceli admitted. "I really wanted to meet this other family, and I talked Abuela into it. I should have realized Paul's wife might be here."

"I'm sorry about how she acted. She's not very nice."

Araceli cocked her head as she gazed at Jessica. "I probably wouldn't be very nice either. I should have listened to my uncle. He doesn't want to have anything to do with the El Paso family."

"Is he still missing?"

Araceli nodded. "We thought he might show up here. He's been so angry since you brought this into our lives. Plus, Robin left him at least one message. I thought maybe he'd come tell her to leave us alone. But he would never come to something like this. He'll be furious when he finds out I brought her here." She nodded toward Mayra.

"Are you staying overnight? I hope you're not driving all the way back in this cold, windy weather."

"We're staying with a friend in Juarez tonight."

"Araceli, you have my phone number, right? Call me if you need anything. Not just while you're here, but anytime. I feel a little guilty about getting your family involved in this."

"Todo está bien. Everything is fine, or it will be. This needed to happen. Tío Abel has been angry his whole life about his father. Abuela has been ashamed. It makes my mother and my aunt sad. Half our heritage is here, and it plays out in our lives. Abuela always demanded we speak English at home, and my mom and my aunt teach English in school. We don't look like our neighbors, lighter skin, hazel eyes. We need to know where we come from, and if we have relatives here, we need to make them family."

Just then, a young dark-haired man walked up to Robin. It had to be her son. He had the healthy look of an athlete, with his father's firm jaw and his mother's ready smile. Robin waved them over.

"Araceli, come meet my son Justin." Robin's voice carried across the crowd.

Jessica sidled away from the group to let the family introductions play out. She surveyed the ballroom. Dick stood in a corner tossing back a drink and glowering in Robin's direction. Sheriff Burns stood beside him. Across the room, Tomás caught her eye and started toward her.

"Mom, Angus and I are going to take off. It's been a long day." Mostly because of this so-called party.

She turned to say goodbye to Robin and the others. Robin wrapped her in a huge hug. Jessica pulled back quickly as Tomás neared. She had to leave before he talked to her again. He was the last person on earth she'd ever work with.

"Thank you for helping me find my family," Robin said. "I know I hired you for something completely different, and I never would have imagined this fabulous outcome."

"Fabulous? That's what you call this?" The gruff voice shot past Jessica's shoulder, and Robin stiffened.

"Yes. I'm thrilled that I have more family, that Justin has cousins."

Jessica took a step back, widening the circle to include Dick, who looked like he wanted to hit something.

"They're not your family. They just want money. I can't believe how naïve you are." The words spewed from his mouth like venom.

Jessica glanced at Mayra and Araceli. For a second time, Mayra took the blame for something Jessica placed squarely at Paul's feet. It sucked.

Robin reared back as if she'd been slapped.

"Let's take care of this right now. How much will it take for you to go away forever?" Dick addressed Mayra, and Jessica heard a slur in his words. Liquor made some men belligerent. It made others dangerous. What category would Dick fall into tonight?

"Dad. Don't." Robin's son put a hand up as if to stop his father, but his words weren't threatening.

"I am not here for your money." Mayra threw back her shoulders, her spine straight in her amber dress. It made Jessica think of a candle, quiet, but containing a potentially dangerous fire.

"Araceli, please go get the car," Mayra said. "Robin, it has been nice to meet you. Thank you for inviting us."

Jessica followed Mayra out of the ballroom, motioning to Angus to do the same. Dick seemed to have the same idea as he creepily followed Mayra to the door. The sheriff waited for him at the ballroom's entrance.

"We need to keep an eye on them," Dick said the sheriff, who nodded in acquiescence. That worried Jessica.

She trotted down the stairs after Mayra, who opened the outside door. A huge gust of cold wind smacked the door wide and flew up the stairs toward Jessica.

She followed Mayra into the icy weather. "Wait. Please."

Mayra turned to her. "I wish you'd never found us. I thought this would make things better, but instead, everything is far worse. Once again, I've proven that I have no judgement when it comes to people."

"Please be careful tonight and get to Juarez as quickly as you can," Jessica said.

"Why?" Mayra asked.

"I don't trust Dick, and he asked the sheriff to keep an eye on you."

"Wonderful. Just one more way I sacrifice my family for my past mistakes."

"It's not you. Really. But be careful. Don't drive alone." Men with guns preying on people in the desert crossed her mind, but she wouldn't share that atrocity with Mayra.

The car with the rounded bumpers Jessica had seen in Mexico pulled to a stop in front of Mayra. "Don't worry, Araceli takes me everywhere. I never learned to drive." Mayra got in, and Jessica watched it depart.

"You must be freezing," Angus said, arriving at Jessica's side and wrapping her coat around her shoulders. She hadn't thought about it when she ran after Mayra, but now she shivered in the chill, although whether from the cold or the ominous feeling in her gut, she couldn't say.

# Chapter 29

Last night, before Jessica and Angus reached home, the first snow flurries had swirled around the car. Now, as she let Tela out the back door for her morning rituals, a light blanket of white covered the backyard. Occasionally, straw yellow spears of Bermuda grass poked through the thin veneer. Tela, a bundle of energy on a normal day, now took mighty leaps across the yard, as if trying to outjump the snow.

As soon as Jessica got her back inside, she hurried to the windows at the front of the house. The mountains gleamed powdered sugar white with undertones of purple, red, and brown. A line of low clouds sliced off the peaks. It typically snowed in El Paso every year or two, but it rarely stuck. Jessica hadn't seen a snow this heavy since childhood.

She took a photo of the view with her phone to memorialize it. The clouds would blow away soon, and the bright sun would melt away the fairytale white and reveal the truth of the desert.

She'd uncovered some of the truth of Paul's story last night, but something still hid beneath the bottom layer. Was it even worth pulling back this final curtain? Forty years ago, yes. Today, the truth threatened to hurt more than it would heal. Yet, her instincts told her the story wouldn't stay hidden.

Her phone rang. She didn't recognize the Juarez number but answered anyway. It didn't surprise her when she heard Mayra's voice.

"Jessica. You have to help me. The sheriff arrested Abel."

No. A chill colder than a blanket of snow wrapped around her as she pictured Sheriff Burns. He'd toyed with her last night, and then likely colluded with Dick. This did not bode well.

"When? Tell me what happened."

"Abel just called. They think he killed Pablo. He didn't. I swear he didn't kill his father." Anguish filled Mayra's voice.

"It's okay. We'll figure it out." Jessica had no idea how, but Mayra's story didn't jibe with what she and Barbara had voiced last night.

"Araceli and I are going to Las Cruces to see him, but we need a lawyer."

Las Cruces. New Mexico. A wash of relief flowed through Jessica. Lefty must have arrested him. While over-eager, he didn't seem corrupt. She couldn't say the same for Sheriff Burns.

"I'll meet you up there. Be careful. The roads may be slick."

Jessica returned to the bedroom and shook Angus awake. "Hey, babe. I've got a conundrum."

He pulled her to him, wrapping her in strong arms. "It's so early."

"I know. The sheriff is holding Abel Gamboa in custody. He's in jail in Las Cruces, and I'm not sure whether to call Lefty or Linda first. And I told Mayra I'd meet her up there."

"Hmmm."

Jessica felt his chest vibrate under her palm. "I promise, I'll come back and make it up to you." She planted a kiss above his heart.

"Call Linda first. She's a badass. It's kind of scary how similar you two are."

"Good idea." She peeled herself off him, even though she'd prefer to spend Saturday morning beneath the covers.

Jessica dressed first, then found Linda's number. Did she really trust her? Jessica didn't trust easily, but despite Linda's connection to the Brown family and the El Paso sheriff, she did trust her. Angus was right, she and Linda had many similarities. They both had taken on male-dominated careers early on, Linda as a police officer and Jessica as a commercial real estate agent in Juarez. That and early trauma had given them both hard edges. Linda probably found it as hard to trust as Jessica did.

Jessica had to turn the page on her skepticism and ask for help when she needed it. She pressed the call button.

Ten minutes later, Jessica called Lefty. Linda had agreed to help and was calling the Las Cruces detention center to learn more about Abel's case.

"Well, hello, Jessica. While I appreciate your finally calling me, I'm not sure I need your help anymore."

Jessica heard a hint of smugness in Lefty's drawl. She tried to extinguish the spark of anger that caused. He hadn't been at the showdown between Barbara and Mayra. He'd probably end up embarrassed that he'd arrested a man who hadn't been at the murder site that night. Unless Mayra had lied.

"I think you've got the wrong man," Jessica said into the phone.

"I don't think so, young lady. He confessed."

It took Jessica a minute to process the words. Either Mayra had lied to her, or Abel had lied to Lefty. It looked like they needed another showdown, this one between mother and son.

"I'm on my way to the detention center, and he has an attorney, Linda Reed, representing him now. Also, his mother is on the way. I'm not sure you have the full story."

Jessica heard a heavy sigh through the airwaves. "I'll meet you there."

"Great. I'll be there in under an hour."

Jessica hit the road. Las Cruces lay forty-five miles to the north on Interstate 10. The snow had melted off the freeway, although she worried about ice on the bridges. The beauty of the drive distracted her from any danger. She caught glimpses of snow-shrouded prickly pear cactus and spikey-armed ocotillo. To her right, the clouds had lifted above the mountaintops, and a few rays of sunlight made it through to light snowy ridges.

The Rio Grande coursed out of sight to the west, but she could see the pecan groves it fed as she entered New Mexico. Her heart gave a little hitch as she thought of her mom ensconced in her cottage with her two dogs. Jessica wanted her mom to be happy. That would take giving up on the anger she let fuel her frustrations. It seemed like something that should be easy to do, but she hadn't found the key yet.

That turned her thoughts to Mayra and Abel. Which one of them had lied to protect the other? She didn't want to believe either of them had killed Paul. Mayra didn't seem the type, although Jessica had been surprised by who turned out to be a murderer in the past.

She wanted to protect Abel for other reasons. No one deserved to be treated like that. He'd been promised a future if he worked for it. And he had. He'd learned English, he'd been accepted to the University of Texas, and then his two-timing father had pulled the prize away. The brutality of that act had poisoned him, just as Paul's expectations for his other son had likely contributed to his drug abuse and death.

Jessica pulled into the detention center, still thinking about the twisted relationships between parents and children. Maybe pitting Mayra against Abel would shed light on her questions. The answers seemed close. Perhaps, if she found the right thread to pull, all would be revealed.

She pulled open the detention center door to find she'd arrived last. Mayra and Araceli sat along one wall while Lefty and Linda chatted near them.

Linda waved her over. "Lefty agreed to let us question him together. I was thinking we'd let Mayra and Araceli wait out here during the initial questioning."

"No." Mayra stood. "I want to see my son. He did not kill his father. He is saying this to protect me."

Lefty looked down at her, his tall stature making Mayra seem smaller than ever. "You killed him? I'm not sure you could have reached his head." A lifted eyebrow cemented his disbelief.

"Detective Griswald," Jessica said, "if you've got a room big enough, let's get everyone together and hash this thing out."

"Might as well. Give me a few minutes." He went through a closed door, leaving the rest of them waiting.

"What do you know?" Jessica asked Mayra.

"Abel called me this morning. I was scared and called you because you warned me about the sheriffs. He was not there that night. You have to believe me." Her voice trembled with panic.

"And no one else was with you?" Jessica asked.

"No. I told you that last night."

"Abuela," Araceli said in a pleading tone.

"Es la verdad."

Jessica wondered why Mayra had switched to Spanish. And why she seemed so desperate to make her granddaughter believe she told the truth. It sounded like Mayra wanted to protect a lie.

"How did you get Paul to meet you at the pecan grove? Last night you said he wouldn't take your calls."

"I called his office and told them if Paul didn't meet me at the pecan grove, I would go to his house and tell his wife everything." Mayra's eyes darted from Jessica to Araceli and back. She looked guilty.

"Who? Who did you tell this to? How did you find out where to meet Paul?"

"I called Mr. Gordon. He's the man who gave us the checks every month. He told me Pablo would meet me at the pecan grove." Mayra bit her lip and seemed to shrink. This looked like the truth.

No wonder Charles Gordon hated Paul Brown so much. His business card might have read partner, but he did Paul's dirty work for him. One thread of truth would lead to another. Jessica just had to keep them talking. "When you reached the pecan grove, was Paul already there?"

"Yes. He was waiting for me."

Jessica had hoped to squeeze in a few more questions before Lefty returned. She believed Mayra would return to lying to protect her child. Unfortunately, she ran out of time as Lefty swung the door open and beckoned them to follow.

He led them down a long hallway and into a room, where Abel sat at a table facing them. Abel scowled when he saw the women entering the room. He seemed to have a special glare reserved for Jessica.

"Mamá. No." The disappointment and fear etched across his face saddened Jessica. He definitely wanted to protect her. "Araceli. Why did you bring her here? I told you not to come."

"I told her she had to. You are my son. You do not belong in jail."

"Excuse me. Abel, I'm Linda Reed. I'm here to represent you." Linda had pushed her way to the front of the table where Abel sat.

"I don't have money to pay you."

"Let's not worry about that today. I've got my own reasons for wanting to find out what happened to Paul Brown."

"Would everyone please sit down?" Lefty entered the conversation and pointed to the chairs around three sides of the table.

Jessica didn't want to do the cop version of having everyone start from the beginning and tell their story. She heard the truth beating at the door and needed to get there as quickly as possible.

Mayra spoke first. "I am here to turn myself in. I killed Paul Brown."

"Mamá. You know that is not true. I was the one who hit him." Abel, voice soft, spoke directly to his mother.

"What did you hit him with?" Lefty asked.

"My fist. He said he couldn't leave his American family. He never wanted to see us again. I asked if he would still pay for my college, and he said no. He refused to support us at all. I was so angry." Abel shook his head as if trying to free himself from the memory.

"No! Abel it was me. You were not there. Don't try to protect me."

Jessica needed to move the conversation beyond competing confessions. "Abel. Did you see Barbara Brown at the pecan grove that night?"

"My father's wife? No."

Mayra and Barbara had seen each other that night. Jessica had seen the memory pass between them at the party. "You and Barbara both admitted to seeing each other. How is that possible if Abel didn't see her?"

"He wasn't there. I went alone, just like I told you. You see, this proves I'm guilty."

"But last night you told me you never learned to drive." Lefty and Linda looked shocked at Jessica's statement. The others didn't.

"Finally," Araceli said in an exasperated sigh.

"Barbara Brown was there?" Lefty asked. "She didn't tell me that when I interviewed her."

"You said she almost drove you off the road? Right?" Jessica asked.

"I remember that truck," Abel said. "I had to swerve hard left to keep from being hit. I thought it was odd that someone else would show up at the orchard that night." Abel stared at his mom. "You never told me it was his wife."

Mayra looked cornered. Jessica tried to picture the two vehicles passing. Abel swerved left. Mayra, in the passenger seat, saw Barbara. If the trucks avoided a wreck by swerving to the wrong side of the road, then Barbara also had to be in the passenger seat. They had both lied.

"Given the extenuating circumstances of having at least one other person at the crime scene, I think you need to let my client go until you sort this out." Linda's voice left no room for argument.

Lefty gave a frustrated huff and stroked his mustache. "Give me a minute. I'll be right back."

As soon as he left the room, Jessica turned to Linda. "Will you handle this?" Jessica swirled her finger around the room. "I need to follow up on something."

"I've got this covered. Good luck."

Jessica flew out the door.

# Chapter 30

Jessica sped down the highway, now black with melted water. Most of the clouds had moved out, leaving a few fluffy trails of white in their wake. The wind had stopped, and her truck sliced through the warming air.

The gorgeous day did nothing to help the appearance of the multistory retirement home. She peeled into the parking lot and practically skidded to a halt.

Instead of the painstakingly goth girl at the desk, a middle-aged woman with waves of dark curls greeted her. "May I help you?"

"I'm Jessica Watts. I'm here to see Charles Gordon."

"I'm sorry, but Mr. Gordon isn't here right now. Would you like to leave a message?" The woman picked up a pre-printed message form.

"He's not here?" Jessica hadn't pictured him ever leaving. He hadn't mentioned any hobbies or family.

"He left about thirty minutes ago."

Jessica rubbed her face with her hands. "Do you know where he went?"

The woman gave her a look like she'd already asked one too many questions.

"You don't keep track of stuff like that?"

"This isn't a prison," the woman said.

Jessica wanted to scream. She'd put money on him driving Barbara to the grove. He knew Paul and Mayra would be there, and he seemed to have an unhealthy obsession with Barbara.

Jessica looked around, as if she'd find some clue in the sterile walls or pinned to the bulletin board. She saw the door to the dining room close. Without asking permission, she strode to the door.

"Hey, you can't go in there. Not without a visitor's pass," the lady at the desk yelled at her but didn't get up.

Jessica gently pushed the door open, not wanting to take down an elderly resident on the other side. She found herself face-to-face with the woman she'd talked to the other time she'd been here. The woman wore the same lime green sweatsuit. The local gossip, the perfect person to speak with.

"Hi. Do you remember me from the last time I visited Mr. Gordon?"

The woman nodded.

"Do you know where he went today?"

"No. He wouldn't tell anyone. Not even Marty, and he borrowed his truck. He must have had some type of secret mission, because he left real quick." Her eyes twinkled with the news.

"That's good information. Thank you. You seem to notice everything that goes on here."

The woman nodded again.

"Has anything unusual happened with him lately?" *Please, please, please*, Jessica thought.

"He had a visitor today," the woman said, almost bursting with the secret.

"Really? Was it someone who has visited before?"

The woman shook her head. "She was a very fancy lady."

Oh, no. "Would you please describe her for me? What was she wearing, and what did she look like? I'd really appreciate your help."

"She wore stockings, a plaid suit, and heels. She'd already put on her makeup and done her hair. Most of us don't have time for that anymore."

Jessica briefly wondered what took up all their time, although this woman certainly kept busy. "How old was she? And did you happen to get her name?"

"I didn't meet her," the woman said. "She might have been my age, but she didn't have wrinkles the way I do. She looks like she comes from money."

"That sounds about right," Jessica said. "Thank you for your help."

The woman smiled at her. "Do you know when Charles will be back?"

"I don't, but I bet it will be real soon."

Jessica strode to her truck, sorry to have lied to the helpful woman. The day now glimmered under a completely sunny sky. She pulled her sunglasses out of the driver's door pocket. Things were clearing up.

# Chapter 31

Jessica's truck hugged the mountainside as she drove up Rim Road. She passed stately home after home, many with snowmen melting in the afternoon sun. By evening, they'd likely be the only vestige of the storm, at least down here. At seven thousand feet, the snow-covered peaks would probably retain their winter blankets for a few days.

Barbara's house came into view. Robin's Mercedes and an old Toyota Forerunner with a dented fender shared the driveway. Jessica parked behind the Mercedes.

She rang the bell. No answer. Knocked. Again nothing.

Robin had to be here. Jessica texted her. Perhaps they couldn't hear the doorbell in the back of the house. No response.

Jessica rang the bell again. The door swung open. Charles Gordon met her gaze, although Jessica's eyes quickly dropped to the revolver he held at his waist.

"Come inside," he said.

"I don't think so." Jessica took a step back.

"Honey, I'm eighty-eight years old, and I'd just as soon shoot you as take my next breath. Now get inside."

Jessica glanced around, but her chances of escape didn't look good. If he had any experience with the gun at all, he could easily shoot her before she could duck behind Robin's SUV for protection. Even if she made it there, she'd be stuck. Generous yard sizes and the sparse trees of their desert locale would make getting to a neighbor's house almost impossible.

She returned her gaze to Charles. He held the gun with easy familiarity. Fuck. She was finally supposed to have a case that wasn't dangerous. Yet here she was again.

She crossed the threshold into the foyer. He matched her progress with his retreat, always keeping enough space between them so she couldn't reach for the gun. Not that she had a death wish.

"Put your phone on that table." Charles pointed to a narrow side table. Robin's rhinestone encrusted phone sat atop it. Was she dead or a hostage? What about Barbara? How the hell was she going to get out of this one?

Jessica slid her phone out of her pocket, wishing she had some emergency button she could push to signal for help. Maybe she could figure out how to do something like that. Plus, she really needed that firearms class. Assuming she made it out of here alive.

She placed the useless phone on the table. Angus was going to kill her. And her mom. Why couldn't Jessica have stopped being an ass to her mom before this? She'd just have to find a way out of this one. Surely, she could outsmart or overpower an eighty-eight-year-old man.

"Get moving," he said. He held the gun steady with one hand and pointed to the living area with the other. Jessica stepped into the room.

"Down the hallway." He'd taken a position behind her.

Jessica put one foot in front of the other, dreading what she might find at their destination. *Please don't let it be bodies.* She'd become something close to friends with Robin and admired her constant positivity. Even Barbara, as angry and mean as she was, didn't deserve this kind of ending.

Jessica slowed as she approached Barbara's dressing room. Wood splinters littered the carpet, and the door handle hung at an odd angle.

"Did you shoot the door?" She turned back to Charles.

"She locked it."

"You could have opened it with a bobby pin."

The standard interior door wouldn't have held up to much. At least Charles had just told her he'd shoot first and think of rational solutions later, if ever.

"Do I look like I have a bobby pin?" he asked. "Now get in there."

Jessica hesitated. "Did you kill them?"

"Not yet. But I'm going to kill you if you don't start doing what I tell you."

Fucking ornery old man. She had to figure out how to get the gun away from him.

Jessica pushed the door open. Robin sat on one of the rose gold sofas with something binding her arms behind her back. Mascara streaked down her cheeks.

Barbara sat at her makeup table. Her face looked perfect, but her hands stretched toward the chair's back. Jessica couldn't tell for sure, but it seemed like he'd used nylon stockings to bind her hands to the cutouts in the back of the chair.

"Jessica. I'm so sorry," Robin said, tears flowing down her make-up-scarred face.

"Go sit on the other couch," Charles said, then pointed at Robin. "And you, shut up."

Jessica took a step toward the sofas but did not want to sit. That would give him a height advantage.

He sidled over to a dresser along one wall, the gun still aimed in her direction. One of the top drawers lay half-opened. Sure enough, he pulled a pair of flesh-toned pantyhose from the drawer. He held them up as he walked toward her.

"Turn around."

Jessica stepped back. "No way. Tell me what's going on here. Did you kill Paul Brown?"

Charles didn't say anything, just raised the gun until it was level with her chest. Her heart. Jessica closed her eyes on the whole sad situation. Who the fuck cared who murdered a man forty years ago? It certainly shouldn't cause more murders today.

"No. I did." Barbara sounded exhausted. "Charles, don't do this."

Jessica turned to Barbara in shock. She needed to figure this out once and for all. "I just left the sheriff's office, and they think Paul was murdered by someone at least as tall as he was." She didn't mention that Barbara's made the third confession she'd heard today.

"He was sitting down," Barbara said. "He'd already been punched in the face. He had a broken, bleeding nose. And he was crying."

"Mom. What did you do?" Robin twisted on the sofa, and Jessica saw how Charles had bound her arms several inches above her wrists. Smart. That would be hard to escape.

"What could I do? He was crying because he wanted her. He told me he wanted to support his children, but you and your brother were his only legitimate children. I couldn't let him get away with it."

"How did you actually kill him?" Jessica asked. She pushed the conversation longer, hoping for some opportunity to get away, get the gun, get the fuck out of this room.

Barbara sat tall, but her eyes squinted as if she peered back to that distant night. "Rage just took over. He couldn't get away with it. I couldn't let him. I walked right up to him and slapped him as hard as I could. Then I kicked him. Then, I was kicking, slapping, punching him. I pushed him over and kicked him again and again and he just kept crying. I remember telling him to shut up, but he wouldn't. Not for a long time."

Jessica shuddered at the gruesome story. "Then what?"

"I don't know. I finally stopped. Somehow, I ended up beside him. Hugging him. That's when Charles pulled me off him. I was crying by that time." Barbara stopped talking. She sank against the back of the chair, probably the way she sank into her husband that night, her world torn to pieces.

"Oh, Mom. Why didn't you ever tell me?" Robin had stopped crying, and she leaned toward her mother.

Jessica took stock of the room. Charles seemed unsure of what to do next, but that wouldn't last. If she could get his take on that night, maybe he'd make a mistake. Maybe not, but she had to try.

"Are you sure he was dead?" Jessica asked.

"He'd stopped crying, stopped moving. I killed him."

"How did you know to go out there that night?" A piece of the story was missing, and Jessica wanted it revealed.

"Charles came by the house. He told me what was going on. I already knew about Paul's mistress and the monthly payments he made to her. I told him he had to stop. He had to choose us. He promised he would." Emotion crossed Barbara's face, showing how her husband's broken promise still shocked her.

Jessica looked at Charles. "So, in a way, you instigated all of this. You let Barbara know about the affair and told her he was going to meet Mayra that last night."

The man stared back at her with hard eyes. Jessica saw a storm brewing in his thoughts. The hand holding the revolver started to tremble. She hoped it marked weakness and opportunity, not anger or death.

"No. He wanted to help me," Barbara said. "He always looked out for me. I couldn't have made it through that night without him. He let me sit in the truck while he buried Paul. He covered for me all these years."

Barbara focused on Charles. "I'm so sorry. I wish I could have given you what you wanted."

Charles shook his head as if trying to bat her words away. The gun moved from Jessica to Barbara. "The only thing I wanted was your love."

"I know. But I loved Paul. I couldn't betray him the way he betrayed me." Tears slid down her cheeks. Jessica hadn't been sure the woman had any tears in her.

"You could have. He wasn't good enough for you. I would have given you everything. I had already given up everything for you."

Enough of this manipulating bullshit. "What the fuck do you think you gave up?" Jessica almost shouted the question. "If you hadn't told her about the affair, everything probably would have turned out fine. Paul would have supported all of his kids. Abel could have gone to college. Robin wouldn't have lost her father. Colby might still be alive. You bastard. You're the bad guy here."

"I gave up everything for her." Charles refocused on Barbara. "I divorced my wife. I haven't seen my kids in decades. She took it all away because I wasn't good enough for her."

Robin slumped back against the sofa as if the information had punched her in the gut. "What is going on?"

Barbara shook her head. "I told you not to divorce your wife, just like I had to finally tell you to stay away from us when I remarried. Why didn't you listen to me?"

The gun shook harder in his hand. It no longer pointed straight at anyone, but if his finger slipped, he could take out any of them. "You should have been mine. It all should have been mine."

"So, you killed him." Jessica kept her voice low but used it like a battering ram against what she hoped was his failing psyche.

"No—" Barbara interrupted.

"What did he use to bury Paul?" Jessica slipped her question in before Barbara could admit to killing him again.

"A shovel." Charles supplied the answer.

"And you just happened to have a shovel with you?" Jessica asked. When no one responded, she continued. "Paul died from a strike to the head with a flat, blunt object. A shovel would have worked. Not a fist, and not a foot."

Jessica looked at Barbara, saw the truth pry her eyes wider.

"You killed him?" Barbara asked.

"I was supposed to use this gun. But when I returned after I got you in the truck, I saw him lying on the ground crying and asking for help. I already had the shovel in my hand."

Jessica couldn't merge the frail man in front of her with the killer who would beat a man to death with a shovel. But perhaps the desperation was the same. Or maybe that one act of passion had followed him all these years like a shadow. Killing again would only make that worse.

"Well, for fuck's sake, put the gun down," Jessica said. "The last thing you need to do is kill someone else."

"She was going to tell the cops I did it." Charles lifted a second hand to the gun, steadied it. The blunt, black nuzzle pointed directly at Barbara. "She came to see me today, for the first time in years. Offered me money to leave town so she could blame me for Paul's murder. She wanted me to take the fall for it because the cops were getting too close."

"Well, you did kill him," Jessica said. This whole thing had become tiresome. She wanted to go home, to scrape all this excess emotion from her memories, scrub it from her skin. The way people wallowed in their hurts and desires, pulling others down with them, ruined too many lives. She'd lived it herself, and it was time for a change.

"Shut up!" Charles turned the gun on her, his voice mad.

"Forty years!" Barbara shouted. "For forty years I thought I'd killed my husband." A high-pitched keening came from the woman. She leaned forward, straining against her bindings.

Charles swung the gun between Jessica and Barbara. Fear crept into his eyes as if he'd just realized what he'd unleashed.

"Every day, I've woken up with my guilt and hated myself for my actions. I hated what it did to Colby. I could have protected him from those nasty rumors, but I was too afraid to admit what I'd done. So, I hated myself more. And I took that hate out on everyone around me." Barbara turned to Robin, her face twisted in grief.

"Oh, Mom. I didn't know." Robin lunged toward her mother.

"Stay put!" Charles shouted in a panic.

"Leave them alone," Jessica screamed back. "Haven't you done enough already?"

"Me? Me? I'm the one whose life was ruined. I haven't seen my kids since the divorce. My wife took them and moved back to Florida. Then I was fired. I lost my whole life over this. And now that my days are almost over, she comes back and offers me money. This should be mine." He swung the gun around the room. "She should be mine. Paul didn't deserve any of this. I did."

What the everlasting hell? Charles had a gun, but Jessica didn't think he wanted to use it. Although he might, out of desperation. She needed to give him the opportunity to escape.

"Charles. All of this has gone too far. You can't fix it with a gun. Just like you couldn't fix things before by killing Paul." Of course nothing would fix anything now. Just like nothing would fix her relationship with her mother.

Only that wasn't true. Not anymore. Barbara had become an instrument of hate because of how much she hated herself. Hadn't Jessica done the same on a much smaller scale? For years she told herself she hated her parents for leaving her, but she'd turned that anger back on herself for being someone they could leave. She'd built a wall of fury to hide behind that had ruled her emotions for years. But she'd been sixteen. She hadn't known any better. Maybe it was time to give that kid a break.

She looked around the room with clearer eyes. Everyone needed to let go of the past. Maybe Barbara could become a different woman now, free from the guilt of killing her husband.

Abel could free himself from the guilt of believing he'd killed the same man. He'd driven his mother there. Finally stood up to his father for being a complete asshole. And never heard from him again. He'd probably spent most of his life steeped in regret thinking he'd killed his father.

Jessica brought her thoughts back to the present and focused on Charles. He'd ruined his life as well. Not just by killing Paul, but by playing the victim instead of taking responsibility for his actions. He lived each day in a jail of his own making, his cell a tiny apartment void of personality where he'd pined for a world he never possessed.

"Put the gun down," Jessica said calmly.

"No. I'm not going to be blamed for Paul's death. I'm not going to jail for that."

"I think you've been punishing yourself for years for his death. Why not face the actual consequences? Do you really think it will be worse? And think of how much more terrible your life will be if you have our deaths on your conscience as well."

"I don't care about you."

"I don't really care about you either. But I care about them. Let them work through their sorrow." Jessica tipped her head toward Robin and Barbara, now straining toward each other.

"You'll call the cops on me."

"I'll give you a head start. Honestly, take as much time as you need. I've got someone else I need to see right now."

Charles glanced over at Barbara and Robin, who stared back at him with teary eyes. He looked at Jessica again. She nodded. Like a cowboy from an old western film, he backed out of the room, still pointing the gun in their direction.

Jessica waited until she heard a car start outside, then padded down the hall and peeked out the front door. The Forerunner was gone.

She locked the door, then went to free Robin and Barbara. Fortunately, a small pair of cosmetic scissors lay on the countertop. She clipped through the stockings and released them.

Robin locked her in a hug. "You saved us. How will I ever thank you?"

"Just take care of your mother. Take her to your house just in case he comes back."

Barbara, once so strong-willed, looked utterly defeated. It would likely take her a while to work through what the last few minutes meant to the sum of her life. Hopefully, she'd land in a better place.

Robin pulled her mother to her side. "I will. We've got a lot to discuss, but hopefully this will let us start over. Are you going to call the police?"

"Why don't you call them once you're safe at your house." Jessica wanted to be done with this case built on secrets.

"I'll call Lefty," Jessica said. "You call the El Paso police. After all, he did hold you hostage."

Robin nodded. She rested her head against her mother, holding her tight. They would be okay.

"We'll talk later." Jessica headed toward the door. "I've got someone I need to see."

She called Lefty from her truck. Linda had already finagled Abel's release, and as far as he knew, the Gamboa family was on their way back to Mexico. Jessica started her truck, glad that they'd get to, if not start over, at least move forward without the past haunting them.

The bright sunshine of the afternoon sky lit the white mountains. A new ease coursed through her body. Everything was terrible, but everything was going to be all right.

She thought about her furious sixteen-year old self. That girl had turned into a woman who leapt from danger to danger, fueled by anger. She hadn't meant to bring all that hurt and rage along with her, or maybe she had. But she could look back at that wounded girl and feel nothing but kindness for her. She forgave her. That girl had done the best she could.

And today, the grown woman could do better.

Jessica pulled up to her mother's cottage. She saw her mom's back through the window, framed by a canvas filled with bright colors. Clarice must have heard the truck, because she turned. When she saw Jessica, her face lit up with a smile.

Hera trotted up to the window, protecting her realm. Jessica saw Sheba pop up beside her, probably standing on her hind legs. The home looked cozy, and complete, and she couldn't wait to get inside.

She burst through the door without hesitation and wrapped her mom in a hug. Relief that she hadn't waited forty years for this moment poured through her, as did the love, unburdened by guilt.

"I love you, Mom."

THE END

———

Visit www.KathrynDodson.com for updates and a free ebook.

Other novels by Kathryn Dodson

*Tequila Midnight*

*El Diablo*

*The Podcast Chronicles*

*Portrait of Deception*

*Five Tries to Get It Right*

# Acknowledgements

In a book about relationships with mothers, I'll start by acknowledging my own. Mom and I never had the tortured relationship depicted in this novel, in part because my mother is a wonderful mom and the nicest person I've ever met. She has always believed in my dreams and helped me achieve them. She drove me hundreds of miles for horse shows. She braided manes before dawn, while I fed the horse, cleaned and polished my equipment, and completed a myriad of other tasks. Eventually, my fingers grew strong and nimble enough to braid manes myself, but she remained my companion and biggest cheerleader. She still is today.

My parents are readers. Like many writers, I grew up reading their books, some of them long before I should have. Soon enough I wanted to create my own stories. But novels don't belong to just one person. They happen because of the many people who help along the way. First and foremost, I thank my critique partners Claudia Arman and Sydney Clark. They give my writing the tough love it needs. I met them through the Women's Fiction Writers Association, an excellent group for writers. I'd especially like to thank Michele Montgomery from that group. She started online write-ins during the pandemic, and they still keep me going. A big thank you also goes to Michelle Regallo for being online at six every Monday and Friday morning and providing a place for creativity and accountability.

My husband Tom delivers fun, love, and support—in whatever order I need them. My son Jack is my biggest fan. He reads all of my books and is my greatest joy.

For those of you unfamiliar with the El Paso region, the Jessica Watts Southwest Suspense Series is a love letter to that wild land. Like a tough parent, El Paso gives opportunities to those brave enough to take them, and embraces visitors with a rich culture and incredible people. But it is also a harsh desert that just might kill you. While I no longer live there, I visit often. It is so much more than what you see from the freeway. Meet me there, I'll show you around.

Finally, and most importantly, if you found this book and read it to the end, thank you. Books need readers to become real.

# About the Author

Kathryn Dodson grew up writing and riding horses in far West Texas. She graduated from SMU with a BA in English/Creative Writing and went on to get an MBA from Thunderbird and a PhD from Clemson.

She has worked on both sides of the US/Mexico border and has held jobs with governments, chambers of commerce, and other businesses. Now she spends her days writing about interesting women in fascinating places.

Join Kathryn for updates and extras at www.KathrynDodson.com.

NOVELS
*Tequila Midnight*
*El Diablo*
*The Podcast Chronicles*
*Portrait of Deception*
*Five Tries to Get It Right*
*Matador*

www.ingramcontent.com/pod-product-compliance
Lightning Source LLC
Chambersburg PA
CBHW020108310726
48970CB00002B/536